FRACTURED TIDE

FRACTURED TIDE

FOUR SHIPWRECKED SURVIVORS.
A THOUSAND WAYS TO DIE.

LESLIE LUTZ

BLINK®

BLINK

Fractured Tide
Copyright © 2020 by Leslie Karen Lutz

Requests for information should be addressed to:
Blink, *3900 Sparks Dr. SE, Grand Rapids, Michigan 49546*

Hardcover ISBN 978-0-310-77010-7

Ebook ISBN 978-0-310-77012-1

Art direction: Cindy Davis
Interior design: Denise Froehlich

Printed in the United States of America

20 21 22 23 24 / LSC / 10 9 8 7 6 5 4 3 2 1

For the DFW Writers Workshop and DFWCon,
and for Russell Lutz, my favorite writer of all time

HI DAD,

I'm going to write you until this pencil wears out. Until all of me wears out. I'm not sure what's real and what's not anymore, but these words, they feel real. Solid. And there's a chance my letter to you will wash up on the right shore.

The wreck, the one that started all this, lies a hundred feet under the Atlantic, close to Key Largo. Ten miles offshore, you'll find a place where the water turns blue-black and the salt spray tastes different, coppery. And you'll feel it as soon as your boat passes over the spot. Something wrong beneath your skin, as if the blood moving through your heart has gone sour, like old milk.

If you feel all that, you keep going. Get to shore. Promise me. The whole point of writing any of this down is to save you.

The last day we saw each other, I lied and said the charter was cancelled because of high seas. Mom never cancelled it. She needed the money, the new captain said it was okay, and we had ten divers with full pockets who wanted to see pretty fish, and, well, you know how it is.

The weather didn't look bad while we were still docked, especially with the wall of hotels and condos that circle the marina like a giant, overpriced windbreak. But once Captain Phil got us out past the Haystacks, the gusts picked up, and we knew we were in trouble. The ocean started up that trick that makes you think your boat's made of balsa wood and Elmer's glue, not tough fiberglass and metal. But you know me, I never get sick; I didn't even when I was little and you took me fishing on black flag days. The tourists spent most of the ride hurling, watching the sea, not the horizon like I told them.

The week before, Phil went out by himself and found the wreck and marked the place with a buoy. When I spotted it, small and white and bobbing about a hundred yards off the bow, the shiver hit me for the first time—that feeling you get when someone walks over the spot your tombstone will go one day. I thought about the water, and how there was just too much of it—too deep, too dark, too cold below the first thermocline. Not a good day to dive.

Phil got up and ambled over to me, which is the only way to describe the way Mom's new captain walked. Like his pilot's chair was his horse, and he was just heading into the saloon. He scratched his salt-and-pepper stubble and ran a sweaty hand over his shirt, a lavender stone-washed wife beater that made him look like a total dirtbag.

"Your mama tells me your job is babysitting the green ones," he said.

"Someone's gotta make sure none of the divers fall over and get a concussion."

Phil eyed me in a way you'd hate. I zipped up my wet suit the rest of the way, wishing I'd chosen the one-piece that morning instead of the bikini.

Phil tipped his head toward the starboard side of the *Last Chance*. A diver, his wet suit new and top-of-the-line, had his head over the side like he was slowly melting into the Atlantic.

A five-hundred-dollar mask, also new, sat in a pool of seawater at his feet.

Phil's face broke into a smile. "Good luck with that one, girlie."

"Like you've never been seasick. Happens to everyone eventually."

Mom passed by and nudged me with an elbow. "Seriously, Tasia. Get the customer in the water."

"Should I hook a bucket to his waist, or just strap it to his head to puke into?"

"Divers who don't dive are bad for business."

I knew what she really meant. No more bad online reviews about a "terrible" experience at Blue Dolphin Scuba Charters. The one time I posted a reply telling the whiner we have no control over the wind and waves and a hair-trigger gag reflex, business tanked for a week. And I got grounded.

Mom pointed at the seasick diver, who was now stumbling toward the head, and then pointed at the water before putting on her mask. She sat on the edge and rolled off backward into the waves, disappearing under the surface like a stone. I waited for her to resurface and give the signal—a fist on the top of her head—to tell us she was okay. There's always a little girl in me who thinks when Mom is gone, even for a split second, she's not coming back.

Too cold, too dark, too deep. Get out and go home.

Our craft bobbed and rolled in the waves like a toy in a bathtub. I stumbled over to the diver, who hadn't made it halfway to the head before throwing his upper body over the side again.

"The horizon, Mr. Marshall." I squeezed his shoulder. "Keep your eyes there. Above the waterline."

He tipped his chin up to stare into the distance, his expression the dictionary definition of miserable. The waves crested white froth that the wind pulled off in ribbons. Then the churning blue-gray waters exhaled and flattened, bit by bit, before the whole show started up again. Beautiful. To me, to you. Not to Mr. Marshall. More crests, swell, and foam sliding over the surface. It was chaos from there to the coast, and he was again watching the sea.

The moon was still out, hovering a handbreadth above the place where blue sky and gray sea met. I pointed at it.

"Fix your eyes on the moon, Mr. Marshall. She'll stay still."

He shook his head, fisting his mouth. "Sia, I don't think I can do it. Go on without me," he said through his knuckles. "Don't want to hold anyone up."

Behind me, another diver splashed into the water. That shiver was still with me, and I fought the urge to tell him he was right to stay up here on the *Last Chance*, that I would join him for a topside vomit party. We would watch the moon disappear into the day together.

Instead I hooked an arm around his neck and walked him over to the bench and his expensive fins. "Once you get in, you're golden. Boat's no good in these waves. Nausea will disappear once you're off the roller coaster."

A touch of hope shone through the green pallor and his embarrassment. "Really?"

"Like flipping a switch."

I hooked the tank to his BC, which he kept calling a "buoyancy control device," like he was a walking textbook of proper diving terms. I didn't bother correcting him. Like the rest of his equipment, the BC was uber expensive, the kind that's made of ballistic nylon and has pockets for everything. I pulsed a healthy shot of air inside—the last thing we needed was this guy to get into the water and sink like a stone—and held it open for him, like a valet with a smoking jacket. "Come on. If I'm wrong, you can get out and lie on the floor for the next hour."

The poor guy listened to me.

And I'm not sure I'll ever be able to forgive myself.

He fit the regulator into his mouth, took a deep breath, and gave me a weak thumbs-up. The other divers were in the drink, only their heads and the bloated tops of their inflated BCs visible as they bobbed in the waves, all watching to see what he would do. The neon-pink mask girl waved him in, and the diver with the navy stripe on his arms gave him an encouraging okay sign. They'd only met him that morning, a guy arriving solo on the docks with a big, shiny bag of gear and a seven a.m. smile, but he was already one of us.

And I remembered something you said to me once: The sea brings us closer. All of us, tiny and vulnerable and out of place in a big, wet world, poised at the top of the ocean, ready to drop, and we suddenly realize how much we need each other.

One giant stride and he was in. I gave Phil a mock salute and followed Mr. Marshall. The warning in my gut was nothing but a murmur, one I could barely hear over the wind. I finned my way over to the buoy that marked the drop line and grabbed it. It felt solid, comforting.

As I purged the air out of my BC and began to drop, I thought about you, Dad, behind bars, what you were doing at that moment. And I felt you there, bobbing beside me in the waves, giving me advice, like you did the first day you dove with me and I was afraid.

We're all in this together, you told me. *We don't leave anyone behind.*

I had done this kind of dive hundreds of times on dozens of wrecks. But the descent felt strange this time, alien. And *I* was the alien, slowly floating through the atmosphere of a new planet, pulled by gravity to a place I didn't belong.

Brave new world, baby, I told myself, brave new world. You may not belong, but you're going there anyway.

It took ten minutes to drop eighty feet and reach the wreck. Halfway down we hit a swift current. I spent a solid minute pulled sideways, like a flag on a pole, moving hand over hand down the line. Marshall followed like a pro, the yellow stripe along his leg making him easy to distinguish from the other divers closer to the surface.

Once the current eased up and we'd dropped another forty feet, the ship appeared within the mist beneath me, two hundred feet long and almost turtled, its hull swelling up from the sand. I pegged it as a Navy destroyer of some kind. A spar in the bow jutted out at a forty-five-degree angle, extending so far it disappeared in the haze, as if the sea was slowly dissolving it.

As I drifted down through the chill of a thermocline, the massive wreck grew. The ship looked different than I remembered. Like it had rolled over in its sleep and was inching its way to the coast.

As the memory floated away with the current, a shiver—that had nothing to do with the cold—ran down my spine. Because I'd never been to this wreck before. I couldn't have a *memory* of it.

No one had been here but Phil, and he'd found the wreck

only last week. It wasn't on any of the maps. An old World War II vessel newly scuttled to make a reef, he'd told us. No blog posts or announcements, and somehow I didn't think about how strange that was.

When my depth gauge read 95 feet, I landed a few feet from the ship. Marshall followed, letting himself fall to his knees, like a man praying on the moon. A warning pulsed louder in me. I had an urge to grab Marshall's arm and shoot to the surface, claw my way back to the boat with this stranger who, for the next forty-five minutes, belonged to me.

I ignored the instinct. I know you think I've forgotten all about your famous daddy-daughter *listen to your gut* lectures. Well, you weren't there, and every year your voice gets softer in my head. And that's not my fault.

Marshall gave me an okay sign, more confident than the last time, and a little head bob as his bubbles mingled with mine.

Mom was already on the other side of the wreck with her group, the neon-green stripe running the length of her wet suit bright and cheery against the gray hull. Easy to spot when you're following the leader. A diver with blue fins rounded the top and joined us. Colette. Probably Mom's idea of keeping me safe with the new guy, sending someone who'd logged over three hundred dives—at least a hundred of them in caves and ships—to bring up the rear.

I attached my orange line to a sturdy bolt and flipped on my dive light. The three of us slid through a wide gash in the hull, a cloud of bubbles dribbling behind.

I unreeled the line, letting it hit the deck so softly the silt barely rose. Pulsed a shot of air into my BC to keep me off the floor. Colette stayed within an arm's reach, her light a smooth circle traveling along the ceiling. Marshall followed, shooting his beam over the walls like an excited firefly. Scared, maybe. No one gets through a shipwreck scuba course without having the risks tattooed on the inside of their skulls.

The first compartment was small, the size of a bedroom—one wall torn open to the sunlit world, the space locked in twilight. We skirted a metal table lying on its side. Marshall's buoyancy was good, his fins a foot off the floor, his movements controlled and small, his hands working their way up the bright orange line I reeled out.

The door to the next compartment hung open, the beginnings of a reddish scale clinging to its hinges. I stopped and pointed. I'm not sure Colette and Marshall understood why. I was watching the beginning of the reef, and if I could speak, tour guide–style, I would've told them nature has a way of taking back everything, even an object like this meant to defend and attack and destroy. Mother Nature, she takes it all into herself and makes it beautiful again.

I unwound more orange line and led them into the silky darkness beyond the door and into the galley. Since the ship was tilted, you know the tables and crates and cooking gear had all shifted to one side. I pointed out objects in the room to Marshall: a single fork on the floor, a glass jar, a can of peaches. At the time, I didn't think how strange it was that the reef program would scuttle a ship with furniture and food still in it, blow a hole in the hull without taking out all the bits first. New life, new reefs, like to grow on bones, not guts. Instead of putting two and two together, I focused on the small black bream darting out of my path, leaving a little gray cloud behind it, and led them deeper.

The darkness thickened, until I imagined it was like hovering in space, in some corner of the universe where the stars have all gone out. I skimmed the light behind me to check on Marshall, and he sent a cloud of bubbles into the beam, his eyes wide and curious behind his faceplate. As I turned back, my dive light caught the brass glimmer of a plaque. The USS *Andrews*. I made a mental note to write the name in the dive log, add it to the post-dive fish and history talk when the three of us got topside.

Two more pitch-black compartments and I found a small octopus. It was time to get my brand-new wreck diver back to the charter, just to make sure we had plenty of time for mistakes, but I hadn't seen one of these little guys in years, so I was ridiculously excited.

Curled up into the size of a basketball, he'd stuffed himself in the corner behind a wooden crate. The creature stilled under my light. Then the tentacles unspooled in slow motion. My breath thundered, fading and swelling. No matter how calm I am, the sound's so loud in my head I always think fish for a hundred miles can hear me breathe.

I reached toward the tip of one tentacle. It shied away, trembling. I pushed off from the wall to give it room to escape. When I turned to watch it float toward the doorway, I realized Marshall was gone.

Oh God. I'd lost him.

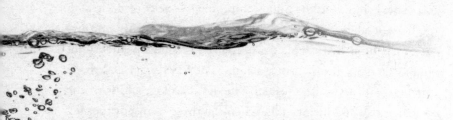

I THREW MY BEAM ALL OVER THE ROOM.
No Marshall. Not at the opening, not anywhere.

A small cloud of silt hovered at the doorway. I swam to the entrance and pulled myself halfway into the hallway beyond. My light picked up nothing. As if the ship had swallowed him whole.

Another beam crossed mine. Colette and I locked eyes, and even behind the mask I could see the shock.

A new diver was off the line. Dad, you don't know that kind of panic. The denial. I was in charge. Me.

And I'd lost him.

Colette grabbed the gauge at my shoulder and fumbled it over. The glass face read 1200 PSI. Her hand stilled, which meant she was calculating, just like I was. In panic mode, Mr. Marshall was probably sucking it down, which meant he was already at 1000 PSI. At that depth, 1000 PSI would buy him maybe twelve minutes of life.

If he was lucky.

I pulled out my slate and golf pencil and argued with Colette for a precious minute. She wanted to go after Marshall. No way was I letting this labyrinth swallow her too. Finally she nodded, her hair floating around her mask. She would find Mom and get an extra tank from the surface. I would stay and look for Marshall. She squeezed my shoulder with her gloved hand, turned, and disappeared through the doorway.

A faint silt trail led me down a long, narrow hallway. I unspooled the line and tried not to rush. Slow, keep it steady, stay off the bottom. My breath thundered in my ears. Bubbles edged to the corner of the ceiling. Everything inside the ship was tilted, the world off-kilter, like swimming through a child's painting of a really bad dream.

Marshall's faint cloud of silt led me, like Hansel's breadcrumbs, into the belly of the ship. And all the things that could happen to him spun through my mind.

He runs out of air, panics, dies. We fish his body out later.

Or maybe he runs out of air, finds a way out, and sprints to the surface, and panic makes him forget he shouldn't hold his breath. The air expands in his lungs. They pop like balloons.

No, he remembers not to hold his breath, but he still ascends too fast. Nitrogen comes out of solution from his tissues. The bubbles that form lodge in his joints, his brain, every organ. He dies on the helicopter that comes to airlift him out, blood bubbling up from his lungs.

I forced the next two scenarios out of my head. Then, honestly, I panicked for a second. Worried I would run out of air too. Pictured myself in scenarios two or three, my corpse floating to the surface alongside Marshall's.

My mask fogged and the world disappeared. I cleared it with seawater so I could read my gauge. The needle had dropped. A lot. I slowed my breathing. I couldn't leave the ship without finding Marshall.

At the end of the hallway, I passed an opening. My hair, which had slipped out of its band, floated in front of my mask.

Through the black veil, I swear I saw a flash in the corner of my eye. At first I thought it was Marshall's yellow-striped leg, but no. It looked like a dive light. As I turned, the glimmer broke in two pinpoints, then disappeared.

Adrenaline made my hands shake. And now I was seeing things, from stress or the pressure or God knows what. Poor Marshall. Where on earth did he think he was going? He was going to get us both killed.

My light revealed two upended cots and a pile of jagged bits in the corner where a grouper floated, its eyes huge and unblinking, its mouth opening and closing as it watched me. I slipped inside the small berth, searching the other corners.

And then I felt it. A rush of something powerful in my blood. A flare of premonition.

I turned. Nothing. A corked glass bottle on its side. The hallway door yawning open, half off its hinges. My neoprene skin felt thinner. And I knew the next thing to swim near me would pierce me with a flip of a fin. The spines would impale me right through.

I kicked, turning in a circle while fire hosing my light around the room. Nothing. But my breathing, my heartbeat, my skin—they told me something different. I unclasped the dive knife strapped to my thigh.

My light moved smoothly up the walls toward the door. I stopped halfway, pointing the beam to the corner instead. The grouper had jammed its body within it, its eyes huge and shining in my light, the little fins moving slow. It wasn't watching me. It was watching the doorway.

You'll think I'm nuts, Dad, but instinct—the weird sense I knew what was going to happen—told me to shut off my light. I didn't argue. Something was looking for me.

Click. The world contracted to the size of a sleeping bag, black so thick, a velvet cloth over my eyes. The chill dropped several degrees. The seconds passed. I breathed. In. Out. Rush of bubbles, heart pushing so hard, a caffeine-like rush. My body shook with the cold, as if my suit was nothing. I've never retained heat well, but this kind of chill went deeper, its tendrils reaching all the way into my lungs. I couldn't see my gauge, but I could feel it, the needle slinking down. And as I was about to give up, to turn on my flashlight and get the hell out of there, suddenly the world wasn't completely black anymore.

A faint glow, deep green. It grew in the hallway on the other side of the half-open door. As I watched it brighten, it felt familiar.

I swam to a corner of the berth, out of sight. The glow grew brighter. A voice inside me said *Shut your eyes. You're walking down death row. The worst of them wants you to look, so shut. Your. Eyes. And yes*, the voice whispered, *the thing out there, it really is that wicked. It really is that powerful.*

I stilled. And then a current came, brushing over my face. A high-pitched scrape started up, long and slow, like something big moving through a tight space. A thrum as a piece of metal fell. The scrape softened, until it faded.

I opened my eyes. Blackness. My hands trembling, I flipped on my light. Gave myself ten breaths before I swam to the doorway to check the hall.

Nothing there. The dread gone, the fear eaten up by the need to find Marshall. I tried to slow my breathing and failed, looked at my gauge—800 PSI. Nine minutes left. If I could calm down.

A cloud of silt swirled in the hallway. I went deeper into the ship, where I thought Marshall had gone. I turned a corner at a T-junction.

Mid-sweep, my light moving into the deeps of the ship, something grabbed my arm.

I screamed a cloud of bubbles.

Dark brown hair caught in my light. A familiar mask, the neon-green stripe running down a black body.

Mom.

My relief lasted only long enough to see what she was dragging behind her.

It was Marshall, floating. His eyes were closed. His reg was in his mouth. But no bubbles.

Mom and I made eye contact. Pure panic. She tapped her oxygen gauge and pointed to the end of the hall.

Out. Now.

I grabbed Marshall's other limp arm and pulled him from the beast. Somewhere close to the exit, I glanced at his face and my heart flipped into overdrive. You won't believe me, but I saw it. His eyes. Something phosphorescent leaked from them, like tears.

I stopped swimming. Mom turned to me. In the crumbling hallway of a shipwreck, eighty feet down and running out of air, she actually took the time to give me *the look*. You've seen it a hundred times. The blame. Then, like a silvery fish slipping away, the look was gone, and she turned to the tear in the ship and swam through.

DEAD BODIES DON'T COOPERATE. They don't grab hold of the ladder rung and pull themselves onto a dive platform. They don't react when a four-foot wave knocks their faces against the boat engine. They don't say thank you when you hold on to them tightly to keep it from happening again. You can't know what it was like for me, struggling to keep him safe. A dead man. Safe. My brain kept trying to square the circle, like a mother arranging blankets around a dead baby.

By the time Mom, Phil, and I had dragged Marshall out of the ocean and onto the wooden platform, I was shaking from head to toe. I think I was crying, but with the salt water streaming from my hair into my eyes, I couldn't really tell. A few divers who'd come up early rushed to the stern.

A tourist dropped her beach towel and kneeled next to him. "Oh my God. What happened?"

"Sia! Wake up and get his mask off," Phil said to me.

I pulled it over his forehead, and Phil tipped Marshall's head back to listen for breath sounds. Felt for a pulse. Started CPR.

The voices kept coming, tumbling over one another.

"Is he breathing?"

"We have to call someone."

"This . . . This is terrible."

"We have to get him to the hospital."

"Is he—"

And that was it. I turned away, leaned over the side at the same spot Marshall had only an hour ago, and threw up. The waves crested and fell all the way to the distant blue horizon, and I felt sick in every bit of my body. Marshall had looked at me and nodded when I told him he would feel better if he listened to me. He believed me when I told him that if he just got in the water, everything would be okay.

By the time I'd finished chumming the waters, an uncomfortable silence had settled over the charter. Phil pulled the tank and BC off Marshall's back and set them with the other gear. The rest of the divers came up one by one, and each time I got to hear the shocked questions all over again.

Marshall's body lay under a blue tarp, close to the benches where we stored the extra tanks. Nothing but a shape under a dark plastic shroud. I sat nearby, my arms and legs numb, my hands like deadwood. If I had only kept my eye on him, none of this would've happened.

Mom put her hand on my shoulder. "You okay?"

I nodded and wiped my face with a beach towel. I was nowhere near fine.

She rubbed a palm over her wet hair and looked east, where the sun hovered three fingers above the horizon. The air thickened with the rising morning heat and the smell of neoprene.

Captain Phil walked by with a tank over his shoulder and gave her the once-over, which would've really pissed you off. How he could switch gears like that, I had no idea.

Mom's wet suit lay in a heap at her feet, and she was wearing the white rash guard you gave her four years ago for Christmas, the one with the O'Neill logo in red and black splashed across the front. Mom has worn that and a pair of black bikini bottoms for every dive since you went away, like it's now her uniform.

She sat down on a bench near me and patted the spot next to her. "Maybe this is a good time to talk about what really happened," she said in Greek. The two guys within earshot at the cooler glanced over at us. People huddled in small groups, half-dressed in beach towels and bathing suits, talking in hushed, funeral home voices. The sound of crying drifted up the narrow stairs that went to the head. There really was no place to hide on a small charter. Mom's fishhook gaze made that very clear.

"Everything was fine," I said, my first language suddenly feeling rusty in my mouth. "Marshall was good, keeping his fins off deck. For a new guy, not bad." I washed the taste of vomit out of my mouth and spit over the side.

"I don't give a crap about how good his buoyancy was," Mom said. "I want to know *what happened.*"

For the first time that day, I really looked at her. The lines of her face were hard. So were her eyes. I knew what she really meant: *How could my daughter let this happen?*

I dropped the gear onto the floor with a clatter. "He took off, Mom. I don't know why."

"Why weren't you watching him?"

I tossed my hands up. "There was an octopus. He was adorable. Colette and I were checking it out. Marshall was behind us. And then he was gone. He swam off by himself, I guess."

"You *guess?*"

"Okay, he swam off by himself!"

She looked baffled. "And why would he do that? No one with even beginner's training does that."

"People do stupid things. You know that." My voice was rising, but I didn't care. No one could understand us anyway.

"You sure you didn't leave him behind, Tasia? I've seen you do this kind of thing before."

"I've *never* left a diver."

"No, but you push the edge of the decompression limits. Penetrate a wreck without knowing where all the exits are."

"I know what I'm doing."

"And what about that shark last week, handfeeding him? That was—"

"The nurse shark? C'mon. They're like puppies."

"Do you want to keep your fingers? I swear to God, just like your—" She stopped and rubbed her face. Calming herself down.

"Like your father? Is that what you were going to say? I think I'll take that as a compliment."

"He wasn't perfect, you know," she continued in a deliberately calm voice. "Once you get underwater, you take risks. That's all I'm saying. He was the same way."

"*Was*? He's still alive, Mom. When did you stop talking about him in the present tense?"

She pointed at Marshall and cut me off. "Look at what happened!"

As her words rung out, the chatter on the roof deck died. She took a breath and stood, apparently done with our conversation. Grabbed a stray mask and threw it in the nearest barrel of fresh water, sending a cold, wet slap against my shins. Her motions were stiff, unnatural, as if she'd forgotten how to tidy up after a dive. I watched her gather gear. Avoid my eyes. And Dad, you don't know how I felt. She couldn't even look at her own daughter.

The boat rocked her off-center as she grabbed a wet suit and switched on the shower, rinsing it down. Some of the water ran across the floor and pooled underneath Mr. Marshall.

"I didn't leave him behind," I said.

"How did he get lost, then? Explain how."

"It was textbook. Everything I did. Until he left us."

She put her hands on her hips, examining my expression. Finally, she exhaled and shook her head. "I shouldn't have let him come with us. Too green. Not enough bottom time."

"Gee, thanks for trusting that I'm not lying to you."

She ignored me and looked west, toward shore. "We're heading to the marina. The cops are too lazy to come out here, so they'll meet us on the dock."

A wave of relief washed over me. I knew I wouldn't get an apology from her—that part of her personality has been broken since you went away—but all I wanted was to start our motor and get as far away as possible from the USS *Andrews*.

"Matt's pretty close," she continued, focused on the western horizon again. Her eyes said she couldn't get there fast enough. I followed her gaze. Nothing in the distance but whitecaps and a few seagulls.

"His charter will be here in forty-five," she said. "Maybe an hour. We'll transfer the rest of the divers to him."

"Isn't Felix with him today?"

She nodded.

I looked away and took a sip of water. "I don't want my little brother to see a dead dude."

"He won't."

"He'll hear about it."

"Yeah . . ." She rubbed the back of her neck with one hand, distracted. "He's seven. He understands death. He can handle it."

"I'm seventeen and I can barely handle it. Call someone else."

The wind was dying, but it still had the strength to carry a mist of sea spray, and I breathed in the sharp tang of salt. That's when the feeling hit me again, so strong I was sure everyone within ten feet of me could feel it too.

Too cold, too dark, too deep. Leave now.

"We should all go in together," I said. "The cops—won't they want to talk to the others?"

"No, they'll just want to talk to me. And Phil."

That didn't sound right, but everything I knew about police procedure I'd learned from reruns of *Law and Order*. And your trial, of course. "Captain Matt can't be the only guy out here. It's a *Saturday*. And it's gorgeous outside."

She shrugged. "His is the closest scuba charter. It has a group headed to the Haystacks, mostly snorkelers, but it'll do." She paused, clearly working the details out in her head. "You can help our people get one more dive in and then head back to shore."

"The cops will *absolutely* want to talk to me. And you really think anyone's going to even *think* about going in the water after what happened to Mr. Marshall?"

Mom moved to a bench under the sunshade and sat, leaning her elbows on her knees and clasping her hands together. She sat there for a moment staring at her hands, gathering her thoughts. I wasn't sure what about my question had her so stumped. It seemed simple enough to me. Everyone would want to go home.

"Tasia, do you remember what happened on the *Spiegel Grove*?"

I'd heard that story from you about a hundred times. But Mom kept going, like she does, not waiting for me to answer.

"Four divers went into the ship, and only one came out," she said.

"Yeah, Dad said the *Spiegel* eats divers."

Most kids get campfire stories about hitchhikers with hooks for hands—but you, your scary stories were never far from the ocean.

"How long do you think it took before people were diving in the *Spiegel Grove* again?" Mom asked.

I took a sip of water and thought. When our apartment manager lost her sister, she wore black armbands for a year. A friend of mine didn't celebrate her January birthday because her brother had died in August. "I don't know, three months?"

"A charter was out there the next day." Her gaze went to the tarp under the sunshade. Most of the other divers were on the roof deck whispering in huddles, too freaked out to be any closer to a dead body. A few stood by the cooler, fishing through the ice for bottled water.

"Life just goes on, Tasia. After everything hits bottom, it just goes on."

She looked away, but the pain I'd seen in her eyes told me we weren't talking about Mr. Marshall anymore. And as I stood there on the boat, two feet away from the biggest mistake I'd ever made, I knew where I was going the minute I got to shore. To see you. If anyone could understand what I was feeling after killing another human being, it would be you. No offense.

The dark feeling that hit me when we first arrived at this spot in the ocean welled up again. I looked at the white buoy and the line leading down to the USS *Andrews*. "We should go now, Mom. Just leave. Together."

And I told her. I did, Dad. I tried to stop everything before it could start. I told her about the weird phosphorescent glow I saw in the ship's hallway, and the strange feeling. But somewhere in the middle of my explanation, her lips started to curve up into a smile.

"You had me worried there for a minute."

"What?"

She put her hands on my shoulders. "You were narced, honey."

"I wasn't. Nitrogen narcosis makes you feel drunk. My head was clear."

"You were narced."

"I was thinking straight."

"You went off by yourself to find him. Risk-taking—that's part of it."

Phil, who was fiddling with a regulator hose, chuckled. "First rapture of the deep. You're a real diver now, girlie."

Mom glared at him, and I hated Captain Dirtbag a little more than usual. "Stop calling me that," I said.

"That's what seventeen-year-old girls get called on *my* boat."

"What are you gonna call me when I turn eighteen?"

Phil gave me an oily smile. "Fair game."

I opened my mouth to tell him off, but Mom got there first, her face flushing. Phil waved her off and walked away like she couldn't take a joke, but all I could think about was the rapture of the deep. Phil and Mom together, it was enough for me to doubt myself and what I thought I saw. But I couldn't shake the feeling something was wrong below our charter.

"Let's cancel everything and just leave."

Mom stopped glaring at Phil, who'd plopped into the captain's chair with his back to her. "No way. You're getting on Matt's charter. I do not want you talking to the cops." Mom glanced at the two divers still eavesdropping at the cooler and switched to Greek. "Tasia, I could lose the business if the police find out someone underage was leading Marshall and Colette into the *Andrews*."

"You want me to *lie* to the police?"

She paused, pressed her lips together as if biting back a sharp word. "No, you're not going to talk to them at all. Your job is to take these ten divers—"

"Nine. Mr. Marshall is dead."

"—to the Haystacks with Matt and show them a good time. Don't tell Dad either when you see him on Saturday. He'll think I'm heartless."

"Imagine that."

Mom drew back like I'd slapped her. "Tasia, that's not fair."

"Our divers all saw me lead Mr. Marshall inside the ship. Did you tell them what to say to the police too?"

She looked at the two divers at the water cooler and then glanced up at the roof where the others had gathered. "They'll all be going back to their hotels and then flying home in a day or so. The police in the Keys are slow. People forget details over time."

I wanted to remind her that they weren't slow when they arrested you, but I kept my mouth shut. So I grabbed some equipment and started breaking it down, letting muscle memory take over. I disconnected a hose on a BC before I realized it was Mr. Marshall's. I almost dropped it, and then turned it upside down instead. A trickle of the Atlantic came out. I wondered if there were bits of *it* in the water. The phosphorescence, bleeding all around the wreck, worming into the seals of the BC. And now pooling under my bare feet.

I told myself Mom was probably right about me being narced. None of what I saw was real. I stepped out of the puddle anyway.

Phil passed by me then, carelessly brushing the edge of the tarp. A corner flipped over to reveal a pale white hand, palm up. The glint of a wedding ring. Captain Phil glanced at me, and the oppressive wave pushed me under again, the same feeling I'd had down below while inside the ship compartment where I'd hid. His barbed stare slipped away and the feeling was gone.

A motor buzz sounded to the east. I would have to take over for Mom soon, as always, and lead a bunch of divers into the deep whether I wanted to or not. On autopilot, I reached into my dry bag and grabbed my phone to check the conditions over in the Haystacks. The rhinestone case I'd picked up for free at Goodwill sparkled in the sunlight. I powered her up and the screen came to life. Then my icons melted down the screen.

I shut it down, swearing, and powered it back up again. Awesome. My OS had picked today to crap out on me.

A vessel appeared on the horizon. Mom squinted into the sun, unwrapped a stick of spearmint gum. She handed it to me, and I waved it off. I knew she was trying to be nice, but I wasn't in the mood to accept anything from her, even gum.

"Matt's charter." She nudged me until I met her gaze. "Don't talk to anyone about what happened." She broke eye contact and popped the gum into her mouth, although she grimaced as if it tasted bitter. "Let me handle everything."

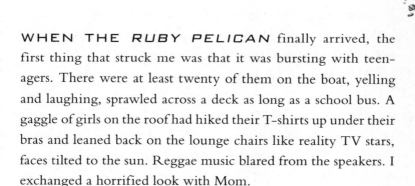

WHEN THE *RUBY PELICAN* finally arrived, the first thing that struck me was that it was bursting with teenagers. There were at least twenty of them on the boat, yelling and laughing, sprawled across a deck as long as a school bus. A gaggle of girls on the roof had hiked their T-shirts up under their bras and leaned back on the lounge chairs like reality TV stars, faces tilted to the sun. Reggae music blared from the speakers. I exchanged a horrified look with Mom.

Matt had responded to our distress call by bringing us a floating kegger.

The boat roared and churned the water as it pulled alongside. The scent of engine oil and tanning lotion blew past me. Up on the roof deck, Felix leaned over the railing, his dark hair wet and stuck to his forehead, his smile wide. He waved when he saw me. I waved back, coming up with a good lie for when he asked about the man-shaped lump under the tarp. Which he would, crazy little Sherlock elf he was.

Someone I didn't recognize threw the bowline to me. Mom and I tied the two boats together, and I got a better look at the partiers. They were younger than I'd thought, and most of them had science books and lab manuals. Not a beer in sight. Apparently, they were high on life, or science, or boat fumes. Whatever it was, I didn't know how we were going to fit more sardines in that can.

Matt appeared from under the sunshade on the other boat, his Orioles cap on backward and his surf shorts hanging low on his hips. He gave Mom a lopsided smile that looked like an apology.

Mom finished tying off the two boats with a half-hitch. "Matt, my friend," she said, shouting over the slosh of the waves. "Not what I had in mind."

Matt spread his arms broadly, like a ringmaster in a circus. "Welcome to the annual Key Largo high school science club summer fun party. Yeah, and it's as fun as it sounds."

The group of girls sunning themselves on the charter's roof all slid their sunglasses down at the same moment to look at him. Each of them wore "Come and Take It" T-shirts, and at first I thought they were NRA or something. Then I saw the microscope silhouette above the words. As usual, after three years of homeschooling, I'm light-years behind on every trend.

Matt stepped up on the gunwale, balanced himself as a wave rocked his boat, and leapt to the *Last Chance* with all the grace of a drunken sailor. "Well, hello there, Miss Gianopoulos. "

"Hi, Matt," I said, smiling. Matt never called me by my first name, no matter how many times I asked him to. I, therefore, refused to call him by anything but Matt, which I think secretly bothered a southern boy like him.

"You ready to get off this rust bucket and ride on a real boat?"

"No way you'll fit us all," I said. "You'll have to bungee the big ones to the side."

Matt shrugged and smiled in that way he always does, everything's gonna be alright, Bob Marley-style. "Your mommy said to come. Here I am." He counted the divers on our boat with one finger, his lips moving silently.

Mom checked her watch and squinted. "Lousy cheap Casio."

She tapped it a few times. "There it is. *Pamé*, sweetheart. Let's get a move on." She glanced at me meaningfully. I pretended to be absorbed in repacking my gear. The police; that's why she was in a hurry. I told myself again everything was an accident. Mom was right. It was best I didn't talk to them.

The diver transfer was easy; Phil and I passed the scuba equipment, piece by piece, from the *Last Chance* to the *Ruby Pelican*, and some helpful science geek with two water PH kits strapped across his chest like nerdy bandoliers helped Mom with the tanks. One of the divers on our boat told me with the saddest voice ever not to bother with hers. She'd lost her taste for diving. Two others asked Mom if they could get their money back. The rest of our divers climbed aboard Matt's charter and started assembling their stuff. I guess Mom was right. Life goes on. At least for some.

By the time we'd handed the science cowboy the last tank, a silence had fallen over the newcomers. Wave song filled the void, stuffing my ears, slapping against the boat. From the looks on everyone's faces, word of the accident had spread. A few of the girls on Matt's roof deck craned their necks to get a glimpse. More than a few of them stared at me, the accusation as clear as a knife's edge in the sunlight.

Murderer.

The word came to me suddenly. I guess it had been there all along, standing behind a half-open door. I wasn't, and I knew I wasn't. But I felt like one anyway. And it was horrible. For a moment I was back in court with you when you took the stand, and I was listening to the hollow sound of your voice. It was an accident, you said. You were drunk. Out of control. Angry. You'd never done anything like that before, and you'd never do it again. And just when I thought the whole courtroom was swayed by the raw honesty in your voice, the dead man's brother stood up and called you a murderer.

Before I could imagine what Mr. Marshall's wife, waiting for her husband back on the docks, would say to me, I distracted myself troubleshooting my phone, trying again to pull an accurate report of the Haystacks out of a suddenly nonexistent internet. The bars are never great that far offshore, but still.

I finally threw the phone back into my dry bag and helped Mom put together some gear for the divers.

We talked about the dive plan for the group. Matt would help me get the gear ashore afterward. The stares from the other boat followed me. I wondered if someone told Felix what his big sister had done. That I wasn't paying attention and that Marshall died because of it. I tightly coiled a hose in my hands, thinking about the strange glow I'd seen in the wreck. What if Mom was wrong about me being narced down there? And if I said nothing, there would be more accidents.

Murderer.

"Mom, I need a favor," I said as I finished stuffing the last of the regulators into a mesh bag.

"All right," she answered, caution in her tone.

"Will you at least wait a while to dive the USS *Andrews* again?"

"You were narced, honey. Here, don't forget defog for the masks."

I took the spray bottle from her and shoved it inside the bag. "Just wait a week or so. Out of respect for Mr. Marshall."

Phil stopped ogling the girls on the roof of the other boat and glanced my way. I got the feeling from his expression he thought I was acting overly sentimental.

Mom picked up another BC and worked a hose stuck in its socket, her face twisting with the effort. "The sea waits for no one."

"This is the wrong time to quote some stupid beat poet."

"Hey, it's what the homeschooling parenting books say to do," Mom said, pulling the hose loose with a snap. "You know, weave it into the day."

"Yes, I'm sure using me as cheap labor is all a part of the homeschooling plan you file with the state."

"Tasia, I would never call you cheap labor. *Free* labor, maybe."

Phil passed by me on the way to the stern and gave me a creepy tap on the shoulder. "Best kind."

I edged away from him. "Mom, I can't believe you're making jokes after what just happened."

She had the grace to look guilty, and we fell into silence for a while, assembling gear, checking gauges, and making sure we had an extra set of everything.

Mom nodded for me to cross over to the other boat, which was sitting pretty low in the water now that it had gained nine scuba divers and a lot of equipment. "Go on, now." She kissed me on the forehead and tucked a lock of hair behind my ear. I was so surprised I pulled back. The last time she'd acted like that, I was getting ready for my first day of high school, back when I went to an actual *school*. "See you at home for dinner."

I nodded, my throat knotting up. She was going to stay and clean up my mess. Lie to the police. To protect the business, she had told me. But the kiss on the forehead told me the truth. This was all about protecting me.

I climbed onto Matt's charter and got settled on a small space of bow cushion. Matt patted me on the back on his way to the captain's chair, as if he'd already been let in on the secret. I flushed. For the first time in my life, I was sick of being out on the ocean. I was ready to go home. I wrapped the beach towel around my waist like a sarong, leaned back, and shut my eyes, letting the rock of the waves lull the stress from my body, and waited for the roar and purr of the engine.

The click of Matt's key in the ignition drew me out of my thoughts. *Click.* One whir. He tried to turn it over again. It caught. Then it died.

IF THERE'S ONE THING you understand better than I do, it's what happens to people when you cram them together and take away their choices. No space. No privacy. No control over whether you get a meal today, or if the state will spring for air conditioning. You've never talked much about what happens in Pine Key Pen, and I'm guessing it's a lot worse than being stuck out in the middle of nowhere with a bunch of sweaty science nerds and a dead body.

We didn't realize what was happening at first. When Matt's boat wouldn't start, everyone climbed off the *Ruby Pelican* and piled onto the *Last Chance*.

And then Captain Phil turned the key.

Click.

Two shocked seconds of silence broke into a wave of everyone talking at once. I couldn't make out much. Some of them acted like a ride at Disney World had just broken down. Others threw F-bombs into the wind. Felix hid on the roof deck, the sound of his crying rising over the panic down below, along with Mom's voice as she tried to soothe him.

Matt told everyone to "stay calm, stay calm." This accomplished absolutely nothing. He tried to call the Coast Guard. The radio didn't work. A girl took out her phone and found it was dead. And then everyone reached for their phones

and discovered the same thing—black screens. Even the flashlights were useless. One girl—I never did learn her name—made
a Bermuda Triangle joke, and the whole lot of us broke into
nervous laughter.

Mom spent another five minutes transferring some of the
passengers back to the *Ruby Pelican*—a really awkward game of
musical boats—and Captain Phil and I poked around the engine.
I put on a rash guard over my bikini top so he'd stop staring at my
boobs. Felix climbed down from the roof and watched us fiddle
with wires and fuel lines. Little circles of conversations started
up behind me, mostly about whether we knew what we were
doing. I was pretty sure we didn't. Neither did Matt, apparently.
The only thing louder than the clank of his tools as he chucked
them onto the deck was the sound of his cursing.

After thirty minutes of troubleshooting on what seemed to
be a perfectly good engine, Phil got up. Once he'd grabbed a
silver flask from underneath the captain's chair, he disappeared
up the ladder.

Felix looked so small standing there in his SpongeBob rash
guard and cartoon board shorts, hair sticking out in all directions, as it always does when I wait too long to get him to the
barber. Mom works eighty hours a week now. I don't remember
the last time she took either of us anywhere but the docks.

"T?" Felix asked in a small voice.

"Yeah?"

"Is he coming back?"

"No, but that's okay." I smiled at him and picked up where
Captain Phil left off, messing uselessly with the thermostat.

"Can you fix it?" Felix asked, wringing his skinny little
hands.

I doubted I could do anything, but I didn't have the heart to tell a seven-year-old that his big sister wasn't good at everything. "Maybe."

While I worked, Felix sat beside me and drew a cartoon shark on his knee. He'd gotten ahold of Mom's good ballpoint pen—snatched it from her clipboard, little thief that he is.

Felix started doing that—drawing on himself—after his art teacher told him last year he "has talent." Mom tries to get him to stop, but as soon as she turns her back, he's sketching cartoons on his body again. Rainstorms on his calves. Superheroes on the tops of his feet. Whales on his forearms. Mom told me she's afraid it's some kind of compulsion. I don't think so. I get the feeling art for him is like diving for me. Not an anchor, really. More like something that sets him free.

Felix looked up at the roof deck, where Mom was still trying to calm a hysterical diver. A couple of guys from the science trip were trying to help, and I silently thanked them.

"You think I'll get in trouble?" He covered the shark drawing with his hand.

"Not today."

"I don't know. Mom gets mad at all kinds of things."

"Well, she's under a lot of pressure."

On the other boat, Matt led a small group in singing "Three Little Birds." The second time around Felix mouthed the words. He caught my eye and I returned his smile. But Bob Marley has always been your thing, not mine, so I played a different song in my head, one I'd picked up on the back patio of Nick's Hula Hut. This super cool singer-songwriter had come through town for the Fourth of July—one night only. Felix fell asleep on my shoulder. Fireworks lit up the skies above the docks, and Vanessa

Peters played her acoustic guitar, singing her heart out, like she knew what my life was about.

> *And I tell myself . . . everything will be okay from now on*
> *If I just close my eyes . . . and believe it . . .*

One of the guys on the roof deck of the *Last Chance* joined in, briefly meeting my eyes. I could feel that moment start to fade—I think we both could. We had a long way to go before we got to *okay*. Then Felix sang "Three Little Birds" louder, his smile widening, and for a second, I actually did believe it. Vanessa Peters and Bob Marley, singing a beautiful chorus in my head.

The song ended, and the splash of waves against the hull took its place.

Felix finished putting a remora on the shark and started drawing on the other knee. A manta ray this time. "Someone on the roof said we drifted into the Bermuda Triangle," he said.

"We're nowhere near it."

"What happens in the triangle?"

"Compasses go wacky, but that's about it."

A voice drifted from the captain's chair. "And it eats planes and boats. It eats everything."

I turned to the voice. Teague. I'd heard his name spoken often since the boat breakdown. He'd been holding court over by the scuba tanks, so I guessed him for the science club president. His blond ponytail trailed over one shoulder, half covering the Stanford logo on his shirt. Advertising his bright future to the world. He doodled in a thick spiral notebook balanced on his knee.

Teague closed the notebook. A sticker across the cover read, *The Universe is made of protons, neutrons, electrons & morons.* I'm sure he thought being stranded in the middle of nowhere was one grand adventure.

"You know what's in the triangle?" He leaned forward on his knees, lecture-style. I sent him a glance that said *Shut up in front of my little brother*—which he absolutely saw—but he went on anyway. "A hole in the Earth's electromagnetic field."

Felix's eyes went wide. "What's that?"

"It's why our electronics are dead."

Felix swallowed and his mouth fell into a frown, the one that precedes a bout of crying. "Dead?"

I gave Felix a side hug. "It's all a big myth. Like mermaids and Santa Claus."

"But Mom said Santa Claus is real."

Oh crap. "Yeah, you're right. He is."

"Maybe the triangle is real too then," he whispered.

Another voice spoke up, a girl with a bubblegum-pink streak in her hair who had been hovering around Teague. "USS *Cyclops*. Left Barbados in 1918, went into the triangle, and was never. Seen. Again."

"A history lesson isn't gonna fix our boat." I nudged Felix. "Screwdriver, please."

That snapped him out of it. He dug around the toolbox and handed me a Phillips.

"What about the *Mary Celeste*?" Teague said, because he obviously couldn't take a hint. Or a break. "Went into the triangle in 1892. When they found the ship, the entire crew was gone. Disappeared." Teague made a *poof!* with his fingers. Felix scooted closer to me. I was about ready to throw Teague overboard.

"Enough with the theories, guys," I said.

"That's gotta be aliens," the girl with the pink streak said.

And the pressure that had been building in me all morning blew. I threw the screwdriver back into Phil's ratty toolbox. "Is this what you do in your stupid science club? Scare little kids?"

The chatter on the boat died instantly. Teague looked both affronted and pleased. Bubblegum-streak girl just looked confused.

"I'm only passing the time." He gave me a smug look.

"Pass it somewhere else."

"I'm not little," Felix said.

I put my hand on his shoulder. "I didn't mean it like that—not like little, little, just young."

My brother got up from his spot beside me, stepped around the tarp to get to the ladder, and disappeared onto the roof deck.

Teague clicked his tongue a few times. "See what you did?"

"What *I* did? What good is it to come up with impossible theories about aliens and wormholes and electro-magno whatever when—"

"Electro-magno?"

"—when what we need is to stay calm, conserve water, and wait for the Coast Guard without scaring"—I lowered my voice—"little kids half to death."

Felix's small head appeared over the railing above. "Shut up, T."

A titter of a laughter moved through the boat.

My mother's low tones floated down from the roof deck. "Tasia."

No follow-up. I was supposed to understand everything Mom wanted me to do from that one word. And I did. *Be the good daughter. Keep everyone calm. Stop antagonizing your brother. Don't lose your cool.*

Matt's voice drifted across the water. "Okay, everybody. Let's sing it again."

So I did. I sang along and hoped to God that Matt was right.

By nightfall, most of us stopped talking about how weird it was, everything dying at once like that. Strange how a crowd gets used to a new normal. They keep thinking *everything will be okay.* But hope, even when it's based on fantasy, is valuable.

At least that's what I'd learn later.

By the time the sun dipped low on the horizon, Teague had disappeared to find a better audience, leaving his snobby notebook behind for my brother to steal and doodle in. Serves him right. And Candy, the pink-streak girl, became my new best friend. She spent the next hour beside the engine, handing me tools and french braiding my hair. I started to relax, sure we'd be home by sunrise.

That's when the guy from the roof deck, the one who'd met my eyes earlier, came down the ladder and introduced himself.

Ben, with the warm eyes and low, honey voice. Ben, looking like a young Lenny Kravitz, his white T-shirt stark against his deep-brown skin. I forgot all about the engine, the warnings, Mr. Marshall. And suddenly I was all thumbs. Navigating reefs and fixing scuba equipment? Check. Talking to cute guys? Not so much. While he and Candy poked around and talked circuits, I alternated between wishing I were up on the roof deck with Felix and imagining what Ben and I would look like in our prom picture.

After all his electrical talk with Candy dried up, he asked me a lot of questions about the engine and why our captain was off drinking himself stupid. All I could manage was a string of one-word answers.

Finally, Ben sighed and tossed the needle-nose pliers onto a bench. "You know what I'm going to do when I get to shore?"

"Leave us a really bad Yelp review?"

"After that."

For one foolish second, I hoped his next words had something to do with the two of us going to a concert. Or sharing a picnic on the beach. But that couldn't be it. "I'm guessing you're going to learn how to actually repair a boat engine," I said.

"You got it." He leaned back against the bench and closed his eyes.

I knew it was super awkward before I opened my mouth, but somehow the words tumbled out anyway. "After we get to shore, maybe we could . . . I don't know . . . Maybe Blue Dolphin Charters can take you snorkeling at one of the reefs. And your family, of course. You know. Gratis. For free. On the house."

Ben must have heard something in my voice, because when he opened his eyes, some of the frustration had melted away. "You want to take me snorkeling?"

I mumbled through an incoherent response—something about how it wasn't *me* taking him, but the charter, although I would be there. Thank God Captain Phil wandered over, stinking of alcohol. For once in my life, I was happy to see him.

He handed Candy a bottle of water. "Share."

"You think they'll send a plane for us at night?" she asked him.

"Nope," Phil said.

"In the morning then?"

"Could be." And he disappeared.

44

Candy watched him go. "Your captain talks like words cost money."

The sun had sunk too low to do much but cast shadows, so Candy fished a Bic lighter out of her pack of cigarettes and held it above the engine while she and Ben gave it one more try. I sat nearby, on a beach towel, and wondered what I would have been like if I hadn't been homeschooled.

I glanced up at the roof deck to check on Felix. Mom had stationed herself at the railing, like one of those sea captains from a hundred years ago watching for ships or storms. You only see her for thirty minutes a week through bulletproof glass, but she's still got the muscle tone that comes from lifting tanks and equipment every day. Makes her look young and athletic and nowhere near fifty. She held an unused flare in one hand, her gaze set landward. Her arm was slung around Felix, who'd forgotten he wasn't "little" and was leaning into her. One hand gripped the edge of her rash guard as if afraid she'd disappear if he let go.

Praying for boat lights, both of them.

The faint glow of the Bic disappeared. "Ugh," Candy said. "My fingers hurt. That's it. I'm done." She pulled out a cigarette and lit it. "Do you mind?"

I shook my head and closed the engine hatch.

Candy lay on her back by the engine hatch and smoked, and Ben and I sat across from each other on the benches. We kept the silence for a while, listening to the waves and the murmur of conversation drifting over from the *Ruby Pelican*. It held at least two-thirds of the crew and passengers now. Turns out nothing clears a boat like a dead body.

"The Coast Guard will find us in the morning," Ben said suddenly, but I got the feeling he was saying it more to reassure himself than me. "I mean, we're only ten miles off shore. It's not like we're in the middle of nowhere."

"Oh, yeah. Of course."

"And we're smart people." He tapped the hard edge of the bench frenetically. "Put our brain power together, we can find a way home."

"Sure," Candy said, leaning against the far side of the boat, taking a deep drag. "I am soooo glad I didn't use up my lighter."

"This ever happen before?" Ben asked.

"Not to me," I said.

Candy flicked ash into the waves. "I mean, it would suck to be trapped out here with a pack of cigs and no fire."

We watched the sun slip below the waterline, its orange glow lighting up the horizon in usual, spectacular Florida Keys fashion. Ben had become nothing but a white T-shirt now, his dark skin and hair blending into the shadows.

Even though I see a Keys sunset every day, it still knocks the breath out of me, and in a wonderful way. And any other night, watching this would've had my heart racing with excitement, because sunset on the water means the same thing to me that it does to you.

"Night dive," I said, mostly because the silence was getting to me. "It's what I'd be doing on a normal night. Watch the sun set. Help Mom play tour guide."

Candy threw the last of her cigarette over the side. "Isn't that scary? Diving in the dark?"

"Nah, the night shift is the best," I said, the scuba talk taking the edge off my shyness.

"Why?" Ben asked.

"You know, the day shift's clocked out—the snapper and

yellow tail, the barracuda that hang above the reef," I said. "In come the lobsters and the other night creatures. A completely different dive. So awesome."

"Sharks, eels, and more sharks," Candy said. "That sounds really fun. Girl, are you nuts?"

"It's not dangerous. Not really."

Candy shivered a little. "No freakin' way. Couldn't do it."

I lay back on the bench and looked up at the stars, so bright the Milky Way was a clear band across the sky. "It's like floating in space."

"You going to study marine biology or something when you get to college?" Ben asked.

"Not going," I said, twirling the end of my braid between my thumb and index finger.

The shocked silence that came back at me was no surprise. I'd heard it before.

"What are you going to do, then?" Candy asked, trying to keep her tone neutral and failing.

"I'm going to run a charter with my family. But not here. In Fiji."

"Fiji, huh?" Candy seemed impressed.

"Yeah, Fiji. But I have to wait until Dad gets paroled."

More shocked silence. I don't know why I told them about you, because it always cools off a conversation. I guess pretending isn't comfortable for me. Or for you. Mom has the corner on that.

"Oh, okay," Ben finally said. "Cool. Family business."

I watched his profile for a bit, wishing I could rewind and start over, not bring you up at all. The best I could do was change the subject. "Why aren't you two over there with Teague and the others? Doesn't the blue tarp"—I pointed to the shadow under the sunshade—"freak you out?" I had stopped thinking of him as Mr. Marshall a few hours ago. Now he was just "the blue tarp," which somehow made it easier.

"Not really," Ben said. "I can't handle crowds. I'm claustrophobic."

Candy huffed a laugh. "No, you're not."

Ben gave her a loaded look. I gave him a questioning one. Then he sighed. "Fine. My ex-girlfriend is over there."

It was my turn to laugh, but I cut it off when Ben gave me a sharp glance.

"That bad, huh?" I asked.

"I don't want to talk about it."

A voice floated over the water from the *Ruby Pelican*. "I can hear you, Ben."

Candy stifled her giggle.

"You'd really rather be around the blue tarp than your ex-girlfriend?" I asked.

"Yep."

Candy fished another cigarette out of her pack. "His parents own a funeral home. He sees dead people all the time."

Somehow that surprised me more than our electrical equipment going out all at once. I'd never met anyone whose parents buried people. Or burned them to ash to put them into an urn. "You're kidding," I said, and then realized I sounded like a jerk, as if what his parents did was creepy—which it was—but I knew, even with my homeschooled social skills, that I had no business saying so.

"That wouldn't be a very funny joke," he said. Not defensive. Matter-of-fact, as if he'd gotten tired of digs at his parents' chosen careers long ago.

I lay back on the bench, watching the stars and thinking about funeral homes and the blue tarp while Candy finished her cigarette. I wondered what that was like for Ben, having death woven into your workday, wondered if it seeped into your shut-eye. Half my dreams were about coral reefs and the inside of sunken ships.

I searched for a topic of conversation, something a cool girl would say. I came up with zip. So instead I put my foot in my mouth.

"Do you help your parents sometimes?" I asked.

"You mean, in the office?"

"No."

"Then where?"

He knew where, but he was going to make me say it. "In the basement, where the bodies are."

"We don't have a basement. And yes, I help out sometimes."

I sat up and leaned against the side of the *Last Chance* and looked out over the water. The moon hung high above us, its light caught on the tips of the waves for miles until the sea gave way to sky. The weird stink that had hung over the boat earlier was gone, and the world smelled good and clean, like salt and brine.

"Does it bother you?" I asked.

"Does what bother me?"

"You know, does it seem weird sometimes, doing your homework and then being called downstairs for 'chores.'" I made air quotes he couldn't see.

"You know what's weird?" he said, his gaze still on the sky. "Pretending we're not going to end up in an undertaker's office once day."

"Good point, I guess."

"You ever wonder about it?"

"Death?"

"No. Wonder who will put you in the last dress you'll ever wear."

A voice came floating over the water from Matt's boat. "Enough, Ben." It sounded like a teacher's voice. "You're freaking everybody out. Things are bad enough without—"

"All right, all right," Ben said, raising his voice. In a lower tone, he said, "That's Mrs. Barnes, our teacher. She's a little sensitive."

Mrs. Barnes spoke again. "The Coast Guard will be here in the morning. Just get some sleep. No more death talk!"

After I'd gotten ready to sleep as best I could—rinsing my mouth out with seawater instead of brushing my teeth, rubbing a beach towel over my face to "wash" the sunscreen off, and undoing the tie to my bikini top so the knot didn't bite into my neck all night, I lay flat on my back. Like a body in the morgue. I turned onto my side, even though it was uncomfortable on my hip.

The clogged drain smell returned, drifting on the ocean breeze. Candy groaned and pinched her nose closed. I tried breathing shallow and through my mouth, but then I could taste it. All those particles clinging to my tongue. The blue tarp, which the darkness made worse, lay only five feet away. So I kept my focus on the east and the moon that had appeared just after sunset, hovering far out to sea. I imagined all the people in the Bahamas, who were lying under the same moon, and wondered if they'd gotten any of the messages Matt had been sending out all day. I wondered about you, if you could see the moon through the little window in your cell.

I closed my eyes. I wouldn't choose a flowered dress for my last outfit, which is exactly what Mom would pick for me. When I die, I want to be buried in neoprene, the O'Brien wetsuit you got me for Christmas.

I guess even then a part of me knew I wouldn't be coming home. That something was happening to me, that I hadn't come out of the USS *Andrews* the same as I had gone in.

I'VE BEEN AVOIDING THIS PART, because it's so hard to write. But I promised you a full account. The nightmare I saw in the ship, the horrible thing that killed Marshall, the creature that now defines who I am and what I want in the darkest corners of myself . . .

It came for us at sunrise.

I woke from a half sleep, a few fragments of a dream about you and me and Grandmother still floating through my mind. Your faces faded, gave way to the sound of girls talking, voices drifting over from Matt's charter. They were whispering about water. *How much can we have? Should we say anything?*

I lay on my back on the hard bench, trying not to listen and failing.

Are you thirsty? I'm thirsty. Do you want your ration?

Someone near the captain's chair of Matt's boat said she could have his if she shut up and let him sleep.

I watched the sky gray and tried to think of something happy. Family beach barbeques, like the time you cooked an entire freakin' lamb on a spit and we shared it with half of Key Largo. Or the day the seas were too rough for the tourists, and Mom and I blew off cleaning equipment and hit the dollar theater. Or, even better, weekends with Grandmother in her little apartment back in Tarpon Springs, when we'd drink tea and watch the sailors unload the sponges from their boats.

But my head kept going dark.

Yiayia and me, sitting by her front window, waiting for the sunset. When she told me a secret, about what it was like when she was little, during the war. How all of Greece went to hell and stayed there for a while. How everyone on her little island got along at first. They shared. Gave each other comfort. Then the bombs kept falling, and the food ran out. My grandmother told me once that humans were great actors, putting on their civilization suits for everyday wear in the cities and for church functions. Put them under God's thumb for a bit, and watch those suits come off.

She never gave me the same details she gave you. I mean, I was *nine* when she told me how the Germans took over Kalymnos, how the Allies bombed it for months and months, and I think she skipped the worst bits. But there was this look. A shiny sort of fear in her eyes, as if she'd pulled a big, ugly seed out of her brain, and it was sprouting in her as I watched, as it had been for the last sixty-four years.

So I thought of Yiayia's stories about water and food and civilization suits. Oh God, I thought. Twenty-five people on our two boats. Enough water to last until noon. And no Coast Guard in sight. For a good five seconds, I thought about hiding a bottle or two for me and Felix and Mom. A hot wave of shame followed.

I got up. Wiped my eyes. The sun was gorgeous, laying its eggs all over the sunrise. Every egg bursting into flight just after it touched down. Orange, yellow, a slow burn of the sky-sea.

Slosh. Slosh. Pop. I was restless, so I stood and straightened some gear, adjusted the bungees that kept the tanks in place, and folded a beach towel lying on the bench.

Ben sat by the engine, twirling a pencil over his knuckles as he watched a small flock of birds floating a little ways off. Candy lay curled up on one side, a burned-out cigarette between her index and middle finger. Phil hunched in the captain's chair, holding court over nothing. I retied the string on my bikini top, tight. Phil was weird, and he was new, and as soon as I got home, I was going to ask Mom to fire him. That felt good, thinking about what I'd do when I got home rather than what I'd do if the Coast Guard didn't show up. And for once I wasn't thinking about what I saw yesterday in the USS *Andrews*. My fear had gone deep and quiet.

Mom was standing at the rear of the boat, her back to me, a silhouette against the rising run.

She swore quietly.

"What's wrong?"

She gestured to the ocean in a throwaway motion. "I left a tank and a reg at a safety stop."

Ben's voice rose from just behind us. "What's a safety stop?" He turned to me, still spinning the pencil, his eyes curious. I got the feeling that was his default setting: curious.

"Before a deep dive," she told him, "we hook a tank and regulator on a rope fifteen feet under the surface. If someone screws up and stays down too long, they can hang out at the safety stop and decompress without worrying about running out of air."

Ben mulled that over a second. "What happens if you don't decompress?"

"Nitrogen bubbles in your brain."

Ben turned his attention back to the birds, away from me. "Nice hobby you got there."

I picked up my wet suit and put a foot in.

"No, Tasia," Mom said. "I'll go."

"Mom, I can't sleep. And I'm bored out of my mind. You stay with Felix." I nodded to the roof, where he was still sleeping peacefully. "He's scared."

"He's asleep."

"No one really slept last night."

"Have you met your brother? That boy snored through the last hurricane."

"I'll get it. No big deal."

I tied my hair back, grabbed my tank, and suited up. Mom looked like she was going to stop me but instead turned and disappeared onto the roof deck. "Don't be long," she called over her shoulder.

Ben side-eyed me. "Aren't you supposed to go with a buddy?"

I attached my regulator to the tank valve and screwed it on tight. "Sometimes it's not practical. Besides, I've been diving three times a day, six days a week, since I was fifteen years old. I know what I'm doing."

"No high school student has enough time to do all that. You'd die of exhaustion."

"Mom pulled me out of school freshman year to help her on the boat after Dad . . ." I tightened a strap, even though it was already fine. "After he couldn't help anymore. I do the homeschooling thing at night. Gives me plenty of time."

"Is that even legal?" he asked.

I shrugged.

Understanding lit his eyes, or maybe it was pity. Ben followed me with his gaze as I made my way to the stern. "Anyway, it doesn't sound safe, what you're doing."

"Somebody drops a fin over the side, and you want two people to suit up to get it?"

"Yeah, actually."

I ignored him and slipped my mask over my eyes.

Three years ago, right before your big exit, you talked me into that midnight dive on the reef. *It'll be like floating in space, Peanut, but with our lights, we'll become the stars.* Maybe it's why I love diving in the dark, or the near dark, the sun slowly staining the waters red. Every time I descend into the black water, with my body hanging over hundreds of feet of nothing like a girl drifting on the dark side of the moon, you're there with me.

I took a giant stride off the platform. The world shifted, became a rush of bubbles. The cold slipped into my wet suit and soaked my rash guard and bikini.

I made the okay sign. Mom waved from the roof deck. Her skin glowed rosy in the dawn light, her shoulders back and proud, her gaze set west, toward land. It's one of my last, best memories of her.

I swam for the white buoy that marked the descent line. The surface of the ocean slapped the side of my head, rippled over my faceplate. And when the sense of unease hit me, the one I'd had the day before in the USS *Andrews*, I brushed it away. Mom was right, I thought. I'd seen nothing but a dream in that ship, a floating, horrific dream that leapt out of my unconscious like a slippery fish. Narced. Imagining things.

I reached the buoy. Purged my BC. The air burbled out of the valves and I sank.

Immediate relief. Nobody tells you how boring it is, being stranded.

Above my head, the early morning light skimmed the surface of the waves. Beneath my fins, the world inked out. I pointed my dive light down, past my feet into the blackness, and sank slowly. Like floating in space.

Fifteen feet down on the ship line, the safety stop gear came into view; a bright pink tank, the reg out of its bungee and hanging loose, pulled sideways by the current. I slipped off my gloves and tucked them into a pocket on my BC. If I could have, I would've lip synced to the Vanessa Peters song playing in my head. That's how much I wasn't thinking about what swam just outside my circle of light.

Untying the knot was awkward while holding the dive light in one hand and kicking against the drag of the current. The light kept falling from my fingers. Dangling from my wrist. Sweeping the depths like a crazy searchlight. I finally took out my reg, held my breath, and stuck the end of my light into my mouth. I've been practicing since you went away, and I can hold my breath for almost two minutes, a few seconds shy of my grandmother's record.

As soon as I pulled the last of the knot free, I should've been satisfied. Headed to the surface. Instead I froze, hanging on the rope like a barnacle.

A prickle on my neck, a brush of current. A sixth sense just outside the poor reach of my dive light. Something was watching me.

I shoved my reg back into my mouth. Then I swam in a circle around the ship line, forgetting about the gear in my hand. My light showed nothing but particles. They glowed under the beam, and then the current swept them away.

I pointed the light down and waited, fins limp. My body

adrift. The cold air dried out my throat. I knew it was dangerous, Dad, I did. I should've surfaced and swam like Michael Phelps to the boat. But like you, I always feel a little pulse inside me that says, *Look*.

Better to be eaten head first, Peanut.

The dive light sliced the dark open. Then a gray torpedo slid through the beam.

I dropped the tank. It plummeted into the depths. My hand caught the rope out of instinct and the tank jerked to a stop. Pulled me off center. The dive light swung in an arc, scanning the depths. My eyes widened until they felt stretched behind my mask.

Gray skin. I checked below again and replayed your lessons. *You're more likely to be struck by lightning on your way to Starbucks than you are to be eaten in the big blue.* But I was alone. It was dark. There was a lot of water beyond the reach of a dive light.

I stayed a moment longer, moving my fins slowly against the current, forcing myself to take stock. Sharks don't want to eat people, I reminded myself. It's always a mistake when they bite. This one wouldn't want 120 pounds of girl covered in a neoprene casing. No way. I fire hosed my dive light around below.

I barely registered the next flash of gray before it hit me. Right in my shoulder. The world flipped on its side, filled with bubbles. I dropped the tank line. The regulator fell from my mouth. A tail as big as my torso swished past.

I shoved the reg back in and bolted for the surface, a panicked bubble in my chest spreading out into my legs, my fins. My head broke the top of a wave. The *Last Chance* came into view thirty feet away. Mom waved at me. Out of habit, I okayed with a fist on my head.

But I wasn't okay.

I swam in a rush for the boat. So exposed, dangling down into the water, closest to whatever was under me. My flesh covered with next to nothing.

A wave splashed across my mask. The world blurred, the boat tipped. The ladder bobbed in the waves twenty feet away. Too far. I was small, weak.

I was food.

I DON'T REMEMBER MUCH from that swim. At least I don't remember moving my legs and arms. I only remember the boat. Fifteen feet away. Then ten. Five. The waves pushing it up like a kid on a seesaw. The red lettering of the *Last Chance* tilting, crashing down.

I reached for the ladder, and something brushed my leg. I cried out, the regulator tumbling from my mouth. A three-foot swell drew the boat up and out of my grip.

I finally grabbed the first rung. Fumbled my fins off and let them fall. A final burst of adrenaline pushed me up the rungs, and I tumbled onto the dive platform and coughed on a lungful of real air.

"You okay?"

I turned to find Mom looking at me as if I'd lost my mind. She raised a bunch of grapes to her mouth and bit one off.

I pulled off my mask and tossed it onto the bench with a clatter. "I dropped the safety stop gear. And my fins."

She stopped chewing. "*All* of it?"

"It was all tethered together."

"What were you thinking, Tasia?"

I started to tell her what happened. And then I realized I had an audience. Candy stood a few feet behind Mom, wrapped in a beach towel, and Ben lay on his side on the scuba bench, propped up on one elbow. Teague, the Bermuda Triangle theory guy, was sprawled out in the captain's chair, one leg over the arm, craning his neck to get a better look. A crowd had formed on the roof deck.

I felt stupid as I said it but did anyway.

"There's something in the water."

Mom turned her back to me, leaning over to peer into the waves, but I'd already caught the shift in her expression, the disappointment. "There's always something in the water. It's why we dive." She took a deep breath, trying to control her temper. "You lost seven hundred dollars worth of gear."

A murmur rose from the boat next to ours.

"Shark!" a girl on the roof deck shouted, and the others laughed.

But she wasn't kidding. There it was, that gorgeous dorsal fin cutting the water like a hot knife.

Mom rushed to the port side. I pulled myself up to a bench to undo my gear, but my numb fingers wouldn't work the release. So I just sat there with my tank growing heavier by the minute and tried to calm down. And you know how Mom is. How she's changed in the last few years. She wasn't about to take it back, not even after seeing what circled our boat. Because I'd dropped the gear. Seven hundred dollars of Mom's—my—hard-earned money, flushed down the big ocean toilet.

Candy held her hand over her mouth, her eyes wide. "*That* was in the water with you?"

"He was just being a little friendly," I said. "I shouldn't have freaked out."

Ben, Teague, and Candy crowded the bench, their eyes lighting up with wonder and fear. "Whoa," Teague said. "This is so much better than Shark Week."

Our morning visitor swam an arm's reach from me, measuring us. Dorsal fin to tail, it had to be at least twelve feet long. It circled the bow and made its way down the narrow alley between the *Last Chance* and the *Ruby Pelican*.

"What kind is it?" Candy asked.

"Probably a tiger shark," Teague said, and I hated that he got it right.

"The ones that eat surfers?" Candy asked.

"Don't sound so jazzed about it," Ben said. But it was in his voice too. The excitement.

You and me, we've seen it a hundred times. People eating it up, the idea of the evil shark hunting humans with a malevolence usually reserved for serial killers and haunted clown dolls. But you know what I know: When it comes to sheer carnage, sharks have nothing on cars. Or guns. These rubberneckers, they sit in their living rooms watching Shark Week, gripping the armrests, while just outside, they've got a death trap parked in the driveway. A few feet away, in the bedroom closet, there's a loaded gun under a pile of sweatshirts. And there they are, watching the nature channel and saying, *Uh-uh, no way I'm going into the water.*

Bunch of idiots.

"Okay, guys," I said, leaning my head back against my tank. "Enjoy your shark porn."

I tried to slip out of my gear, but my hands shook, and the release at my waist was really jammed, damaged when I slammed against the ladder. I gave up, exhausted, and watched the top of the food chain swim on by.

The tiger rounded the bow of our boat and disappeared, then popped back up on the port side. Something about the way it moved caught my attention. Swimming in jagged patterns, jerky and fearful. Not at all the way sharks act.

Captain Phil stood on the sunroof, watching, still wearing that purple stone wife beater, which now had wide, dark pit stains. Mom climbed the ladder back to the roof to wake Felix from his pile of beach towels, leaning close to his ear to give the science lesson, pointing at the show. He smiled wide and leaned over the railing.

I closed my eyes, thought about what Felix and I would do when we got home, and how maybe I'd use tip money from yesterday's dive to take him for milkshakes at Amy's Cafe, let him ask his big sister little kid questions about sharks. And I remembered something you showed me in a magazine once, the images of a surfer's leg. The creepy indentation where it had healed up without a pound of flesh. How you closed the magazine when Felix toddled by, showed him the picture of the clown fish instead. That's become my job since you went away—flipping the page to show him beautiful things, hiding the ugly bits.

Out of the corner of my eye, I caught movement. The water buckled a few yards from our engine. As if something large pushed from below. Before I could turn toward it and see it full on, it was gone. My imagination, I told myself.

More shouts from Matt's charter. The girls who'd been suntanning yesterday were huddled together on the roof—scared and loving it.

Slosh, thunk. Against the hull. Driftwood, I thought. Or sea trash. Something that fell off a container ship ten thousand miles away riding the currents toward our shores. *Slosh.* But for some reason my body didn't believe it. Adrenaline kicked in as I searched the water for the source.

The tether between Matt's boat and ours tightened and groaned.

The sun slanted its light over the water. The waves slapped the boat. The passengers on the *Ruby Pelican* and the *Last Chance* watched the tiger circle. The line groaned again. *Splash*. Some doofus had thrown a Coke can and pegged the dorsal fin.

An odd instinct in me rose, like bubbles from a regulator, telling me we were all dead. Sudden and irrational, hitting me hard, like the shark had earlier, knocking me off balance. I struggled to get the tank off my back, fighting with the stubborn release.

One of the girls on the *Ruby Pelican* called out, "Look!"

The tail of the shark flailed in the water.

Teague stood near Ben and watched it writhe and thrash. "It's eating something," he said.

Next to the stern ladder, a ridge appeared in the water, and I stopped fiddling with the releases on my BC. Something moving just below, pushing up the top layer. A faint glow pulsing in dim morning light. Green. Phosphorescent.

The feeling of unease, the thing that had dogged me since we dropped our anchor here, that's when it opened up. I saw what was inside. Just for a second. And it was ugly, and terrifying, and inside my chest hard as stone roots. I couldn't breathe for a full ten seconds. So I leaned against my tank, gripping my knees until my knuckles turned white.

Wrong. All of it. My body felt light. Another weird thought hit me—I'd left some important part of myself in the wreck. Or worse, brought something up with me.

A cry from Matt's ship. The shark had stalled in the channel between the boats, thrashing its long gray body in a frenzy. The sun slanted rays on it. A cloud of blood bloomed in the water.

Teague stepped up next to me and leaned over the side to get a better look. "What's it doing?"

Something thick wrapped around the shark's massive body. A clear rope of some kind, cutting into it. My first thoughts were seaweed, then tentacles, both wrong. Two more strands wrapped around it, one around the shark's jaws, near its gills. More blood. And then, before any of us realized what was happening, the cords pulled the tiger shark down. Pulled deep until the gray of its skin faded into black and it disappeared entirely.

A shocked silence settled over both boats.

Movement again, to my left, near our dive platform. A flash of something whitish gray. I turned, and in my memory, that turn took forever. My gaze had been fixed on the red cloud in the water, and then I pivoted toward the little flash of gray-white, past the silver cleat on the gunwale, past the ice chest near the stern. The smell of a clogged drain drifting through the scent of sea brine hit me before I could focus on what it was.

As thick as a rat snake, but almost see-through, its tip rose from the water and reached across the diving platform. Three more came with it, long and thin, like filaments of a jellyfish, trembling pink as the light of the rising sun hit them. Past the ice chest, the silver cleat. The moment I screamed, the thick one whipped up and wrapped around Teague's thigh.

He cried out, high-pitched, as the thing yanked his feet out from under him. I stepped back, my gear throwing me off balance. I fell. My head slammed into my tank, stars exploded in my vision, and the world flipped. Teague flailed out, his fingers scrabbling across the slick deck before grabbing on to my head, my hair, and then my gear, my face. Yells came from all around me. Ben. Candy. A thunder of feet on the roof deck.

Teague screamed again, and I slid with him, gliding across the slick fiberglass deck. Toward the water. Toward the thicker part of the root snaking out of the water to take whatever it could. Hands clung to my tank, my hair. I caught the edge of the bench, but my wet neoprene greased right over. Someone grabbed my arms to keep me from going over, but Teague held on, screaming. My shoulder popped, and I cried out. Pulling me apart, I remember thinking, until I'm in pieces.

Candy dug her fingers around the tentacle and the filaments circling Teague's thigh. Then she jerked her hands back as if she'd been burned.

Teague and I slid another foot and slammed against the edge of a bench.

And he screamed, the same thing over and over. *"Pull it off!"*

I couldn't get enough air. The world blurred into a panic of high-pitched voices and pain in my shoulders as my rescuers pulled me apart.

Another tentacle, wrist thick, whipped out of the water and wrapped around his waist. Three filaments followed. Tightened. His eyes went wide, and he stopped screaming. The hand he'd threaded into my long hair tightened, and God, the white-hot pain as a fistful came out by the roots. Out of instinct, I grabbed for his T-shirt. Mom rushed past me, catching his wrist. He slipped to the edge of the platform. My grasp slipped, and he tumbled over the side.

And he was gone.

Mom pulled me back from the platform, asked me something, but the words jumbled and reeled, made no sense. Choices spun through my head. Hide down below. Hide on the roof deck. Get away from the ocean. A scream echoed across the narrow alley of water between our boat and Matt's. The scream multiplied, and then all sixteen of the passengers on the *Ruby Pelican* rushed to the side closest to us, away from something we couldn't see. Their boat tipped dangerously. One of the girls got an elbow in the face and fell overboard. She treaded water for a second and disappeared.

More tendrils snaked over the side of the *Last Chance* and grabbed the girl next to me. A gray tentacle slipped around her head. A crawling mass of filaments followed. She jerked and stumbled. A red welt appeared on her neck, her cheek, eyes impossibly wide, head tipped back as if she were searching the clouds. I remember reaching out for her. A pop, and blood sprayed the deck, the water, and me. I stumbled and fell again. Struggled, trying to wrestle myself out of a thirty-pound alba- tross slowing me down.

A cry filtered down from the roof deck. Felix. Another whip rose from the water and slid up the side, where my brother stood. Ten cups of coffee in my bloodstream, all at once.

Before I could get to him, Mom rushed for the ladder. I'd never make it up with the tank on my back, so I went for the spear gun instead, the one Phil kept cinched to the wall. It wasn't there. I grabbed the orange case attached to a bracket under his seat, thinking maybe a flare gun could wound it, burn it. Then I remembered the gas can. We'd left it by the captain's chair the night before.

More panicked cries, and I was half aware of screaming com- ing from the *Ruby Pelican* before an unnatural wave tipped the *Last Chance*. I stumbled toward the back of the boat, hands shak- ing so bad I fumbled with the latch on the case.

Splash. Another overboard. Someone I didn't know. A

horrible feeling welled up. Gratitude, that it was them and not me. Not Felix. And maybe the thing swimming beneath us was full now.

Candy grabbed my arm, her eyes full of helplessness and panic. "Sia! What—"

"The gas can! Dump all of it over the side!" I pulled at the latch of the flare gun case, but it didn't budge.

As she stepped toward the gas can, a tendril as thick as my calf snaked up and over the gunwale and wrapped around her waist. She flew backward and plummeted into the waves. Cried my name once before she disappeared.

A few seconds later Ben was in Candy's place, dumping the gas into the water.

A flash of silver zipped by, coming from the roof. Mom, with a spear gun, reloading. Felix held on to her thigh. The spear disappeared into the murk, uselessly passing by whatever horrible thing spread out beneath us.

I worked the latch on the flare gun case, digging my water-soft fingernails under the plastic as Ben dropped the now-empty fuel can into the water. The cries from the other boat cascaded around me. I didn't want to look. But I did, for one horrible second. A dozen tentacles and a thousand filaments snaked up the sides, cradling the *Ruby Pelican* like a bath toy.

Ben wrenched the flare gun case from me and smashed the latch against a cleat twice. The gun spilled onto the floor and I grabbed it. Fumbled a shell into the chamber just as Ben cried out, a filament wrapping around his thigh, slicing through the skin.

I should've grabbed my dive knife. Cut through the rat snake and set him free. But I didn't have time.

The slick of gasoline over the water shimmered in the rising sun. I tilted the gun up, hoping the flare had enough time to catch fire before it hit the water, praying I would hit the slowly widening patch of fuel. I didn't think about the consequences of what I was doing. Fire. Boats made of wood. People made of flesh. I just pulled the trigger.

I watched it arc slowly, then drop into the waves.

The world around us erupted into heat and fire. The sea buckled as something enormous thrashed beneath, its writhing rising high above the flames. I caught a horrific glimpse of an eye, huge and unblinking, through the orange glow.

And then the sky tipped as our boat capsized and the world went dark.

FLAMES. That's what burned through my mind when I woke on the shores of the island.

Rough, wet sand on my face. The other side baked in the high noon sun. My body felt stretched and snapped back into place. Everything ached. My fingers tingled. My eyes felt full. Ready to burst.

I pushed myself up to a sitting position, and the world swam. My arms wouldn't lie flat against my sides, and I looked down to find I still wore the inflated BC. A small part of my brain registered that's why I wasn't at the bottom of the ocean.

The rest of me was just thirsty.

I struggled with the clasp on my gear for five minutes before I finally broke the stupid thing with a rock and slid the heavy tank from my back.

I sat for a bit, watching the blue sky, water moving, rolling, waves cresting and falling. God. I closed my eyes at the nausea. My throat stretched like a rubber band. The flames leapt up in my mind again. And the eye of that thing, looking at me through the glow.

I listened to the surf crash and tried to remember. So hazy. I remembered shooting the flare into the water. The fire spreading, people screaming, and my last thought, before we capsized.

Felix.

I stood in a rush of memory and scanned the beach for him. I searched the water for him, for his small head bobbing in the waves, terrified I would have to see my brother pulled under by whatever had destroyed our boat. But there was nobody out there.

I was alone.

When things get bad, we tell ourselves all kinds of things to stay sane. You do it too, I'm sure, lying on your bunk, staring at the stains on the ceiling of your cell. You tell yourself that everything will be okay, and the people you love are alive and well. On the other side of the island, I remember thinking. They're on the other side, waiting for me. So I started walking.

I made my way down the beach. The island, which I could swear didn't exist on any of our maps, stretched out for a mile in both directions, its coves smooth white sand, studded with shells and stones and an occasional boulder of black rock. Ten feet up from the water lay a dark line of seaweed from high tide. Another forty feet back, the palm trees began. The gaps between trunks were eaten up by shadows. This will sound totally irrational, but the shadows *watched* me trudge through the sand, like they were alive or something. I tried to make sense of that feeling, but then the thirst hit again, and I couldn't think about anything else.

When the sweat made the inside of my wet suit slick, I peeled it off and left it in the dunes. The rash guard kept my torso and arms from cooking, but the bikini bottoms did nothing to protect my legs. My shoulder ached, a reminder of how close I had come to slipping over the side of the *Last Chance* and joining Teague and Candy and all the others.

I walked for a long time.

Mom. I had to find her. Felix. Where was he? Around the

next curve? Maybe Ben, Candy, and Teague made it here. And then I remembered what happened to two of them. But Ben? He could've made it. And Captain Phil? An ugly part of me hoped not.

I peered out to sea as I padded barefoot across the wet sand, shading my eyes. The sun bounced off the froth of the whitecaps, glinted across the expanse. No weird ripples or swells like I'd seen just before that thing attacked us. Was it gone?

A quartet of birds, a hair smaller than gulls and whiter than sand, waded in the shallows down the beach, pecking at fiddler crabs. All of it postcard perfect. But there was no tiki hut selling sunscreen here. I swallowed, and my spit tasted thick, like a sprinter's mouth. The thought of water put an ache in me. Oh God, how I wanted it, ice cubes and all.

Forcing myself to go into the shadow of the palm trees, I looked for a stream or a spring or even puddle of rainwater. I stepped over masses of roots, through the cool, moist air trapped beneath that canopy, and got the feeling again I was being watched. Once I thought I saw a shape, a person walking toward me, but I blinked and he was gone. A mirage.

I stumbled back out into the light, emerging at a different spot on the beach, around a curve. I left the thick palms, crunching through the fallen fronds, and the damp scent of that place gave way to salt and seaweed. The sun against the sand was so blinding I almost missed the shape down in the surf.

A white craft. A charter. Forty feet long, blackened up one side, beached and listing starboard.

The *Last Chance*.

"Holy God," I said to no one, and sprinted, kicking up sand. When I reached the side and stopped, I was winded and woozy.

"Mom? Felix?"

No response from the shadows under the canopy. Waves swelled and faded and beat the shore. All around drifted the smell of engine oil and suntan lotion and neoprene wet suits, which were still bungeed to the benches, life-sized dolls with all the bones removed. Tanks too. BCs—most of them had stayed in their tethers.

I searched for water bottles and found none. No food either. I sat beside a tank and ran a hand over one of the tethers. You always taught me to keep the bungees tight so we didn't lose our gear in rough seas. Take care of your gear, you said, take care of yourself. A lot of good it did me, I remember thinking.

I didn't appreciate it then, all the stuff that had made it through. No one does, I guess. Appreciate what's left, I mean, after a storm takes your life and flips it upside down. So I was thinking about all the cell phones and the ice chest full of fruit and the flare gun. Kinda like you, lying in your bunk, missing your ceiling fan and your reggae playlist and your minifridge. But at least you still had us, across town, waiting for you.

Another sound came to me over the waves. At first I thought it was Felix, crying. But a deep breath cut off the sound.

It was me. Crying like I hadn't cried since you went away, huddled in the shade of our ruined charter. And I wasn't crying for the people who'd died that morning, who were dragged screaming into the ocean like fish bits. No, I was too selfish to think of them. I was crying for what I needed most, my family back again, more than water or a rescue. I was crying for Felix. My mother. And you. Always you.

Click.

My eyes snapped open. That sound had a direct line to my

heart. I knew it, from the time you took me into the woods to shoot beer cans.

I inched around. My instincts told me no sudden movements.

A man's shadow blocked the sun, which had dipped a good five feet. It burned a corona around his shape. I squinted, shifted. A Colt pistol in his hand, the kind you first schooled me on, before we moved up to the Glock and the rifle.

The gun shook, barely. That much I could see. Maybe tremors meant he'd lost his nerve. Or maybe it meant he was out of control.

"Hey," the man said. "Get up!"

I didn't.

"Do you speak English?"

"Of course I speak English."

"Well, get up, then. Now."

I rose to my feet, and the corona behind the man with the gun disappeared.

He wasn't so much a man as a boy, around my age if I had to guess. Acne covered both his cheeks—speckled red and faint, like it was just clearing up—where it wasn't covered with a poor attempt at a beard. His dark hair brushed the collar of a dirty white shirt. His eyes were wide-spaced, which gave him a sort of peaceful, farm-boy look, as if he was used to staring out over grain fields instead of holding a gun.

I kept my voice calm. Soothing. "You were on Matt's boat, right? The science trip? I was on the other one. I'm one of the dive masters."

His expression stayed blank.

"Remember? Your boat was going to take our divers out to the reef at the Haystacks"—I spoke slowly as if he had sunstroke, which at the time I thought likely—"because of the accident."

"Yes, I remember the accident," he said, his face hardening. He said *accident* with such venom I would've backed up a step if there hadn't been a boat behind me. We watched each for a good minute, both of us barefoot in the sand, while I figured out what had happened.

I put my hands out, palms up, and he flinched.

I took a step forward. "We're both stuck here, and we both have to get home, so put the gun down."

"Home," the guy said, the gun wavering an inch.

"Yes, home," I said, reaching out to push his gun hand down, toward the sand. He let me, and I exhaled.

"Home," he said, running a palm over his face. "I hadn't considered it." He looked me over again, calculating. Considering something. I had to keep myself from bolting. The look in his eyes . . . I felt like I'd just glimpsed the underside of a rock.

I watched him struggle with himself, as if he didn't want to cry in front of me. Behind him was a long stretch of thick palms, up off the white sand beach. They moved like seaweed caught in a current, and I blinked, because I was imagining the trunks bending, as if they'd been caught in a Category 5 hurricane. And then I blinked again, and they straightened up, like I'd dreamed it.

Dehydration. That's what I thought then, but of course I was wrong. I just didn't know it yet. And I had the weird feeling yet again, that I—no, *we*—were being watched, and I also felt something else. Even if this guy was losing it, at least I wasn't alone anymore.

He tucked the pistol into his waistband. Now that I could focus on something other than a gun in my face, I noticed the stains on his clothes. Patches of soil that must've come from the forest. His shirt used to have sleeves. He'd apparently ripped them off, exposing his broad, wiry shoulders. That shirt had once been white. Pants too.

Despite the full sun, cold rushed through me, and I wanted to sit before I fell down. Because I was wrong about him. He'd been here on the island more than a few hours. He'd been here at least a few weeks. Which meant one thing.

The guy with the gun wasn't from the science trip.

The man-boy took a few steps back in the sand, his gaze on mine, as if he expected me to go for a knife or a bomb or a garrote wire.

He took the gun from his waistband again and waved it at me. "You tell anyone you saw me, and I'll come back. I'll kill your whole family."

And then he turned and walked toward the trees, disappearing like a fish slipping back into the kelp forest, and then into the deep.

YOU WOULD'VE FOLLOWED the mystery guy into the palm trees. He had water, if he'd been here long enough for his clothes to fray and his beard to grow half an inch. You would do what had to be done.

That long summer reading list you made for me last year rose up in my head, full of stories like *The Tempest* and *Moby-Dick* and *Life of Pi*. Always you picked the ocean for me, preparing me for this moment, I guess, although that makes me sound like I believe in fate or something, which I don't. And after seeing the man-boy with the pistol, I couldn't stop thinking about *Lord of the Flies*. And the last thing I wanted was a replay of Piggy and a bloody rock, with me holding the rock.

I decided to find water another way.

I spent the next hour in the palm trees, looking for hydration. The air, once I stepped into the shadows of the forest, dropped fifteen degrees, oddly, as if I'd just entered a basement, the kind old ladies use for roots and mushrooms and other things that shy from the light. The forest floor gave underfoot, as if made of flesh rather than roots and earth. Palm fronds, green with brown edges and some paper-thin ghosts of leaves, lay in drifts against trunks and in hollows made by their thick roots.

This place seemed not so much a forest as a vast cave. I know that sounds strange, but it's what I kept thinking as I tromped around, mouth begging for water.

Water. People describe being thirsty as burning. A burning thirst. But it's so much worse. You aren't thirsty. You *become* thirst. It takes over your whole being, that drive for a cold swallow, the glass beaded with drops snaking down the sides, and yes, you can remember how good it is to drink. The whole glass. And another. So here's my next confession.

After a while I stopped thinking about you. And Felix. And Mom.

It shocked me later, to remember how easily thoughts of my family had been replaced by a single basic need.

After an hour search, I'd found no puddles. The few coconuts I came across broke easily and were black inside. I picked up a shell and dug in a moist spot. Nothing.

By the time I made it across the hot sands and back to the boat, the heat had stretched me thin, and my gums felt like they were pulling away from my teeth. I don't remember being afraid of dying then. Just all the stuff that came before it.

And then I remembered the lessons you taught me on those camping trips. How to start a fire, how to navigate by stars.

How to make fresh water from salt water.

Most of the contents of the charter had been lost when the thing attacked us, but I took stock of what was there. An emergency kit with a penknife, bandages, and Neosporin. Ten wet suits, ten tanks, ten masks, all tethered to the benches. Ten slates with little golf pencils attached. Teague's sopping wet notebook with the snobby sticker on the front, hidden by my clever little brother in a bench seat. Your small plastic toolbox, *Gianopoulos* written with Sharpie across the lid—Mom's catchall for anything she didn't want sliding around the deck—screwdrivers, a hammer, a small box of tampons, and some no-run pens. Underneath it all I found a Tarpon Springs key chain, the one you bought a thousand years ago when we all went up to see Yiayia for one of your "family-togetherness" weekends. The ignition key was useless, and the happy scene on the fob—flip-flops and palm trees—felt like it was making fun of me somehow, so I dropped it into the box and kept searching.

And then I found what I really needed—an empty water bottle wedged between the broken radio and the gunwale.

I used the penknife to saw open the water bottle. I kept the top, in case I found a use for it later. I only needed the bottom half. Once I filled it with seawater and set it inside one of the masks, I put another mask upside down on top of the makeshift cup. Marshall's was the best choice, a crazy-expensive thing that wasn't flat, the glass coming to a point to give him a five-hundred-dollar view. I set it all in the sun, far back from the tide line.

A strip of neoprene I cut from a wet suit served to cover the sides of my contraption. The medical tape held it place and kept the water in, evaporating and beading on the top mask and sliding down the sides to drip, nice and fresh and salt-free, into the bottom mask. In a few hours I would have a glass of desalinated water, courtesy of physics, Mother Nature, and the big ball of fire in the sky.

I sat in the shade of the *Last Chance* and waited.

The sun peaked, burning high above me, and my shade disappeared. The sand gleamed, stretching in either direction for a mile before curving into the palms. The forest shadows were cool, but my body recoiled at the thought of going back in.

Something was wrong with that place. And the guy with the gun . . . Out in the open, I could see him coming. Thirst was bad, but whatever could happen to me in the palm tree cave was worse. Besides, a part of me still believed someone else from the charter had survived. Felix, Mom. Anybody. I was more visible out here on the beach.

After an hour of watching the waves for swells or ripples, wondering if that horrible thing had enough reach to snag my ankle and drag me off the beach, I got up to check my desalinator. Water beaded thickly on the underside of the glass. I prayed it wouldn't drip back into the saltwater cup, so I watched it, the sun beating the back of my head, until a drop finally rolled to the lowest point and dripped. So beautiful, this small miracle. At this rate it would take several hours, but I would eventually have enough to keep me alive.

I marked the time with a stick in the sand. After two hours, I'd stopped sweating, which was a bad sign. Staying visible on the beach no longer seemed important, so I lay on the deck of the *Last Chance* under the sun shade, tilted, and listened to wave song. Breathed in the salt breeze. Tried not to die.

The third time I got up to check the water, my head throbbed. *Drip.*

One bead at a time.

Drip.

I couldn't wait any longer. I peeled it back and drank it all, a little less than a tablespoon. I topped off the cup with seawater and reassembled it. I returned to the shade.

Three hours, staring out into the big blue and waiting.

This time when I got up to check, my joints ached. The heat and dehydration working against me. I rounded the stern and stopped. There was a bird that favored one leg standing next to the mask and container, pecking at the glass.

"Hey!" I tried to run, but my legs gave out. I struggled to sit up, and the world tipped. I threw a handful of sand and seashells at him. "Get away from that!"

The bird hopped away and side-eyed me, then ducked its head and edged toward it again, holding one foot off the hot sand, and I noticed it was missing a toe. I got to my feet and made my way toward the desalinator, swaying like a drunk girl. The bird blurred. "Touch that and you're my next meal."

It took off in a flurry of white feathers. I knelt beside the mask to inspect the damage. Thank God, the neoprene strip was still intact.

I forced myself to leave the thin layer of water that coated the glass—not near enough—and returned to lie in the cool sand on the other side of the boat, where shade had appeared as the sun sank.

Four hours. My mind felt foggy. I forgot about keeping an eye out for my feathered friend and watched the ocean, the bits of seaweed floating in the white froth. The world smelled of salt, and suddenly I was with my grandmother again, learning to swim on the beaches near the sponge docks.

I could even *see* her, as real as the sand or the waves or the burning hot sun. Yiayia stood in the surf, dropping her silver stopwatch into my little palm. I remembered how it felt seeing her disappear beneath the waves, hair trailing out and mixing with foam and seaweed. The awe and terror of that moment, when a part of me thought she wouldn't come back.

It was always my job to keep my eye on the second hand, and once the silver needle had rounded the face twice, she'd pop up, wave at me, and yell, "Your turn!" I'd toss the stopwatch onto the beach and dive into the waves headfirst, then hold my breath for a whopping ten seconds before sputtering to the surface.

You don't remember this—you were working one of those live-aboard dive charters, the kind that took you away for a month at a time—but I reached the one-minute mark right after I turned twelve, just before Epiphany. Afterward Yiayia and I sat in her window overlooking the sponge docks, celebrated with mountain tea and her famous braided cookies. She talked about what life was like back before the war, back on Kalymnos, when her dad worked the sponge fleets. Gone for months, like you. How much she missed him and wished on stars that he would come home and never leave again.

And he did come home. Men from the sponge fleet came, carried him into the house and laid him out on his bed. He'd stayed down on the bottom too long, they told her. What my grandmother called "the sickness" had taken the use of his legs. She said every family on the island had lost someone that way, or had come back with pain they couldn't shake, or a limp that kept them from work. That's when she stopped wishing on stars, she said. And she swore she would never dive with anything except her own breath.

I remember covering my ears and telling her to stop. You were so far away, living life underwater. Yiayia pulled me against her, said she was sorry. You'd be home soon. You'd be okay.

A week later, just before she died, Yiayia told me something I'll never forget, sitting with me watching the fishermen come into the harbor at sunset, with their piles of sponges. She said that when people died, their spirit left not from the heart or the brain, but the lungs. One exhalation of breath, and their whole selves slipped out. "Not a bad way to go," she said.

I sat beside the *Last Chance* eying the small buoy in the distance, the one that marked the USS *Andrews*, and thought about my grandmother and all her talk about breath. The thought of Felix slipping under the surface, that hot coal of want burning beneath his sternum until he drowned . . . that horrible thought punched right through the thirst, and at that moment—but for only a moment—I wanted to see him more than I wanted water.

Five hours. My tongue was dry as old leather. My body ached, and my mind felt slow. And I was pretty sure I smelled. Like a rotting barnacle. I laughed to myself then, wondering what Yiayia would say if she could see me, breathing like a fish out of water here on the sand.

Six hours. The sun dipped low above the palm trees. The glare off the beach dimmed. When I stood to walk to the condenser, my legs shook. I forgot my name. I was only thirst. Afraid I would fall on my contraption and spill everything, I crawled the last few feet. My hands shook as I peeled off the tape, unwrapped my mask like it was made of eggshells, afraid one breath would make it all disappear.

I pulled off the top to look inside.

Nothing. I blinked, afraid my mind was gone. Where was it? Not a drop. I sat back on the slowly cooling sand. I would've cried, but tears were impossible. I screamed. So loud it must have woken every dead sailor within a mile.

I picked up the mask, hands shaking, and examined it. My vision blurred, but I could see the seal had failed. The sun, the heat, so many hours, my own stupid impatience, the little bird I now hated—they had all betrayed me. The fresh water had leaked out and filled the sand with glorious honey.

I threw Marshall's five-hundred-dollar mask into the water,

rising now with the tide. The ache and the fog joined up in my head. The palm forest, its long stalks darkening, bled into a mass of gray. I watched it, my hands in the sand, my knees digging in. A flutter of white wings rose from the edge of my vision and disappeared into the dusk. A surge of regret moved through me. I'd expected a bigger finish, for the end to mean something. But I was just fading, like all things fade. My last thought was whether I'd be awake for it, the last moment. When my spirit slipped out of my mouth, whether I'd feel it. Whether I'd have one last glimpse of the ocean before it all ended.

I WOKE TO THE FEEL OF WATER on my mouth. Sweet and delicious. And voices hovering above me like birds, the vowels wings, the consonants sharp beaks. A tumble of sound. At first, I thought it was you, here on the island to rescue me, but I couldn't muster the strength to open my eyes.

"Hey, hold her up."

Not you.

Someone else.

"I *am* holding her up." A guy's voice. Familiar. "It's like trying to pick up a dead body."

Dead. The stranger's last words dropped in my head like a stone. Dead. Was I? Am I? Maybe I was in the next world, wherever that is. And it was hot, so much hotter than I expected. I started to worry.

A small cry, a voice higher and younger than the others. "T, wake up! Wake up. You're okay, T, come on, you're okay." That little hitch in his voice when he called me T . . .

Please, I thought, please be real.

I took a deep breath, to see if I still could, and opened my eyes. There he was, Felix, his small, round face hovering over me, the panic in his eyes turning to relief. That smile broke out, the one I know so well. The one I bet you miss.

"T, you're okay!" Felix threw his arms around my neck and

FRACTURED TIDE

put his head on my chest, like he did when he was a toddler and Mom had me take over bedtime. I put a hand on the back of his head. It felt greasy, sweaty. He really needed a bath, but we could deal with that later. Right now the sight of him was almost as good as the capfuls of water someone was rationing into my mouth.

Two figures kneeled on either side of me, but their images swam. Sunlight strobe. A flash of blue, like the world had become a grainy screensaver. The scent of coconut sunblock filled my nose. A familiar dark-skinned face leaned close.

Ben. Yes, thank God, it was Ben. Even though I'd only known him a day, if I had to be stuck on a desert island with anyone, he'd make my top five.

I tried to say his name, but my lips had turned to rubber, so it came out as "bean." In my head, the word sang. Ben, Ben, Ben is alive. Ben is here with me. He smiled, looking to the girl across from him, someone I vaguely recognized, but I couldn't put a name to the face. Someone who didn't return his smile. The song died a little in my head.

I sat up with some help and shook the sand out of my hair, spit it out of my mouth.

"See, Steph?" Felix said to the redhead. "I told you she was tough."

I locked eyes with the girl named Steph, and she looked away first. From the science trip, I guessed, although I had the feeling I'd seen her around Key Largo somewhere. Small, like me, but red-haired and pale-skinned. Her spaghetti strap top was dirty, her shoulders sunburned. She shielded her face when she talked. Really not the best genetics for a desert island. I didn't envy her.

But then I was the one who'd almost kicked it. I was the one who almost died because a survival technique went sideways. A smell wafted up. Me. Ugh. This was not what my fantasy of stuck-on-an-island-with-a-hot-guy looked like. Not that I had those fantasies regularly. Or ever. Sorry, Dad. I don't have an eraser.

Steph helped me sit up against the *Last Chance* in the shade. Felix leaned against my knee, his damp rash guard cool. Ben collapsed on the other side of me, grimacing. He'd torn off the bottom of his T-shirt to make a bandage for his thigh. The image of the whiplike filament wrapping around his leg hit me full force, and I felt a little sick. His scream, how the blood flowed. Then I imagined how his leg would feel once it became full-blown infected.

I searched the horizon, the blinding sunlight shattering on the waves. Endless. Empty. Not even a seagull. Definitely no ships. "We need the Coast Guard," I said, my words still slurred.

"No kidding," Steph said.

"Or to find more survivors," Ben said. "Somebody with a satellite phone." He leaned his head back against the *Last Chance* and closed his eyes.

More survivors, I thought. Mom. She had to be alive. She just had to. Out there in the palm trees somewhere, wandering and looking for us.

Just as Felix ducked out of sight, into the cabin of the *Last Chance*, I remembered who I'd run into yesterday.

"There's someone else on the island," I managed, although I sounded a little drunk. "With a gun. Went into the palm forest. Scary guy. Almost shot me. I could see he wanted to. He's out there in the forest." Along with all those eyes watching me, I thought. Or maybe I said that last part out loud.

Ben side-eyed me. "Don't worry about that."

"But—"

"He's gone now. We'll keep an eye out for him. Just drink. Rest."

I was too woozy to figure out what that meant, but I found it vaguely reassuring. Felix came back to feed me capfuls of water, each one making me crave a gallon more.

Felix started to bring the whole bottle to my mouth and Steph stopped him.

"Uh-uh. We've only got one more," she said. "Stick with the capfuls." She held out her palm. "Hand it over."

Felix pulled a bottle from behind him and reluctantly handed it over.

"Where'd you get it?" I asked, staring at the magical, beautiful half bottle.

"In the filthy head of your charter," Ben said.

"Ugh," Steph said. "So gross."

She didn't know the half of it. And she probably hadn't cleaned a toilet in her entire life.

"We've got to find more soon," Ben continued. "And make a signal fire and get out of here."

I checked both ends of the beach, hoping for a glimpse of Mom's familiar form. "Where are the others?"

"There aren't any others," Steph said. "They all went down with that thing."

Felix's expression slumped. He capped the bottle and put it on the sand beside me, then stood to take a couple of steps away from us. Arms crossed, he checked out one end of the beach, then the other.

"Don't say that," Ben said, glaring at Steph.

Felix looked from Steph to me. "They might be here," he said, his voice breaking. "We just haven't found them yet." He swallowed, took a breath, and held it for a few seconds. I've seen him do this on the playground when the bigger kids push him around. Trying to stop the tears.

Steph threw her hands up. "I'm just—"

Felix cut in before she could say another word. "You told me my sister was dead. And look at her!" He pointed at me. "Mom's somewhere on the island, looking for us."

Steph opened her mouth to speak, but I held up a hand to cut her off. She didn't know my little brother from Adam. And if she said one more thing about my "dead" mother . . .

"Come here," I said and patted the cool, wet sand next to me. Felix sat cross-legged and I put my arm around his small waist, hoping he was right. The thought of Mom gone forever made it hard to breathe. "We'll look for her. But we need to find more water first, okay?"

"We need to find *her*." He swallowed again and held his breath for a few seconds before blowing it out.

"We will, but we need to get water for her."

Felix nodded and wiped his nose with his hand. I reached up and finished the job with the sleeve of my rash guard. Steph mumbled "gross" under her breath and tried to hand me a beach towel. I waved her away. The look she gave me was beyond irritated, and again I got the feeling she knew me somehow. And really didn't like me.

Felix sniffled, his eyes welling with fresh tears.

"Why don't you go pick up some driftwood?" I told Felix, pointing down the beach where a few pieces lay baking in the sand. "Like we did last year when we camped out on the beach with Mom for her birthday. Bring it back here and we'll make a signal fire."

He sniffed and looked toward the driftwood, but it was clear he wasn't listening.

"Felix?"

"What?"

"Did you hear me?"

"No."

I repeated the whole request, slower this time, ending it with, "Don't go near the water. And stay off the big boulder, the one jutting out over the water. It's too deep on the other side."

He nodded, his eyes widening a hair. We were both imagining the same thing, that tentacle snaking up the rock face, pulling him over the edge and into the waves.

"And don't go into the palm forest."

"Why?"

"Just stay where I can see you."

"But why?"

It's always this way with him, more so over the years you've been gone. "Do you really want to go into the forest?"

"No."

"Then don't be a butthead."

His face darkened into a scowl, and he moved off in the direction of the driftwood.

"Just be careful!" I yelled. Or tried to yell.

I stood with Steph's help and leaned against the gunwale of our broken boat. The ocean stretched out, whitecaps, blue sky, forever and ever. The salt scent here was clean, green like seaweed. It hit me then. This place didn't smell familiar, the way the Keys do.

"I feel like we're . . ." At the end of the world, I almost said, but didn't. It was strange and poetic and something a home-schooled kid would say.

Ben looked like he'd just survived the apocalypse, in his torn T-shirt, a nasty-looking bruise on one side of his face, his band-aged leg oozing blood. Shell-shocked is what you'd call him. Somehow that made me feel better. That the guy I'd sat next to on the charter—the distant, curious, perfect boy who wasn't afraid of anything, even a dead body—wasn't that perfect after all.

A dead body. The tentacled thing. The island appearing out of nowhere.

"Ben, how on earth did we get here?" I asked.

He turned to the waves, searched the horizon. "The current. It dragged the anchor while we slept."

"That doesn't happen."

He gestured to the beach with an open palm and a little flourish. "Let me present Exhibit A."

"I've been out on these waters a billion times. I know all the Keys. The Dry Tortugas. All of them. There is no island here." I rubbed my face.

"The ship dragged the anchor," he said. "It's the only explanation."

I pointed to the buoy. "That's the wreck we dived on."

"No way. There are buoys everywhere in the Keys. It's a crab trap or something."

"It's our buoy," I said. "I'd know it anywhere."

Ben didn't respond, and I wanted to shake him, tell him to listen to me. He played with the half-full bottle of water as if he couldn't stop thinking about what was inside. Suddenly, neither could I.

"Ugh, Ben, stop," Steph said, watching the water slosh in the bottle. "You're making everyone thirsty."

"Fine." He handed it to her. "You hold it."

"That makes me more thirsty."

Ben sighed and closed his eyes. Holding his tongue, I realized, the way you used to when you fought with Mom on those first few visits, until you both got used to the new normal.

I took the bottle from Ben's hand to stop the argument. "You've been here for a grand total of one day and you're already fighting. That's great."

They exchanged a loaded look, one with history. It was only then I put it all together. Who she was to Ben.

"She's the ex you were telling me about, isn't she?"

Steph crossed her arms and glared at me. Ben pursed his lips and looked away. And I burst out laughing.

"Sia," Ben said, "it's not funny."

"Yeah, Sia." Steph crossed her arms and gave me a wounded look. I laughed harder.

"Come on. It's a little bit funny. Trapped on an island with your ex."

A ghost of a smile touched Ben's mouth, and for the first time since I'd met him, I didn't feel awkward.

"You done poking around in my personal life?" Ben asked. "'Cause we need water."

We worked for the rest of the afternoon making fresh water converters out of whatever we could find. Beach pollution usually makes me sad, especially after Felix came home from school one day talking about all the plastic swirling around the Pacific.

His little face so earnest as he told us we had to take the charter out and clean it up. If you were out of prison, you would have probably agreed with him, organized a beach cleanup fun run or something. Mom would sigh and go along with it—as long as Blue Dolphin Scuba Charters was splashed all over the charity swag. A big Gianopoulos family "save the ocean" day on the streets of Key Largo.

So you're gonna hate what I'm about to say. At that moment, searching the beach for trash that would save our lives, I'd never been more grateful for how wasteful human beings can be.

While Steph, Felix, and I collected and sorted, Ben rested his leg in the shade of the *Last Chance* and made the most ingenious converters I'd ever seen. They looked a thousand times better than mine. Turns out it was him and not poor Teague who was the head of the science club.

Steph unloaded another armload of trash into the back of the boat and brushed off her hands. "Gah. I'm so sticky. I think I'm done."

"I saw some more in the other direction." I pointed down the beach.

"Why is there so much?" she asked, frowning.

"No cleanup crew."

"What?"

"The people who take it all away before the tourists come. So we can all pretend this isn't happening."

"Huh. I never thought about that. Must be a suck job." She put her hands on her hips and sighed as if she'd accomplished something amazing by picking up one armload of trash. Then she peered down the beach with a curious expression. "This island looks big."

Ben leaned against the hull, making a desalinator out of an empty can of beans and a scratched-up scuba mask. "The island is big. Wow, you're a real Sherlock Holmes, Steph. Thanks for that."

She ignored his dig, kept looking down the shoreline. "Like, Hawaii big."

"Uh-huh."

"Maybe we'll find a beach house or something. Maybe someone lives here."

"Someone does live here," I said, peering into shadows between the trees again. "The gun-toting Robinson Crusoe who almost shot me yesterday."

Ben caught my eye and tilted his head toward Felix.

"Someone has a gun?" Felix said, his gaze going to the palm forest. "Here, on the island?"

"It's just an expression," Steph said. "When people are thirsty. They call it gun-toting Robinson Crusoe."

Felix squinted and scratched his head. "No, they don't."

"You're seven. There's a lot of stuff you don't know." She patted him on the shoulder, her usual scowl softening.

Ben and Steph were right. I had no idea what they'd done to make him "gone," as Ben put it, but if they didn't want Felix to hear about it, neither did I.

I kneeled next to him. "Can you look down in the head of the *Last Chance* to see if anything useful survived?"

As soon as he was out of earshot, I turned to Ben and Steph. "So?"

Ben looked up from the desalinator he was assembling. "There's no guy."

"You said he was gone."

"You were out of it," Ben said. "I was humoring you."

"No, really. A guy *lives* here." I looked from Ben's face to Steph's. "He pointed a gun at me."

"Uh-huh."

"He said he'd kill my family."

Ben gave me a measuring glance. "You. Almost. Died. Your synapses cooked up a psychedelic treat for you. There's no one here but us. Unfortunately." Ben looked back at the converter, his long, slim fingers fitting medical tape along the edge. "Let's just focus on clean H_2O."

"But—"

"Sia," Steph cut in, "just stop. Really. Before you scare your brother half to death. Pull yourself together." Then she turned and wandered down the beach in search of more manna from garbage heaven.

Worst luck ever. Wrecked on a desert island with a hot guy (you heard right, Dad. Hot. Your little girl is all grown up), and he thinks I'm nuts. As does his horrid ex-girlfriend.

I don't know if you've ever questioned your sanity during those long nights listening to the rats in the prison walls. I like to think you have. Does it make you blush and stammer? Make you feel like your body isn't yours? Like it's just something you're wearing, clothes that don't fit?

Yeah, I know. Totally irrational. But it would all start making sense soon, why I felt this way. Why *all of us* felt this way.

Felix came out of the charter waving a first aid kit he'd found. Ben's bad mood disappeared long enough to high-five him—when Felix is happy, it's contagious—and I kissed the top of my brother's sweaty head. Then I wandered away from Ben and Steph and spent my time keeping an eye on Felix as he played a few yards back from the wave fingers and the wet sand. I searched the surf for sea monsters, scanned the palms for a sign of the strange, shipwrecked man-boy. The one with the gun. The one nobody believed existed. I wondered: If I had told them before their little nerd club cruise that sea monsters exist, would they have believed me?

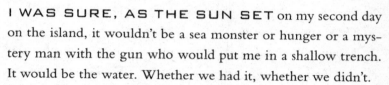

I WAS SURE, AS THE SUN SET on my second day on the island, it wouldn't be a sea monster or hunger or a mystery man with the gun who would put me in a shallow trench. It would be the water. Whether we had it, whether we didn't.

By nightfall, Ben had made three more converters. We had enough water to barely keep three and a half people alive, about eight ounces each. I gave Felix a little of my ration, and he didn't argue.

Felix and I made a camp not far from a string of three boulders that sat in the surf. We made a fire, castaway-style. In the three years you've been gone, I've taught him everything you've taught me, and you would've been proud. He was the one who got the first spark. Some dry driftwood, a good stick, and some coconut fuzz, and we had a raging bonfire, right there on the beach. Our glow slicing through the dark so high, so big, I was sure they could see us in Key Largo.

Steph pulled a cushion from the boat and sat cross-legged on it by the fire. She was wearing shorts, and her pale legs glowed in the warm light. Ben lay on one side in the sand, twirling a smooth piece of driftwood between his fingers, the way kids do in class when they have a problem sitting still. He and Steph had apparently signed a truce, as they actually exchanged a few weak smiles. Ben even cracked a joke that was good enough to make Steph and me laugh together for a rare second. I was starting to feel hopeful that everything, as Matt would say, gonna be alright.

Felix had fallen asleep on the other side of the boulder, next to the spiral notebook he'd pulled from the charter. His legs had apparently run out of doodling space. His mouth was slightly open, his arms splayed up above his head in a surrender position, the way he always sleeps. Mom and I joked about it sometimes, that he got this one from you. No offense, Dad, but we always laugh, because it's not too soon anymore.

I mounded some sand behind me as a makeshift pillow. It felt cool and solid. The stars peppered the blackness above the island. The crackle of the fire drowned out the ocean swell. A beach cookout sound, like the one we had the night before my first day of high school. Mom, smiling as she pulled hot crab legs out of the stockpot and piled the plates high. Then you, chasing her with a crab claw and a fake horror movie voice until Mom wrestled the thing out of your hand, giggling like a little kid. Me, holding my four-year-old brother's hand and laughing on the beach with my family.

I rubbed my eyes with the heels of my hands, my mouth watering at the thought of hot crab, my heart aching at the picture of the four of us, together.

Ben put the stick down and tipped his head up toward the ceiling of stars. It hadn't taken me long to realize he looked at home beside a campfire. And the way he surveyed the beach from time to time, like a seasoned hiker who's always orienting himself. One more mental checkmark on my list of reasons why Ben would make the top five list for desert island companion. I tried not to stare, but even in torn clothes with a bloody bandage on his leg, he was one beautiful dude. And his eyes . . . Intelligent, warm.

Watching him, my heart stopped aching over that perfect picture of us, one week before you went away. Then, between beats, I felt it constrict. Actually squeeze. I guess that's why they call it a crush.

Steph's next words swept the good mood right out of me.

"We ever gonna talk about what happened out there?" she asked.

Ben lay down on his back and folded his hands over his stomach. "I'd rather not."

"Why?"

He didn't answer at first, his gaze still on the sky. "Weird," he finally said.

"Weird what?" I asked.

"I can't find any satellites."

We fell silent and I looked up too, searching the sky for those unnatural pinpricks of light, hiding there among the constellations. Before I could think about what their absence meant, Steph spoke again, her voice small.

"I'm worried it'll come for us. Here."

"I'm still trying to figure out what 'it' is," Ben said.

Steph picked at her peeling sunburn. "I don't care what it is."

Ben turned to look out at the dark water, lost in thought. "Lot of weird stuff in the Mariana Trench. Maybe it came from there."

"I saw it when we were diving," I said.

Both of their gazes fixed on me.

Steph looked incredulous. "And you waited to tell us until now?"

"I've been a little busy staying alive, thank you very much." They waited for me to go on, and the spotlight made me nervous.

So I kept talking, homeschooled-style. Babbling, really. "So yeah, that morning before you guys showed up, I saw it down in the USS *Andrews*." I swallowed, although I didn't have much spit left. "That's what happened to Mr. Marshall, although it didn't cut him. Just . . . drowned him or something, I don't know . . ."

I choked down a lump in my throat and went quiet. Saw Marshall in my head, his blond hair floating in the current, giving me the okay with his gloved hand. He was on the bottom now, along with everyone else, littering the ocean floor. Or inside that thing. I put my hands over my face as the grief swept over me. Mom. All those people. Oh God, Mom. I would never see her again.

"Captain Matt said it was a diving accident," Ben said.

I wiped the corners of my eyes, trying to remember the last thing I said to her. "That death wasn't an accident," I managed. "I didn't get a good look at it, but I saw something."

Ben tilted his head, the firelight playing over the planes of his face. "And you let them call our charter out there?"

"My mom said I was narced. Made sense at the time."

Their blank stares reminded me most people don't dive twice a day, three hundred times a year, like you and I do. Well, like you used to.

"Sometimes, when you go deep," I said, "and the USS *Andrews is* deep, some people get this thing. Nitrogen narcosis. Divers call it being narced. Makes you see phantom lights sometimes. Makes you take over-the-top risks."

Ben watched me for a few uncomfortable seconds. "Do the effects, you know, hang around for a while?"

"No," I said, although I couldn't remember if I was telling the truth.

He exchanged another loaded look with his ex, and I bristled. But at least he left off blaming me. I hadn't yet. I should've pushed Mom to pull anchor and head home, rather than wait around for another charter. I threw a stick into the fire and watched it burn.

Steph wrapped her arms around her legs and stared at me across the flames. "I didn't get a good look at it, you know, when it was . . . Not really. Just something gray, and moving . . ." She shuddered.

Ben shifted with a grimace and threw his arm over his forehead. "None of us did. We were too busy dying."

"I saw it glowing in the hallway of *Andrews*," I offered. "It's phosphorescent."

Steph gave me another blank stare.

"It glows in the dark," Ben translated. "You should know this, Steph. And that means my Mariana Trench idea's not far off. A ton of creatures down there have bioluminescence."

Steph let out a tired sigh. "Have you met me? In case you've forgotten, I hate the ocean. Why would I bother learning about what swims in it?"

I blinked a few times, trying to process that thought. She *hated* the ocean. I felt like she'd just slapped my mother or something. "What kind of person *hates* the ocean?" I asked.

Steph turned her eyes on me. "I can hate anything I want, and I don't have to explain myself."

The look on her face suggested her feelings didn't stop at the ocean. "Do we know each other or something?" I asked.

"Really? You don't remember?" She shook her head slowly, her expression indignant.

"No, I . . ." I searched my memory again, but before I could ask her anything, she turned to Ben. "And despite what you think, I didn't come on the trip because of *you*, Ben, or to learn about the *ocean*. I came because Mrs. Barnes is my cousin. She told me it would be fun." Her voice lost all its sugar on the last word.

Ben must've caught my confused look. "The teacher," he said, his voice softening.

I turned back to Steph to say something. A knee-jerk "I'm sorry" for whatever I did that I couldn't remember. She was digging her toes into the sand and staring at the troughs, trying not to cry. Suddenly all the nasty thoughts I'd been having about her felt really heavy. I hadn't considered that they'd lost people too. Truth was, I hadn't thought about anyone but me and Felix and Mom. And well, okay, Ben.

"Maybe she's okay," I said. "Maybe on the other side of the island. I mean, none of you knew I survived, and I did."

Steph stood up and walked toward the surf. Quick, like she had something to do there.

"What?" I said, turning to Ben. "It's possible."

"She's not Felix. You can't lie to her."

"Mrs. Barnes could be alive."

"The thing got her. We watched it happen."

I followed his eyes to where Steph stood at the edge of the surf. Her white tank top glowed faintly under the moonlight, her skin only a shade darker. The big, black ocean stretched out in front of her, endless. Her shoulders shook.

"I'm sorry, I shouldn't have said anything."

"That's right, you shouldn't have."

"I got knocked out when the boat capsized." I paused, scared to ask but dying to know. "Who else?"

Ben shifted his leg and winced. "The waves were high, so I couldn't see most of the people." He looked out, his voice blowing back to me in the wind. "But I heard them."

Hope washed through me. He didn't see Mom die, not like he saw Mrs. Barnes. "So tell me what you *could* see. Anything. Maybe I can figure out which direction everybody else drifted. We could look for them tomorrow."

He shifted gingerly until he lay flat on his back. "I'm not reliving this right now."

"Please?"

"No."

And then I said something that rose up out of a memory. You and me, hunting beer cans in the woods, the day before you went into Pine Key Pen. Setting them up on stumps and blowing them to oblivion. You knocked can number sixteen off the log and gave me the gun to reload. And what you said, it's always stayed with me.

"When things get bad, you have to look at it, right in the face, and when you do . . ." I trailed off because as soon as Ben turned his head, your voice faded, drowned by the venom in his eyes.

His next words came quiet, as if he were measuring them, one spoonful at a time. "You think because I dress dead people that I can handle this better than Steph? Than you? A bunch of my friends *died* yesterday. Prepping caskets for strangers isn't the same as losing people you love." He broke eye contact and passed a shaking hand over his face. "Why am I even talking to you about this? I mean, maybe this kind of thing happens to you all the time, seeing how your dad's in prison. God knows what you've seen. But to me, this is a friggin' nightmare. I need it to end."

And with that little punch to my gut, he stood with difficulty and limped down the beach. No "sorry about your mom" or "we're all in this together." He just disappeared into the darkness.

The fire crackled. I sat in its heat, the smell of wood smoke making me dizzy and burning my eyes. Apparently, I wasn't Ben's first choice for desert island companion.

I lay back in the sand, looked up at the sky, and tried to shrug it off. I didn't need them, and I didn't care about them.

My eyes welled up anyway, tears pulling the pinprick stars into streaks until they reminded me of shore lights, the way they look through a mask when you've just surfaced from a night dive. I watched the stars waver and bleed. Felix snored a few feet away, and I imagined Mom on the other side of the island fashioning a spear out of driftwood to get us some fish. That thought pulled me apart, turned the sky into a pool of swimming light.

I have this memory of Mom that I'm not sure is real. That once she was a mommy mom, all lemon bars and goodnight kisses filled with sugar. And then you went away, Dad. The sweetness in her dissolved until all that was left was: You hungry, Felix? Cut the food yourself. You bored? Entertain yourself with this cardboard box. You want a coloring book? Make your own.

Basically, she took all your tough talk about independence and made it her new normal. Sink or swim, baby. Stand up for yourself. Fail and learn. Look fear in the face, and when you do, you make fear small. But she doesn't soften it like you do, with a quick side hug, or a just-the-two-of-us fishing trip, or an ice cream at Amy's. No way. She left her soft side on the courtroom floor three years ago.

I guess Mom would say I don't sound grateful, but I want you to know that I am. If I live through the next week, it's because she made me a survivor. And survivors don't need people like Ben and Steph.

The tears washed the smoke out of my eyes, and I knew, just knew, Mom was close by, looking for me. I lay on my side and fell asleep, my back warmed by the fire, my mind drifting somewhere in the palm forest, where I was sure she was hunting wild boar and finding hidden springs.

I HAD A DREAM THAT NIGHT, I think. Or that's the real world, and I'm having a dream right now. Sounds like some kind of delusion, I know, but you don't understand this place, how the island gets inside your head, then shatters. So I wake most mornings with broken glass for thoughts.

In my dream, if that's what you want to call it, I stood on the roof deck of the *Last Chance*, white-knuckling the railing, a storm raging all around me. Gray clouds, rain hitting my face like a wet fist over and over. The *Last Chance* was floating out to sea, and it was sinking.

A sting. On my ankle. I can still remember the white-hot, searing pain. Not like a dream at all.

I reached down and grabbed the thick cord that had wrapped around my leg and pulled. The agony of that, oh God, it was like I'd pressed my fingers against the surface of an iron set on high.

Captain Phil lay on the other side of the roof deck, his eyes wide open and staring. Gray filaments snaked over his face, his stomach, his purple muscle shirt. There was a gun in his hand, an old-fashioned pistol.

I let go of the cord as the sound of my name rose up over the storm surge. My brother's voice.

Felix ran down the beach toward the water and me, past Ben, who lay on his side, clutching his stomach. Even in the lash of rain clouding my vision, I could see the blood pouring from between his fingers.

My mind numbed, because it couldn't be Ben. Not him.

It was only when Felix reached the roaring surf that I realized what he was about to do. I yelled out to stop him, but he dove in anyway, to get to me, to save me.

I reached for Phil's gun, and before I could wrench it out of his death grip, pull it free and shoot into the sea, into the body of that thing that was about to kill me and my brother, another thick gray cord snaked around my arm. I can still feel it breaking through the skin, cutting through flesh until it hit the bone. What that felt like.

One second. Two. Three. My eyes on the waves near the beach. Then Steph surfaced with Felix, and my heart leapt. And as the thing rose all around me, snaking over the edge of the ladder, over the railing—ten, eleven, twelve filaments, like slow-moving roots, pulsing in the gray light—my fear gave way to gratitude, that sometimes people do the right thing.

That's when an inferno rolled out from the center of the island, flattening the thick palm forest in a wave of light and sound.

I woke, still seeing the image of my blood flowing over the roof deck of the *Last Chance*, the way your eyes hold on to the sun when you stare at it too long.

I dragged myself out of my makeshift bed and cleaned up in the surf, trying to get the taste of blood out of my mouth. My flesh ached where the ropes had cut into me in my dream, which made no sense.

I said nothing to Ben and the others about the "dream." None of them looked like they'd had a good night's sleep either.

"I'm hungry," Felix said.

Steph looked toward the forest. "There's gotta be some food in there."

"Finding food in the ocean's a better bet," I said.

"What, with that thing lurking out there?" Ben said, and when I glanced at him, I stopped breathing. One second he was sitting on a piece of driftwood, his leg stretched out. Then came a shimmer, and a girl was there, *right there*, next to him. Someone I'd seen earlier on the roof of Matt's charter, blond and thin, her arm in a sling. And then the shimmer faded, and she disappeared. A dream, I thought. I was still dreaming.

"Sia?" Ben said, and waved a hand in front of my eyes. "You with me?"

"Yeah," I said, studying his face, the chin, the shape of his eyes. Seemed like him. Real. "You're right. I'll go with them into the forest."

As the three of us slipped into the shadows between the trees, leaving the blinding sun behind, I glanced over my shoulder at Ben, wondering about the girl I'd seen. A hallucination. Had to be. But as I took in all the details—him leaning against the driftwood with one forearm slung casually over a knee, and his serious expression as he watched the little flock of birds down the beach—all I could think about was how much I wanted to be sitting there beside him.

Steph followed my gaze and gave a little snort. "He started a bird-watching club this year at school." She gave me a conspiratorial smile. "One of the many reasons I broke up with him."

When I responded with a blank stare, she narrowed her eyes and moved a few paces ahead. I stopped in my tracks, because that expression finally did it. A fractured memory of who she really was flooded back.

About a year ago, I'd just come off of a four-tank day and a night dive that didn't go well, what with a new diver hyperventilating and then losing her fin, which Mom then ordered me to find. The last thing I wanted to do was to go into Nick's Hula Hut, on St. Patrick's Day of all days, looking like I'd washed up on the beach and dried out in the sun. But Felix was starving, so in we went.

The crowd was an ocean of green, bobbing and dancing and shouting. We made our way through the press, the air thick with the yeasty smell of spilled beer, the blaring "Margaritaville" following me all the way to the end of the bar. You know Nick, how extra sweet he's been to us since you went away, adding an extra piece of fish to our order, or throwing in a side of fried pickles for free. How he always gives me a big side hug and ruffles Felix's hair and calls him Nugget.

That night was different, though. St. Patrick's Day, Nick's least favorite night of the year, the night he asks regulars to avoid. I didn't get a "Hey, Sia!" or a side hug. Nothing but a quick chin nod before he turned to yell our regular order through the window.

A redhead wearing a plastic "Birthday Girl" tiara, who had evidently been to the face painting booth given the slathered-on green starburst around one eye, leaned on the bar, ID held casually between two fingers. She watched Nick pour tequila into a silver shaker, her big beauty queen smile lighting up the room. A group of girls buzzed nearby, a gaggle of perfect makeup and perfect hair and ninety-dollar flip-flops. They fluttered around Birthday Girl, laughing and giving each other sideways glances, as if they all shared the same secret.

I remember how exhausted I was, leaning against the bar

near the cherries and the olives, my last birthday flashing through my head. My big party? A cupcake that I wolfed down between dives. In my dive bag I found a picture Felix had left for me to discover—the four of us holding hands under a rainbow. He even added little gray bars across your stick figure body. I think Mom got me a present, but I don't remember what it was.

The girl one barstool away gave me the quick once-over, and then looked away without another glance. I wasn't in her zip code.

As Nick salted the glass and shouted out drink orders to the other bartenders, I started to recognize a few of the girls. They'd been in my class freshman year, back before you went away, when I still actually went to school. The girl who'd dismissed me and my Walmart flip-flops was in my homeroom.

Which meant Birthday Girl wasn't even close to twenty-one.

You know what I had to do.

She looked so happy and confident waiting there, leaning against the bar with one hip, her broad smile sunny, lipstick perfect. The clothes came from a bank account that always had fresh juice in it. The birthday girl. I didn't even hesitate. Just leaned over the bar to whisper in Nick's ear. As I pulled back, the redhead and I met eyes for a split second. The smile faded.

It was for Nick. It *was*. After what happened at spring break last year, one more slipup and they'd pull his liquor license for good. When Nick snatched the ID from her for a better look, and she turned her attention on me for real, her face full of the shock of betrayal, I was too tired to look sorry. I just gave her one of your favorite gestures, an empty-handed shrug that says, *This is on you, sweetheart.*

Nick's loud cursing was pretty much my cue to leave. But as

I made my way to the door, I chanced a glance back. Her friends had already dispersed, and an officer I hadn't even noticed lurking in the bar now loomed over her, examining the ID. Birthday Girl was about to have Minor in Possession on her permanent record. And the narrow-eyed look she sent me across the crowd was the kind that leaves a welt.

As I fell asleep that night, my belly full of fish and chips, I wondered if maybe, just maybe, I could have let it go. But if I'm honest with myself—and I guess that's what I'm doing now, stuck here on hell island until I die—maybe a small part of me was just too tired and bitter to care about anyone who had a life and friends and the joy to wear a plastic tiara to Nick's Hula Hut on St. Patrick's Day.

No wonder she hated me.

"Sia," Steph said, snapping her fingers in front of my face. "Pick up the water and let's get moving."

We made our way through the trees, and I could swear the trunks somehow leaned in on me, no matter what side I took, stealing the air from my lungs. All those invisible eyes. I told Steph *again* that the coconuts were rotten. She tipped her head, swung her hair over her shoulder, and gave me her back. I thought about fessing up and telling her I was sorry, but a bigger part of me wanted her to apologize, for her to feel horrible about what she had done, putting Nick at risk like that.

I cracked open coconuts, one after another, and showed her the insides, debating what I should say. Steph dug into the soft earth, swearing when she found nothing to drink. Felix stuck his fingers into every nook and cranny. As I raised my rock to crack one more coconut open, just as I decided I shouldn't even let on that *I* knew that *she knew* who I was and what I'd done to her, a flash of white caught the corner of my eye. I dropped the rock and turned, but it was gone. Or should I say, *he*. Robinson Crusoe, disappearing like the slippery eel he was, deeper into a palm forest, away from Ben.

I didn't tell them what I saw. Maybe they were right and it wasn't real.

Steph stepped back, brushed the dirt off her hands, and looked to the top of the palms. "Maybe the good ones are still up there."

I peered into the canopy. It was a three-story climb to the crown of the tree, with no real handholds, and I had bare knees.

"Can you climb that?" I asked.

"No way. That's all you."

I eyed Steph's tank top and shorts, tilting my head.

Steph pulled back. "Why are you looking at me like that?"

Two arguments later and a promise to give her most of my water, I was halfway up the tree, her tank top tied onto one knee, her shorts secured around the other. Steph had forced Felix to "go play behind a tree and don't look at me," and I'd twisted my rash guard into a sapper's rope, one end held in each hand and looped around the other side of the trunk. Gripped the tree with my knees, scooted the rope up and leaned back so it didn't slip. And like a caterpillar, I inched my way up. But not for coconuts, like Steph thought.

My leg muscles trembled, the sweat pouring off me making the climb near impossible. Halfway to the top, just as I thought the rash guard would grease right out of my grip, I glanced down. Steph stood in her underwear and bra, arms over her chest, shoulders hunched. One more reason for Birthday Girl to hate me, but it couldn't be helped.

"Will you please hurry?" she shouted up.

I wanted to. Wished I could let go and swim through the air and kick my way to the top. And not just because every muscle in my body burned with every inch I climbed. I knew, deep down, when I finally reached the peak and had a view of the entire island, that I'd see a plume of smoke rising from the far side. Mom, making a fire. Then together, we'd figure out how to get us home.

I reached up and grabbed a shaky handhold on a couple of fronds. Managed to pull myself one foot higher, then forced my head through the last barrier between me and the sky.

The entire island spread out around me. At first the world spun with vertigo and the pure thrill of it. Like perching on top of the world. But I had a feeling, something gnawing inside me, as if this wasn't the first time I'd had this view.

Steph called up to me, commanded me to tell her what I saw. And what I saw was amazing. The island was a massive emerald teardrop, too big to get a good view without hovering in a chopper.

A flock of birds burst into flight, drawing my eye.

A dark patch, there in the center of the island, among the sea of fronds, constantly moving in the sunlight. It took me a bit for my brain to figure out what I was looking at. The trees there were gone. A flash of hope told me maybe there was a house in a clearing, some off-grid hippie with a chicken coop and a SAT phone. Or a spring and a waterfall.

Or a man-boy with a gun and a tiger trap.

Those navigation skills you taught me kicked in, and I figured it'd be an hour's walk to the clearing. To the phone. Maybe to Mom. If I was lucky, I wouldn't get lost. But I'd need a weapon, just in case. And I didn't have one.

"Sia!" came a sharp voice from below.

I slipped on my perch, swearing under my breath. "What?"

"You see any coconuts?"

A diseased-looking clump lay directly under my hands. I twisted one off, just in case it still had something worth eating inside. "Incoming!" I yelled before dropping it. Two seconds later a thump, followed by a yelp.

I turned to check out the coastline and spotted the three big boulders near our camp, sitting in the surf where the water went deep blue. Ben was there, a tiny figure down by the boulders, arms crossed, staring at the horizon. Offshore to the northwest, where the water turned an even darker blue, I spied the white buoy of the *Andrews*. Beyond the buoy was nothing but ocean, full of whitecaps and endless all the way to the far horizon.

No other islands, no ships, and no mainland. A beautiful prison.

"Is that it? Really?" came her voice again from below.

I twisted off another and let it fall. When I glanced back toward the *Andrews*, I almost lost my grip.

There it was. A telltale hump in the water. Big, as if something huge moved just beneath the surface. The buoy rose in the swell as it passed.

That thing, out hunting.

What I saw next made me wonder if I was dreaming again. Either that or I was losing it. A shimmer appeared in the water, like the one I'd seen on the beach when the girl showed up next to Ben. The whitecaps near that unnatural swell in the ocean *bent* somehow—I don't know how else to describe it. Then the shimmer spread toward the island. I watched it ripple past me, heading straight for the dark clearing, turning the sea of fronds strange and warped.

My stomach plunged and I shut my eyes. And laughed. Because for the first time in my life, I'd gotten seasick. At least that's what I thought it was at the time.

"Sia! Get down here!"

"Little busy right now."

"I'm serious."

"What's wrong?"

She paused a hair too long. "I need my clothes."

I took one more look at that dark spot in the jungle before I slithered down the trunk into the dim quiet below. When I finally put my bare feet on land again, I untied my knee guards and handed Steph her tank top and shorts.

"Happy now?"

She took the clothes without looking me in the eyes. "Felix is missing."

My mouth went dry. When I turned to check behind the nearest trunks, my head swam. The same thing I'd felt inside the USS *Andrews* when Marshall went missing. But this time it was Felix.

I ran through the trees, calling his name, then looped back to Steph, who stood in the clearing, her face in her hands.

"Don't just stand there. Look for him!"

I ran in the other direction, leaping over tree roots and looking behind every bush and trunk. Mom's harsh lesson on the boat sounded in my head.

You sure you didn't leave him behind, Tasia? I've seen you do this kind of thing before.

I ran faster, so fast I tripped over a root, my shoulder smashing into the ground, but I got up and kept searching, calling out his name, the sound of Steph's cries and mine echoing in the trees. The panic swelled like a bubble in my lungs. Then I rounded a thick trunk and found him curled up in a hollow in the roots, sobbing.

He threw himself into my arms and squeezed me tight. I can't remember the last time he clung to me so hard. Maybe the day you left, when you didn't show up for dinner. He stared at the empty chair and wouldn't eat, then hung on to me and cried until bedtime.

I kissed the top of his head and rubbed his arms, which felt cold, as if he'd been sleeping on the ground a long time. "I would never leave you behind."

"Where did you go?" he asked.

"Just looking for coconuts."

"All night?" he asked, his face still buried in my neck.

"No, it only felt that way." I couldn't get any sense out of him and figured he was still shell-shocked from the boat, so I didn't put two and two together. I still had no idea what the island really was.

"Sia, I'm hungry," he said.

"I know, little man. Me too."

Over Felix's shoulder, I met Steph's eyes. We were both thinking the same thing. No coconuts. No wildlife except for birds, which were too fast to catch. Until I had a weapon to deal with the man-boy, I wasn't heading to the clearing. The forest held nothing for us but shadows.

A breeze moved past me, bringing the briny scent of the ocean with it. And at that moment, I knew what I had to do.

Thirty minutes later, I stood on the beach, in the sunlight, the water lapping my ankles. Steph had taken Felix down the beach so he wouldn't see. Ben stood a few feet from the water, staring at me like I'd lost my mind.

"You don't have to do this."

"Unless you want to start in on each other's fingers, I'm getting us some grub." I fit my mask over my face.

"Come sit with me and we'll work this out. I've got a plan."

"No, you don't." I waded into the waves.

"You're gonna catch a whole lot of nothing with no fishing gear," Ben said.

A wave slapped my waist. "If I'm not back in ten minutes, order pizza."

"Would you please get out of the water?"

I dove under the next breaker.

Waves moved above my head. Froth, chaos. Below, clarity. It's the way it's always been for me, and you. Get away from the world of light and air and enter the world of light and water, and suddenly we're home.

The slope of the sand was gradual, and beautiful, like brown sugar spilled in a clear glass bowl. With sunlight beating down directly overhead, the underwater world felt safe, because I could see for a hundred feet. Tourists would pay double for this kind of visibility. I had to remind myself the safe feeling was an illusion, my search for food a gamble. I had to get what I needed fast and get out.

The sugar sand slowly gave way to shallow rock formations, and soon I was swimming over the healthiest reef I've ever seen. Bubble coral and fire coral, all in brilliant shades of red and orange. White brain coral as big as a beanbag. Sea grass sprouted in clumps between the black rock, swaying in the current. And then the fish. The fish! Yellow butterflies, silver-striped jack, snapper, all swimming in thick schools that blocked out the sun. Long gray trumpetfish and the wildly colored parrots. A huge grouper hunkered down under a shelf of rock, opening and closing its mouth, waiting for dinner to pass too close.

But as I swam above the labyrinth of the reef, looking down on the show, my nerves started firing. The fish were beautiful and healthy, but a little strange, all of them. I recognized the shapes and the species, but the colors were off, the stripes on the bannerfish too close together. And then I swam above a school of snapper that looked just—well, wrong. The island, I thought. It's not what we think it is.

My stomach growled and I brushed my thought away. Figured the low blood sugar was messing with my head. I needed food. I didn't care what color it was.

It didn't take long for me to find what I was looking for. Lobster. A big fat slow one, a kind I'd never seen before in the Haystacks or around the sunken ships in the Keys, scuttling just underneath a rocky shelf. Its flat tail dragged along the bottom, spindly legs tapping a rhythm on the ocean floor as it searched for bits of dead fish. Under its spotted shell was a whole lot of white flesh. If I hadn't already been wet through and through, my mouth would've watered.

One deep breath and I went under, scissoring my way down into the avenues of reef city. My body felt stronger than it did on the island—fast and agile. And you'll think it strange, considering everything that had happened in the last two days, but gratitude swelled in me. How much better life is underwater, I thought, even now. Away from the annoying feel of solid land under my feet. Here I get to slip through the currents like an eel, spin and twist and laugh at gravity.

The lobster hadn't gotten far since I'd first spotted it, and I hovered a few feet behind the tail, reminding myself of your lessons about where to hold it without getting sliced. I grabbed it by the back, getting a good hold near the antennae. The lobster convulsed, the tail curling violently and straightening out again. Strong little monster. It was not about to go quietly.

I swam back to shore and surfaced ten feet away from Ben and Steph. Deep in conversation, their heads close together, neither of them saw me in the waves, so I threw dinner onto the beach next to them. Both jumped and yelled out, scrambling back from the water.

"Good God, Sia!"

"Son of a . . ." Ben winced, his hand on his leg. "Mind giving us a little more warning next time?"

Felix's giggle drifted over the waves, and I saw him, head peeking out from around the bow of the *Last Chance*. "I knew she was there."

I laughed, and the sound of it surprised me more than it did them. I don't think I'd allowed myself to unclench the fist around my heart for even a second since I'd arrived on this island. But seeing Felix relaxed and unworried, and knowing there was baked lobster in our future, had my hopes soaring. And after what Ben had said to me last night, I was determined to give him a hard time.

Ben settled himself back on the sand, trapped the lobster with his heel before it scuttled into the surf.

Steph gave me an accusing look. "Two minutes ago he was bawling his head off for his sister, and now it's all hilarious."

Felix looked away from Steph, his smile fading as he pushed his toes into the wet sand. "She came back. She's okay."

I thought about leaving the water then, and I should've. A little voice warned me it was time to get dry, that inner mother who says, "Get out of the rain!" when the lightning starts up, or declared to "Stop at two beers!" at that kegger I went to last year, the one I never told you about. But the voice was soft, and the waves were loud and beautiful. I was doing something other than waiting, and it made the worry fly right out of me.

No way I'm sharing one lobster with three other people, I thought. And Felix needed more food. I turned to swim out again.

"T!" Felix's voice followed me, his panic thick, all good humor gone.

"Be right back," I called over my shoulder, and dove under the next breaker before I had to hear him freak out.

Near shore the pickings were slim, mostly fish darting out of my way, so I swam back into the reef, skirting a large black rock encrusted with glorious coral in reds and yellows, and another brain coral the size of a farmer's prize pumpkin. The sand under me had that undisturbed quality you find at hidden beaches in the middle of nowhere, white and rippled to catch the patterns in a perfect shot. A part of me wished I had my camera. The other part of me prodded my stomach again.

I swam out a little farther, looking for lobster and crab, telling myself the thing that attacked us was asleep in the hold of the USS *Andrews*. Logic told me it was too big to come into the shallows. I surfaced for a breath and dove again. Movement, on the sand farther out, as the shelf deepened and the water beneath took on a darker hue of blue. A huge crab. The thought of it cooked over flames overruled my caution, and I swam for it.

Still too shallow for the big creatures, I told myself, as I rounded a rocky cluster of coral and reached for the sweet spot on its back. The crab scuttled away deep under a shelf and disappeared. So close, I thought, to a hot crab diner.

I paused at the bottom, looking one last time into the crevice, and contemplated what would happen if I reached my hand in there.

And that's when it happened.

A slow buzz of electricity in the water, through my toes, my fingers, down in my spine. I'd felt the same thing before I led Marshall down into the USS *Andrews*.

Too cold, too dark, too deep.

I backed away from the crevice's dark maw, pulling myself hand over hand in a zigzag pattern up the rock face, avoiding the sharp coral. As clear water gave way to a haze in the distance, more mountains of color and shadow rose from the pale ocean floor. The USS *Andrews* was out there. That thing was out there too, nesting somewhere inside.

My lungs burned and I surfaced for a breath. Looked toward the buoy, where the wreck lay. Still far. I tread water and looked out to sea, adrenaline's rush rising in my blood—fuel that would get me home. It's usually a comfortable place for me, nuzzled in that little pocket of risk, buzzing on the thrill of what if. But this time it was too much. Something swam beneath. Something would rise and swallow me whole.

I tread water for two more strokes and turned 180 degrees, putting my back to the buoy, to the wreck, and whatever was living inside of it. And my breath caught in my throat.

The island was gone.

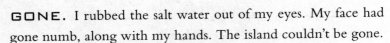

GONE. I rubbed the salt water out of my eyes. My face had gone numb, along with my hands. The island couldn't be gone.

I swam in a circle, kicking at the great nothing underneath. I searched west again. Was that the way I came? Was that even west? I tipped my head back and squinted. The sun hung at high noon. The buoy bobbed not that far off. When my body rose with the ocean swell, I scanned the distance for a glimpse of a low-lying island.

Your navigation lessons came back to me then, thank God, because otherwise I would've started screaming at the sky, begging for a rescue that would never come. I dipped my mask underwater and checked the slope of the sand, observed the ripples to see which way the current moved. Then I swam toward an island I could no longer see.

Strange thoughts came with my panic. The ocean behind me was an open wound. The world was bleeding, she wasn't going to stop, and I was caught in the current. That thing surfaced in my mind, slipping through the waves, defying the laws of gravity better than I ever have. Faster. Stronger. Hungrier. And then I thought of Felix on the shore, crying for his sister. Of the sun setting and him standing at the edge of the surf for hours, waiting for me to come back. And it was that last thought, of him forever waiting, with no one but strangers to take care of him, that pulled me apart. Took the lid off all the panic I was feeling, until a sob caught in my throat and I couldn't breathe.

A thousand years later, I found the shallows again. The reef thickened beneath me, and my heart felt light and empty, my arms weak and useless. But the island wasn't there. Just open ocean. I would never find it. I would tread water out here for hours until I drowned.

Two more panicked strokes later, I crossed a threshold, an invisible line in the sea. My stomach buckled, and a razor moved across my mind. I gasped and stopped swimming.

In an instant, the island appeared only thirty yards ahead. The beach. The trees. The *Last Chance*, broken and lolling in the rising tide.

Voices burst into life. Ben and Steph and Felix, all standing on the beach, screaming. Ben's face was a mask of panic as he waved me in. Felix's mouth an open *O* of shock. Steph's gaze was on something behind me, her eyes wide, her hand over her mouth.

The wind took the words from Ben's mouth, but I made out the shape of his lips moving as he said the same word over and over.

Swim.

I didn't look. I just swam. Churned the water in a full-out sprint for the beach.

Your voice came to me, what you said when you threw me into the pool for the first time, before I knew what to do.

Swim to shore, little fish.

It tore my lungs apart, crawling through the water. My feet. I couldn't stop feeling them back there, closer to *it*, whatever it was. My calves; one bite and it would have me, slice through the muscles and tendons until I couldn't kick anymore.

My hands hit sand. Too shallow to swim, and Ben was there, knee-deep, grabbing my arms and dragging me out of the surf and across shells and gravel and up onto the beach. He stopped ten feet from the waterline and dropped me, then fell beside me with a cry of pain, holding his leg. I looked back, panicked we hadn't made it far enough, out of its reach.

But behind me the ocean was calm, waves and whitecaps moving underneath a cloudless sky.

Steph stood behind the *Last Chance* holding Felix by the upper arm in a vise grip. Ben glared at her.

"What? You think I was going to lose him again?" she said. "He was trying to go in after her!"

I looked at Felix's stricken face, and then hers. Then I turned on my side and threw up.

Cooking that lobster was the longest ten minutes of my life. And hunger has a way of putting its heel on other thoughts, grinding them into nothing. That rubber band pop in my stomach when I crossed that invisible line suddenly seemed like my imagination. Just a hunger pang. The disappearing island was a mirage. It had to be.

Ben and Steph couldn't stop staring at the smoking shell, and Felix kept asking when dinner would be ready. To distract ourselves, we discussed our dilemma. We needed food. None of the coconuts were edible, and the only food was in the ocean. That thing was in the ocean too, hunting.

Steph contemplated the waves as if trying to solve a math problem. "It took a while to sense you were there. Smell you or whatever. Maybe we can set a time limit, and make sure you get back before that."

I noted her use of pronoun. *You.* "I can teach you how to catch them," I said, turning the lobster on the coals. "Where they hide in the reef."

"Maybe I can make a fishing net with stuff from the charter," Steph said, a tremor in her voice. She quickly cleared her throat to cover. I pretended not to notice.

"I hope so." Ben shifted in the sand, grimacing. "I don't want either of you going into the water every day with that thing."

"I doubt we have enough good scraps to make a net," I said.

Steph looked down at her shirt and held the bottom out. A moment later she eyed mine and Ben's.

"Uh-uh," I said. "I'm not walking around this island naked so you can make a net that probably won't work."

"Oh, so it was okay to ask me to strip down to nothing, but you get to keep your rash guard on?"

Ben gave each of us a curious glance, and we both waved him off at the same time.

He shrugged and shifted his leg, wincing. "God, I hate being benched like this." He turned to Steph, who gave him a desperate, pleading glance. Then he turned to me. "It's a lot of risk, Sia. And finding that lobster was probably pure luck."

"Nuh-uh. It wasn't luck," Felix said. "My sister's, like, a really, really good free diver."

"Still," Ben said, "it's—"

"No, really. The best. Just like our grandmother. Back in Kalymnos, when Yiayia was a kid like me, she could hold her breath for *ten* minutes—"

I poked at our lunch, which was red and smoking. "More like two."

"She used to free dive down to a *thousand* feet—"

"Eighty. It's eighty, Felix."

"And bring home treasures—"

"Sponges, Felix. Sponges."

"They'd sell it to *pirates*."

"They sold it at the market."

"She and her mom supported the *whole family* with the stuff she brought up."

"That part is true."

Felix turned his bright gaze on me. "T's just like her. She's *amazing*."

I shrugged. Ben looked at me with a new level of respect, and I blushed. Steph hadn't stopped watching the ocean, afraid it would reach out its salty hand and snatch her from the beach. I'm not sure she'd even heard our conversation.

"I'm a good swimmer too!" Felix said. "I know how to grab lobster without getting pinched. And crab! We can all take turns, and I—"

"No!"

Felix startled as if I'd slapped him.

I took a breath and evened out my tone. "No, Felix. Steph and I will do it. Ben can't swim with his leg like that, and you're too little."

I wanted to take the words back as soon as they were out. My last few sounded like Mom, and not the good part of her. The tough-as-shark-skin part of her that suddenly appeared when you went away.

Felix's face stiffened and he looked at his feet. He didn't want to hear his least favorite phrase right now. Too little. Smaller than the other kids, smaller than you were at his age. Just small. He turned and walked down the beach.

"Hey, Felix, I'm sorry," I called after him. He didn't turn or stop.

Steph stretched out in the sand and rested the back of her hand against her forehead. "Real nice, Sia. Best big sister ever."

I started to tell her off, but the insult died in my mouth. You would have handled it better, told off Steph, ran after Felix to apologize, but suddenly all I could do was stare out at the water and think about what Steph and I had to do. Go out there and fish with that thing hunting us. Every day. And maybe what I'd seen earlier wasn't a mirage, and the island would disappear again. And next time maybe I wouldn't be so lucky.

"There's another option," Ben said, scratching his cheek and looking out into the waves.

I held up a hand before he said it. "We can't eat fiddler crabs. They're practically all shell. And they're salty."

"And NO insects," Steph said and shuddered.

"No, that's not what I mean. What if—" Ben paused and searched the waves again. "What if we kill it? Then we'd have all the time in the world to fish the reef."

"Sure thing," Steph said. "Let me just get on the SAT phone and call in an air strike."

Ben rubbed the top of his thigh, his expression looking more and more determined every second, his gaze on the sea.

"Oh no," Steph said, watching Ben.

"What 'oh no'?" I said.

She pointed at his leg. "Ben's going all Ahab on us. Wants revenge."

"I just want to eat," he said, clearly irritated with her. But something in his face told me maybe Steph was right. And part of me was starting to like Ben's idea.

When he turned to me, a new spark lit his eyes, a side of him I hadn't seen since we first met on the charter. "This is the plan. We study its behavior. Take our time, figure out its—"

"Study it?" Steph said. "The thing eats everything it touches. Field study over."

"No, it doesn't," I said. "It's not mindless. It didn't just grab everything that wasn't nailed down. It has a purpose, and some intelligence."

"Look," Ben said, "I know you're still freaked out—"

"You mean almost dying?" Steph stood and pointed to the *Last Chance*. "Did you see what it did to our boat? And you want to try to kill it. I'm sure that will go well."

Steph went quiet and splayed herself out in the sand like a surfer at the end of a good run. I had the feeling that after one day together on the island, she was giving up.

Ben struggled to his feet and limped toward the water, like he could find the answers in the tumbling surf. I watched him for a while, wondering if he was right or just desperate. Then movement down the beach drew my eye. A group of birds pecked at a fiddler crab, fighting over it, the wind ruffling their feathers. I had a weird sense of déjà vu while watching them. Or maybe it was the lingering effects of my near-death experience.

I tore my eyes away and joined Ben at the water's edge, far enough from Steph. His chin was up, his shoulders set. He glanced at me, and a flash of hope lit his eyes. I don't know why, but he needed this. So did I.

"All right," I said.

"All right what?"

"We should try to kill it."

That was all the permission Ben needed to launch into an

eight-step plan that involved field research, reconnaissance, and beta testing several traps he'd already been thinking about.

"You two will have to do most of the searching," Ben said, "but I'll take field notes. Make a clock with a stick in the sand. Where's that notebook your brother has been doodling in?"

I watched him slowly limp in a circle, scanning the beach for my little brother.

"I just figured something out," I said.

"What?"

"You're the guy at school who asks for extra homework."

His only response was a smile, and the sight of it warmed me all the way to my toes. God, he has a beautiful smile. Then that weird feeling hit me again, full of teeth and scales and all the things that might be, knifing through that moment of warmth and light, darkening the sunshine bouncing off the crashing waves. I don't know how I knew, but something terrible would happen to him. Soon.

His smile started to fade as he took in my expression. "What's wrong?"

"Nothing."

"You're upset. I mean, more than usual."

I sighed and pushed the hair out of my eyes, which the wind had turned into a black veil across my vision. "If we do come up with a plan, it's just me and Steph putting it into action. No seven-year-old kid. No guy with a bad leg. That's the deal."

The last of his smile faded. He turned away so fast I almost didn't see it. A hint of shame there in his eyes, that he had to stay on the sidelines.

"I'll come up with a good plan, okay? Minimum risk," Ben said.

"*We'll* come up with a plan." I poked him in the shoulder with one finger. "You're not in charge of the island."

"Okay, *we*."

I had a sudden urge to feel his hand on the small of my back, let him slip it around my waist and draw me in for a hug. And then his gaze caught mine, and for a second, I had this weird feeling he was thinking the same thing. I had to stop myself from reaching out, stop my hand halfway to his, let it fall by my side, palm empty. Funny how I spend most of the day with my hands empty, but suddenly I couldn't stop feeling that nothing.

I looked over my shoulder to find Steph watching us, her expression curious rather than angry. I guess the relationship was really over for her. So if Ben and I . . .

I looked away quickly, a blush hot on my cheeks. What was I even thinking? There was no Ben and me.

Ben kept his gaze on the horizon. "We're going to get home. I can feel it. A few days from now, I'll be back in my bedroom, watching TV, like none of this ever happened."

He took a breath and let it out, and I felt a part of me deflate as well. Ben didn't really know me, and I didn't know him, I reminded myself. It was just the island pushing us together.

"Everything's gonna be alright," Ben said.

"Thank you, Captain Matt." I was surprised to hear my voice break on the last word. The Bob Marley song rose in my mind, along with Matt's face, and the faces of the others I wouldn't see again. And then my mother's face, and then yours, and I had to hold my breath to keep from crying. God, maybe Ben wasn't the only one who was desperate.

I could have imagined it, while I watched the horizon for hints of a rescue or the thing that put us here, but I thought I felt Ben's hand for a half second, touching mine. Then the warmth left, and he limped away in search of my brother and the notebook.

Later, after the sun dipped into the sea and the island winked out, we ate the lobster's legs too, crunching them like pretzel sticks. Licked the inside of the carapace. Salt and meat and, God, it tasted so good. Two days, and only two hundred calories each. For the first time in my life, I thought about your prison food, dropped like slop onto your divided tray, and my mouth watered. I thought about the homemade spanakopita Mom used to make, when she still cooked, when she didn't have to go it all alone. And the baklava, dripping with the thyme honey she ordered from that little shop on Kalymnos, the one Yiayia used to talk about. How good it all was then.

Steph wouldn't meet my eyes; both of us knew we had a slim chance of killing that thing, and she knew I'd be asking her to go into the shallows in the morning. Nervous, biting her nails like she was trying to make an Olympic sport of it, watching the horizon for lights, for the Coast Guard to top the horizon like a freakin' flock of Valkyries and save us all.

Ben limped into the darkness near the palm forest to change the bandage on his leg, probably because he didn't want us to see him cry. When he came back, I was laid out by the fire, sucking on the remains of my last lobster leg, which was pretty much a straw now. The wind whistled through the skeleton.

Ben settled in the sand and put his hands behind his head. "You know what I want?"

"Food," I said. "Just a guess."

"No, a movie."

Steph groaned. "I just want water that tastes like something other than a five-hundred-year-old Christmas ham."

"I feel ya." Ben rolled onto his side, a hint of a smile on his face. "So here's a question for you."

"Shoot," I said, sucking on my lobster straw.

"If you were trapped on a deserted island, and you had—"

Steph held up a hand. "Oh please."

"—any movie, but just one, what would you pick?"

We threw movie titles around for a while. *Mean Girls* for Steph (figures), *Transformers* for Felix (of course—his taste in movies sucks), *Princess Mononoke* for me (blank look from Steph), and anything Star Wars for Ben (so adorable). Then Steph had to go and ruin it all.

"It just hit me. That is such a ridiculous question, what movie would you bring to a desert island."

"It's fun," Ben said. "Can't a question just be fun? This is exactly why we broke up. You take everything too seriously."

"What three books would you take if you were trapped on deserted island?" Steph asked, an edge in her voice. "Hmmm. What tool, if you could have only one? What food, if it was the only thing you could eat?"

"It's just something to pass the time."

"It's ridiculous because you don't get to choose what you have on a deserted island. No one does. No movies. No books. No beachside resort full of tiki huts and margaritas."

I remembered that night again, her leaning against the bar at Nick's Hula Hut with her fake ID between her fingers. We exchanged a glance, and I could see she was thinking about it too.

"You know," Steph said, turning to me. "Now would be a good time for an apology, since we're stuck here, like, forever."

"Sorry for what?"

Her eyes narrowed. "For what you did to me at Nick's Hula Hut."

Ben looked from her to me. "What did she—"

She turned to him. "Remember my infamous grounding?"

Ben's eyes widened. "Oh, yeah." He turned to me. "No way. That was you?"

The rock in my stomach grew an inch. "Steph, you were going to get the owner in trouble, make him lose his liquor license again."

"No, I wasn't. How would the cops even know?"

"They were watching him. Probably."

"Honestly, Steph," Ben said, "you shouldn't have done it anyway. You could've gotten an MIP, and then it would have ended up on social media, and then your chances at getting into a good—"

Steph held up her hand, palm out. "Don't lecture me. And if you're wondering, that is the *real* reason we broke up, your 'I know everything' attitude, not me taking everything 'too seriously.'" She turned to me. "What you did was humiliating. On my *birthday*."

"Oh, was it your birthday? I hadn't noticed."

"You're really not going to apologize?"

It would have been so easy to just say I was sorry, but something in her eyes made it almost impossible. "I'm sorry you decided to break the law at the same time my brother needed fish and chips. I'm sorry I ran into you that night. Really. But I was protecting a friend of the family, so no, I'm not apologizing for what I did."

We all fell silent. I picked up a rope and tied some of my

favorite knots. Felix got up and wandered out of the fire's light. Steph's gaze followed him until he was too far to hear, the hurt in her expression showing.

"I want to change my answer," she said. "To the movie question."

Ben kept his gaze on the drawing he'd made in the sand. "I thought you didn't like the game."

"*Shawshank Redemption*," she said. "You know, the one about the guy who goes to prison."

My hand stilled on the rope. And I felt a little sick, because I knew where this was going.

"What do you think, Sia?" Steph asked. "Have you seen that one?"

"I don't remember."

Of course I had, and it had given me nightmares. About you.

I tied a sheepshank, and the name reminded me of the movie, so I untied it. And I thought about Ben, what it must've sounded like when he told her about you. Probably recounted our first conversation on the charter. Spilled it all, while I was out getting them food so they would last another day. *Hey, Steph, do you know how messed up she is? Listen to this.* Such a mistake, telling him that night on the boat.

Ben glanced at me. "Leave her alone."

"Why? Maybe it runs in the family. Maybe we should know what happened."

"Steph—"

"That's what you told me, right?" Steph asked.

Ben wouldn't look at me. The silence drew out between us, like the mooring line of a ship about to snap.

"So you want to know, huh?" I asked him.

He met my eyes. My shark-skin tone had hit a nerve.

I picked up a piece of firewood and drew with it in the sand. The lie came to my lips, that you didn't do it. Got thrown into the slammer anyway. Like a movie.

"If you don't want to tell us, that's fine," Ben said, but he kept his eyes on mine, the question still hanging between us. And I thought about all the times I covered for you, remembered all the excuses, a thousand of them. And for once in my life, I didn't care about helping you save face.

"Sometimes I say it was a white-collar thing," I said. "You know, insider trading. Tax evasion. I've told that lie a couple of times."

Ben scratched his beard stubble, mulling over my answer. "If it hurts too much to talk about, you don't—"

"He killed somebody in a bar fight. Three years ago."

Ben's expression froze. Steph had a glint in her eye. I could swear it was satisfaction.

"Not with a knife or anything. He's just strong. Used to carry one tank under each arm when loading the charter for a dive. When he taught me to swim, he could throw me so high above the waves, it was like being at a water park. Once, I saw him pick up the back end of a Volkswagen bug, held it a foot off the ground just to make Felix laugh."

Steph looked genuinely shocked. "He killed someone . . . with his hands?"

"His fists, actually."

"Why?" Ben asked, and he looked sorry for me, which made everything worse.

I thought about that night, standing outside the police tape, listening to the cops talk to Mom about you. How you didn't mean to, how you usually took out your bad temper on things that couldn't die—punching bags and walls and an occasional barstool. How you and alcohol didn't get along. I started to tell Ben and Steph what your attorney said at trial, that it was an accident. Manslaughter isn't the same as murder. People make mistakes. I'd repeated all these lines before, once to the boyfriend you don't know about, the one I dated for a month last year. And I'd said those words to a friend I used to hang with down at the arcade, over my first and last cigarette, also something you don't know about. Making excuses for you, that's what I was doing. But instead of telling Ben and Steph my rehearsed lines, I peered into the fire and thought about what movie you would choose if you were here.

Felix came back with Teague's notebook and plopped down in the sand to draw. And it was as if someone had flicked a switch in the conversation. Steph started talking about her favorite theaters in Key Largo, and how much she missed buttered popcorn, and the three of them went on for the next two hours, the fire warm and yellow and crackling, Steph stoking it with wood to keep it high.

Before the flames burned low, while we could still see, Steph made twelve little divots in the sand and taught Felix how to play mancala. Ben fell asleep with his back to us. And I took Felix's notebook, tore Teague's snobby sticker off the front, and opened it to a fresh page. Maybe you'll never read this, but I had to talk to you. Visiting hours, dear Daddy, are officially over.

As I sharpened my golf pencil from time to time, Steph eyed my dive knife. I felt a little pulse of satisfaction, right in my sternum. One thing you're good for: keeping people at a safe distance.

The fire burned until the moon swung around the ceiling

of our island and disappeared below the trees. Without it, we melted into the dark. When the pile of logs was nothing but coals, when I was the only one left awake, I felt civilization snuff out. Movie houses, schools, hospitals, and warehouses full of gadgets and air-conditioning units and faucets—they didn't exist out here. As I drifted, the world became nothing but stars and the surf's swell and release.

The breeze shifted, became fresh and green again. I rolled over onto my back. Maybe civilization was an illusion, I thought, a piece of candy to suck on while we waited for the inevitable. In the end, someone would still be choosing the last outfit I would ever wear, no matter how many plastic insurance cards Mom had in her wallet. I thought about poor Mr. Marshall and his insurance card and what movie he liked the best. And then I thought about what I'd seen past the police tape the night you went away, the black plastic shroud and the hump of a shape underneath. And for that second, lying there by the fire, I felt closer to you than ever. Trapped with you on this island in solitary confinement. We were alike, I thought. Exactly the same.

The tears came up out of nowhere.

I let them wash everything away until I felt all wrung out, and Ben's movie question popped up in my brain. Mom. She was alive. Somewhere on the island. I could feel it, as if there was a spider silk tether joining us. If Mom could bring only one movie to a deserted island, what would she bring? I drew a blank. I know what you would say. *The Godfather*. But Mom? Three years ago, she would have picked a Kiyoshi Kurosawa flick, something emotional and painful and hopeful. Maybe *Tokyo Sonata*. And now? I had no idea who she was anymore, and I wanted to find out. I had to.

I looked at the stars, breathing in the scent of seaweed and wood smoke, and told myself I would look for her tomorrow. She was somewhere on the other side of the island. I knew it.

The salt breeze shifted, turned rotten, and a chill spread through me. I turned my head toward the ocean, its immense darkness. A faint green glow appeared, about fifty yards offshore. I watched it, breathlessly, for a long time. Or maybe it was watching me. I kept my eyes on the water until the glow faded, and the creature slipped back into the deep.

THAT NIGHT I DREAMED of my grandmother.

We sat on the sponge docks in Tarpon Springs, like we used to do when I was little, watching the Easter fireworks. Bursts of color bloomed in the sky, scattering light on the waves, like shook tinfoil.

Out of the dark came red comets, shooting above the faint silhouettes of sails clustered in their slips. A golden willow next, curving like the moving skin of a jellyfish. Then pink chrysanthemum and a green dragon's egg, and when each burst faded to black, the fireworks left bits burning in my irises.

Yiayia turned to me, looking just like she had in the pictures she'd showed me long ago, images of her when she was only fifteen and still dove the waters off of Kalymnos. But pictures and memories and reality and dreams are all the same here on the island. When you find this journal, maybe you'll be the one to figure out which world is real.

"There," she said, pointing across the river, where the fireworks fell into the sea and turned into candles, floating on the water toward us. "That's where the others are."

"What others?" I asked.

She put her fingers to her lips and her eyes sparkled, as if she were holding back a joke.

Yiayia handed me the end of a leash. At the other end was

a black cormorant, its neck slender and serpentine, its eyes wild with fear. A snare circled its throat, and I felt sorry for it.

"Let it go, Tasia," Yiayia said, and I released it. The bird flew off, a rush of feather over black water. A burst of fireworks lit up the night again. Fire on water.

It dove and came up with a gorgeous fish. The narrow snare around the bird's neck kept it from swallowing, forcing him to save it for us.

I reeled it in.

"Cormorants won't fish for you if they aren't hungry," she said. "So you keep them that way and let the hunger milk the world of one more morsel." She took the fish from the cormorant's mouth. "What vanity this is, to think we are above them."

The bird's eyes rolled and glinted in the firelight. A knot tightened around my throat. The ring. So tight I'd never be able to swallow. A burst of green lit the air, a stunning peony, falling into the sea to become candles on the water, the glow changing into phosphorus, into the beast, rising from the dark water just off the docks—and somehow, in my dream, I didn't care that it was coming. Because I was hungry, hungry in a way only my grandmother could understand.

"Sia, wake up!"

The voice came from the fireworks. And then I did wake.

The smell of brine. The beach, not the docks. The soft breeze coming up from the waves breaking not far away. The moon had slipped into the ocean hours ago, so I couldn't see much.

"Sia!" A hushed whisper. Ben, kneeling beside me, a shadow in the dark. Something in his voice made me sit up.

"Look," he said, pointing out to sea. "Look at the water."

At first I saw nothing, still caught in the funk of my strange dream. Night had swallowed the world, except the stars. I felt so tiny under the big show. The ocean swelled in the dark, whooshed back out to sea. The wind moved through the palm trees, sounding a crackle from the dry underbrush in the forest, as if the world were on fire.

Ben's hand was tight on my arm, so tight it hurt. "Get up. Come on." He led me to the water's edge. "Watch."

"What's wrong with you?" I said, and I wasn't whispering.

His other hand in darkness, on my shoulder. "Shh!" A harsh whisper. "I don't want to wake Felix. I don't know how to explain. Just. Look."

And there it was. A flash in the distance. Orange. Then white. Like an explosion at sea. But without sound, as if God had pressed the mute button on the world.

"What on earth is that?"

Another explosion, and the flames lit up the shape of the thing in the water. It was a ship. Had to be. And not a little scuba charter like ours. Bigger than something the Coast Guard would send.

I covered my mouth to keep my insides from spilling out. Along with my crushed hope.

The fire burned so far out to sea that if I held up my hand, I'd snuff out the light with my palm. I watched it burn. And then it winked out.

"Was that what I think it was?"

"If you think it's a ship exploding, then yes."

I stood listening to the swell, staring into the dark, and I couldn't breathe. "Well, there goes our glorious rescue."

He whispered something, but I wasn't listening. I walked knee-deep into the surf, useless rage filling my chest until I wanted to hurl something into the ocean. I was about two inches from an ugly cry, and I've never needed an audience for that.

I couldn't see him, but I could hear Ben come into the waves to stand next to me. "Wait, Sia," he said. "Watch the horizon."

Still fuming over our near rescue, I didn't even try to understand what he wanted me to see. A minute passed in silence, until my heartbreak disintegrated into a feeling of uselessness, focused on the absolute hopelessness of our situation. Felix, Mom—we were all done for. Ben stood so close I could feel his warmth, and before I could think about it I was searching in the dark for him, feeling through the air. I grasped two fingers and a thumb, and his hand fumbled awkwardly into mine. I remembered you saying the sea brings us together. And that thought, of you, your voice, made the tears come.

We could've been on board in a few hours, drinking sodas and eating roast chicken and rice and strawberry Pop-Tarts. They probably didn't have any of those things, just simple rations, but it was my fantasy.

"Just wait," he said, his voice low and full of a sort of awe. "It's better if you see."

I sniffed in the darkness and wiped my face with the back of my hand, embarrassed I had lost it in front of him. "What are you talking about?"

"Wait and watch."

"Why didn't you wake up Steph for this?"

"You understand weird better than she does."

Something in his voice made the hair rise on the back of my neck. "What's going on?"

"Sia, in the last two hours, I've watched that ship explode and sink five times."

"You mean five boats have come for us, and the thing got all of them?" I imagined the Coast Guard mobilizing a whole armada to find us. It figured. No one would cry much over me and Felix and Mom. But the science boat? Twenty teenagers? That's a lot of panicked parents on the mainland calling Florida senators.

I put a hand over my mouth. "Oh God, Ben. All those people."

"No, Sia," he said, his voice a strange sort of whisper, as if he were having trouble convincing himself. "It was the exact same light show five times. Same explosions. Same seconds between the flares. I counted. That's what I've been doing for hours. I was watching the water, looking for that thing to light up, seeing if it knew where we are, what it did at night, wondering if that was the best time to trap it and kill it, when we could see its glow. And then it started, and"—Ben's words ran into one another—"it's the same event over and over."

I stood on the wet sand, shivering in the cool breeze. Ben had to be hallucinating from hunger. We weren't on a loop, over and over; it would be like the same wave hitting the beach. And that just didn't happen.

He pointed into the dark. "There," he whispered. "It's beginning again."

An orange light lit the horizon.

And we watched a ship out on the black water, our only hope. The vessel flared as if hit by a torpedo. An explosion. Over the next minute, the fire slowly shrank until it winked out of existence.

It wasn't the same, I told myself.

You told me once the mind is an ocean, and most of us

live on the surface. But the currents beneath, that's what moves everything around. The currents make the boats shift position in the night, push the waves against the shore just so. And you told me most people are so foolish they actually think they're in control of who they are and where they're going.

That's why I couldn't believe, in the beginning, what I was seeing. Because I've got a current in me that's all about denial. *This is not happening. Dad's not in prison. Mom loves me unconditionally. Felix is safe. Everything will be okay from now on. If I just close my eyes and believe it.*

We watched the whole thing start up again, and again, until my theories all went out like candles on the water. That current within me pushed a few more times and then stilled.

I took Ben's hand again, leaning close to him for warmth, and watched it over and over, until dawn approached and the fires melted into the day.

Once the sun had risen enough to wake the others, Steph wandered off with Felix to scavenge, and Ben limped down to the water with Felix's notebook and a golf pencil. He sat a few feet into the wet sand, his bad leg stretched out, his curious gaze on the horizon. Hunting for Moby Dick, I guess.

I watched him for a while, his back to me, his arms wrapped around the knee of his good leg. My face burned hot just thinking about the night before, crying like that in front of someone. You always taught me to keep breakdowns private. As I've gotten older, I've started building a pile of "things Dad was wrong about." That crappy piece of advice belongs on top, consumed by flames. Still, old habits are hard to ditch.

I wandered down to the surf to rinse my face and mouth with seawater, and he caught sight of me and waved me over before I could scurry back to the fire.

I covered the distance slowly and stopped a few feet away, keeping my toes in the water. The cool rush over my feet calmed me, as it always does. "Good morning," I said, and started to put my hands in my pockets. Then I remembered a bikini and rash guard don't have pockets.

Ben didn't seem to notice my mood. He pointed northeast, out to sea. "It surfaced over there about an hour ago."

"What did it do?"

"Ate a bird."

"Well, that's fun."

"It's helpful."

"I'm sorry about last night."

I started to add, "For falling apart like that," but stopped myself. I already sounded awkward enough. If I could have reeled my words back in like a fish on a line, I would have. Because he acted like I hadn't said anything.

The notebook was open and flapping in the breeze. I sat beside him in the sand and flipped through a few pages, my face burning.

FIELD NOTES: MAY 19 (20?)

7:00 a.m. (approx.) began observations of northeast side of island, one-kilometer strip.

7:15 a.m. Creature consumed a fairy tern. Encounter lasted approximately 5 seconds.

"A fairy tern's a real thing?" I asked.

He flipped the page and pointed to a small pencil sketch he'd made. "It's a type of seabird. A new one for me. Number eighty-seven."

"It had a number on it?"

"No, that's the eighty-seventh bird species I've seen."

"You're keeping a list?"

He shrugged, but I could see how excited he was, which was pretty cute, I had to admit.

"And it's not supposed to be out here," he said. "Usually lives about halfway around the world. Maybe introduced somehow? I don't remember reading about that, though."

"And you know ALL the birds."

"Yeah," he said, matter-of-fact, not catching my tone.

He started rambling on about the weight of the bird, how it paddles its feet in the surf, where it's likely to do most of its floating, and my eyes did actually start to glaze over a little. Which lack of sleep and a lecture on birds will do to a girl. "Ben, that's great. Really. But how does this help us? We already know that thing's a meat eater." At the sound of my last words, my stomach turned. Meat. That's what we were to that thing.

"Now we know it can detect really small things, not just boats and"—he gestured to me awkwardly—"people. Which means . . ."

He looked at me as if expecting me to finish the sentence.

"That it's . . . really hungry?"

"No, that if we set a trap, it won't be that hard to draw it where we want it."

I thought about yesterday. "Yeah, I already knew that."

We fell into silence, watching for more terns. I pretended interest, pointing out random feathery things as they landed in the water, searching for minnows in the shallows. After it was too awkward to bear, I turned to go, but Ben's voice stopped me.

"I'm the one who needs to apologize."

"For what?"

"That conversation about your dad."

Oh God. That. "It's no big deal."

"I was curious, but I . . ." He looked down at his hands, which were resting on his knees, then he settled his gaze back on me. "I shouldn't have pushed. And I'm sorry you feel like you have to apologize for something you didn't do."

"We were all out of it. Tired and hungry. I didn't take it to heart."

"Uh-huh," he said, and I felt a strange vibe, like he knew a secret about me, even though we'd just met. "You're made of titanium, right?"

I blushed and looked away. The palm leaves rustled in the ocean breeze, filling the space between us.

"And thank you," Ben finally said.

"I get an apology *and* a thank you. Wow."

"What you did to get us food, it was really brave." He turned to me, his brown eyes warm. "You're pretty awesome. Especially with this survival stuff." He quickly glanced down at his leg. "Usually I am too."

I shrugged and forced myself to meet his eyes. "My dad taught me everything I know."

Ben's mouth curved into a slow smile. "Sounds like he did a good job."

Maybe you'll think it strange, but that was it for me. The moment I trusted him for real. The moment the crush became something more.

I stood and brushed the sand off my bikini bottoms, smoothed my hair back behind my ears, suddenly self-conscious.

He held out a hand. "Here, help me up. My leg's stiff."

When I took his hand, I had a weird feeling—that I'd known him all my life. Or maybe that I *would* know him for the rest of my life. A sense about us that went beyond just me getting an apology I really needed. As he steadied himself, his other hand on my shoulder, something brightened in his eyes. Maybe he felt it too.

"You want to walk down the beach with me?" I asked. "Watch us fish?"

He tilted his head, like we were both in on the same joke. "Us?"

"Just wait and see. I'm gonna get her into the water."

"Good luck." He looked out into the waves. "Nah, I'll stay here. See what else happens."

"Have fun . . . watching for birds." I made it only a few steps down the beach before he called me back.

"Sia?"

"Yeah?"

"Let's not tell her about last night."

"Last night?"

"What we saw." He tilted his head to the ocean. "She wouldn't understand."

I held his gaze and nodded, thinking about apologies and how it wouldn't hurt to give in, tell her I'm sorry. Again that pulse hit me, the kind that comes when you push through a wall you didn't even know was there until it's gone.

When I found Steph, she was dismantling the canopy of the *Last Chance* for some mysterious reason. As soon as I reminded her it was her turn to go in, she clutched her stomach. Gave me the whole "I'm too sick to go in" routine. I told her to get into the water. Her response—a dramatic dry heave into the crook of her arm. Then she gave me the saddest eyes I've ever seen. Looked at me like a blobfish caught in a tuna net.

Still feeling like a jerk from the night before and my famous non-apology, I left without trying to bully or shame her. Truth was I wanted to be in the water, to get *me* out of my head. But her playing hooky wasn't cool, and I would find a way to make her eat her excuses. No way I was going to dangle myself like fish bits for that thing because Steph thought she wasn't built for this kind of work. Total BS anyway. We are what we're taught to be. And you may have your faults, Dad, but letting fear control you was never one of them.

As I swam out, I started my count. I had ten minutes—that's what we'd agreed to. To distract myself from the fear, I planned a conversation, thinking about how you would handle Steph's weak excuse. Necessity, sweetheart. That's what you would say. After all, we'd all agreed. No one wanted to go out, but better a quick death from a beast in the ocean than a slow death from hunger on land.

I thought about Felix hearing my planned speech. Reminded myself to send him on an errand first.

The water was cool, the air salt-scented and fresh, and the sun low on the horizon. I took a breath and went under, the world below dim, the ocean at sunrise; the time for sharks to cruise and feed, the time we nudge tourists from, just in case. I kicked my way to the white sand bottom, fear rising in me, and hit the sweet spot—that place between wanting to head back to shore and swim farther out. You know what I chose. Your voice, always in my head. *Necessity, sweetheart.*

I stayed on the shallow side of the reef, surfacing a few times to check topside for disturbances in the water. I stayed out too long, but the lobster was worth it. Medium-size. Dragging his claws under some orange coral growing on the side of the black rocks. I snagged it and swam to shore. With each stroke, I imagined the sting of a jellyfish on my ankle. The rope wrapping around my calf and pulling me under.

By the time the fear had worked its way through me and bled out into the water, I was mad again. So pissed at Steph that when I came up from the surf, I was ready to bust. Steph stood with her back to me, talking to Felix. A miraculous recovery. Why had I felt bad for her and her sad little birthday gone wrong? A few feet away was the sun shelter of the *Last Chance*, in pieces. A beach towel lay on the sand, torn into strips and partially knotted together. The beginnings of a net. A really crappy one. A colossal waste of time and resources.

Felix looked up at her, smiling, as she played a clapping game with him I'd never learned as a child. Somehow that made me even madder. I threw our breakfast with perfect aim at the middle of her back.

Bull's-eye.

She squealed and fell onto the sand. Felix laughed at first, but when Steph stood, her eyes full of venom, his smile fell away. He looked from her to me.

She kicked the lobster away and it scuttled toward the surf. Felix grabbed it before it reached the damp sand, the creature flipping its tail and bucking in his hand.

"Put it in the ham tin, please," I told him. "Why don't you go help Ben?"

He ran off without a word.

Steph took two steps toward me, stopping at the wave line as if afraid to touch the water. "What'd you do that for?"

I took off my fins and stepped onto the beach. "I dunno, Steph. Maybe because you don't do anything."

"I'm making a net."

"It won't work."

"I'm making a shelter for us too."

That was actually a good idea, but I wasn't about to say so. "You should be in the water, fishing."

"I do a lot."

"It's not enough."

"Not everyone has the same skills, Sia. I've got mine, and you've got yours."

"And mine put me in mortal danger. Not really equal, Steph." And then I delivered my speech, the one you would give. About necessity. She listened quietly until I was finished, her eyes on the sand. When she met my gaze, the wounded look she'd worn since I first hit her with the lobster had given way to something else. Something hard.

"You know, Felix has been telling me a lot about you, and your family." She put air quotes around *family* in a way that made all the blood rush to my face. Her voice took on a mean girl lilt, the kind that sounds nice but isn't. "I feel really sorry for him. What it's like to visit your father in a room full of murderers and child molesters. With Dad behind bars and Mom dead at the bottom of the ocean, he's got nobody now."

I couldn't come up with a response to that. At all. Her smile became a shade sweeter.

"That's why I've been so nice to him. You should thank me."

I held out the fins and my mask and snorkel. "Your turn. Take your time."

She pulled her hands back, afraid to even touch my radioactive gear. "I told you, I'm sick."

"You don't look sick."

"The sunburn is so bad I have a fever."

"The water is cool."

She raised her eyebrows. "Water amplifies the sunlight."

"You can wear my rash guard," I said.

"It won't fit. My boobs are bigger than yours."

Is this what life would've been like if I'd kept going to public school near our apartment rather than done the homeschooling thing? People like this, times one hundred, all making little digs at me in that special language I don't get. Or maybe I'd be able to break the code if I'd grown up with them, or if I hadn't been yanked out of school after only a few weeks of being a normal freshman. Maybe I would have understood their clapping games and the way they think. But it wouldn't have been worth it. All those times I told you I wanted to go to pep rallies and football games, and asked why Mom made me miss out on all of it?

I take it all back.

Steph and I went quiet, standing on the wet sand, staring at each other. She couldn't go join her horde of girlfriends and their ninety-dollar flip-flops, and I couldn't get into my beat-up truck and drive away. We were stuck. On a beach. In the middle of nowhere. Together.

Steph sniffed and tossed her hair over her shoulder, but the strands were so tangled they caught in her ragged nails. She finally got her fingers out of the mess and looked out over the waves, rising and then curling, breaking into a shock of sea-foam. "I can't believe we're fighting," she said, her voice suddenly quiet and small.

I could. I *knew* we would. Because I had this sense now. I could feel what was about to happen. The feeling had built in me for days without me realizing it. No, not that I knew what was going to happen. I was remembering *what had already happened.* A part of me was able to touch that now.

"I can't go," she said, making fists, but she was trembling. She wouldn't look at me; instead she dug her fingernails into her palms and watched the buoy in the distance. The fear was actually *shaking* her, like a dog with a rag doll.

"You really hate the ocean, huh?" I asked.

"Who said I hated it?"

"You did. Our first day. You looked out into the big blue and said, 'I hate the ocean.'"

"I don't *hate* it. I deeply dislike it."

"Did you have a bad experience in it or something?" I asked. She sighed dramatically. "No."

"Almost drowned once?"

"I can swim if I have to."

"You saw *Sharknado* and swore you'd never get into the water again."

"Seriously?" Steph said.

We stared at each other, the roar of the surf taking up the space our words had left behind. Maybe it was low blood sugar, but all the fire in me went out. I broke eye contact and sat on the sand. Steph followed suit, which surprised me. She picked up the tiny shells scattered around her feet, giving her hands something to do. Her eyes were glassy, tired. Ready for a good cry. And it hit me why she was losing it, other than the dead cousin and the hunger and the fear. Since we'd all washed up here, Felix was the only person who'd been nice to her. I knew what that was like. Odd man out. It sucked. Just because she was a jerk with a capital *B* didn't mean it didn't suck for her too.

Steph shaded her eyes, peering out into the waves. She had the look of someone trying to read a foreign language for the first time. "Why do you like it?"

"Love it. I *love* the ocean."

She sniffed out an almost laugh. I followed her gaze. The white-tipped waves rolled in, crashed against the shore. The truth came out before I could stop myself. "The big blue is immense. Endless. It makes me feel small."

"That's exactly why I hate it," she said.

"Small in a really good way."

"There's no such thing."

I picked at my cuticles. Scratched at the grit in my hair. Thought about being small. "My mom can't run that charter without me there," I said. "She needs me to pick up Felix from school. Help him with his homework. Load the tanks. Return phone calls. Do everything."

"Poor baby."

"I'm just tired of being a lynchpin in the family," I said. "Take me out and everything spins out of control."

"You certainly are full of yourself."

"You know, Steph, I'm just trying to talk to you like a human. What's wrong with you?"

She scattered the handful of shells she'd collected. "I have no idea what that feels like."

"Being human?"

She shot me a look that stung. "No, being a lynchpin. If I weren't around, there'd be one less place to set at the dinner table, and that would be about it." She paused, as if thinking. "I'd probably get a spot on the mantle, though."

"For your urn?"

"My picture." She made a little half-snort laugh. "Mantle space is very high rent in our family." She gave me a weak smile and looked at her toes, which she had been burying under a clump of seaweed. "You know what happens when the lynchpin goes?"

"Disaster. Anarchy. Hysteria."

"Ha, ha. No. The family finds a new lynchpin." She tossed her hair over her shoulder—more successfully this time—and met my eyes. "You're a lot less important than you think you are."

Like you, I'm opposed to eye rolls. Hate it when other people do it. But that comment, it deserved an eye roll. "Look, you can wait a bit, maybe an hour to pull it together. But we agreed. We share the risk. That means you need to get in and get us a lobster."

Steph bit her lip and looked over her shoulder at Ben, who studied the water, the notebook in hand, twirling the golf pencil between his fingers.

"Steph, his leg is getting worse. And if he doesn't eat . . ."

I stared at her until she looked at me. She closed her eyes, a martyr with her face upturned to the sky.

"Okay, I'll go in. Once. For Ben. And Felix." She held up one finger. "But waaay down the beach, around the curve."

"Why?"

"To confuse it." She looked out into the surf. Trying a different spot on the island wasn't a bad idea, although something in her tone told me I should go with her.

She got up, took the fins from my hand.

"I'm coming with you."

She froze, composing her answer carefully. "Your brother is terrified. And you'd rather hang around babysitting me? Real nice, Sia."

When Steph turned to leave, I didn't follow. "Steph?"

She turned back, her eyes expectant, as if she thought I might apologize or thank her or something.

"I'm glad we're finally talking. Really. But if you ever talk about my family that way again, you'll have a lot more to worry about than a sunburn and a—"

Click. It came from behind us.

BOTH STEPH AND I FROZE.

"Don't move," a voice said.

The wind changed, and I smelled sweat, heard someone shift in the sand.

Robinson Crusoe was back. Definitely *not* a figment of my imagination.

I exchanged a quick glance with Steph. The soft push and slur of his feet reached my ears as he tromped closer. Toward the lobster in the ham tin. I cut a quick glance to my right, and I saw my brother far down the beach, his back to us as he talked to the small things that lived in the surf. Ben was nowhere to be seen.

The footsteps behind came closer, circled us, and stopped.

Mud-spattered feet. Dirt encrusted under his toenails. He'd rolled up the white pants to his knees. I thought about tackling him. It's what you would do.

"On your knees, both of you."

Both of us dropped without a word.

I finally looked up. The guy looked more haggard than the last time I saw him, his face not much cleaner than the rest of him. So young. A baby under all that grime. The desperate glint in his eyes sent a pulse of fear through me.

He moved the gun from my forehead to Steph's. In his other

hand he held the ham tin. The lobster scratched and tapped against the corrugated sides.

"What else you got?"

"Nothing," I said.

He turned the pistol back on me. "I'm asking the redhead." He pressed the barrel between her eyes. "Your food. Where is it." A statement, not a question.

"You're holding it," Steph snapped back.

"Hey, dude, everything we get, we get from the ocean," I said.

He pushed the gun into my face again. "I didn't ask you!" He turned back to Steph. "Equipment. All of it. Show me."

Steph hesitated a moment. "But we only just met."

I almost smiled. Almost. But I was hungry and scared and a scary guy with a gun wanted our lobster. And then the Sense came again. The feeling I knew what was going to happen, or what had already happened. It scrambled my brain, made the world swim. It also told me what I needed to know. Odds were this guy wasn't going to kill us.

"Desalinator. Knives. Weapons," he said as he glanced around the area, looking for our stores. "Where's the guy you were with?"

Neither of us answered. The glint in his eye sharpened. Maybe I was wrong. Maybe I was losing it. Maybe I needed to channel you and try to wrench the weapon from his hand and end him. Then a flash—dark hair, dark skin, ratty T-shirt, bloody bandage—entered the corner of my vision.

Ben. At the edge of the palm forest. He made hand gestures I didn't understand, like a cop communicating with his partner in an action movie. Totally incomprehensible. But I got the gist. Distract him.

"Weapons?" I asked him. "My mom hates guns, so she'd

never let them on the boat, and this girl"—I gestured to Steph— "came here with a bunch of science geeks. The best she's got is a PH kit and a microscope."

Steph had seen Ben as well. "Both at the bottom of the ocean. Sorry."

Ben crept up from the forest shadows, limping far too slowly. He held a fist-sized rock. I kept talking, fast and loud to cover his steps. "Look. I know you're hungry. I am too. But that doesn't mean you go all *Lord of the Flies* on us."

"Lord of the what?"

"Really?" Steph said, in a tone she usually reserved for me.

Robinson Crusoe decided at that moment to clock her on the side of her head with the butt of the pistol. Steph squealed. Ben stumbled, shock registering on his face.

"Enough! Weapons, now."

Steph held her head and moaned loudly to cover Ben's approach.

"I swear we didn't have weapons on the charter," Steph said. "Things have gotten bad in Florida, but they don't let us take guns on school field trips."

Robinson Crusoe blinked as if recalculating. "Florida?"

Ben limped closer, rock ready.

I raised my voice and babbled to give him cover. "Well, technically, we might be in the Bahamas now, because we might've drifted off course because of the currents, which were really pushing us around, and—"

Our captor waved the gun. "What are you talking about? We're nowhere near Florida."

Steph and I exchanged a glance. Ben was only steps away, the rock raised high, ready to strike. Robinson Crusoe pushed the gun into my face.

"I don't know who you people are"—he said this in a quiet, rational voice—"or how you got here. But this here is the South Pacific, and I don't give a rat's—"

Thunk.

Steph let out a short scream. And Robinson Crusoe slumped to the sand.

I FOUND A SLIMY LENGTH OF ROPE in the cor-
ner of the *Last Chance*, and Steph began some weird Girl Scout
knot that she half remembered. I ripped it out of her hand and
started to tie that handcuff knot you taught me. And yes, you're
right, the one I said I'd never need. She glared at me and pulled
the rope out of my hands. I yanked it back.

"So I was hallucinating, huh?" I said, finishing my wrap-
and-cinch double-column knot. Robinson Crusoe lay on the
sand like a dead fish.

"Can't blame us for not believing you," Steph said.

"Sure I can."

The sun was behind Ben, so I couldn't see his expression.
Then I stood up, and the corona around him disappeared. He
was watching me with a half-curious, half-amused expression,
the kind of look he gave me back on the *Last Chance* when he
first met me.

"I'm sorry I didn't believe you," he said.

"Two apologies in one day," I said. "Wow."

Steph looked from his face to mine, trying to figure out
what she'd missed.

Ben broke eye contact first, lowering himself carefully onto
to the sand while gritting his teeth. The blood seeping out of his
bandage was hard to miss.

I kneeled beside him to get a better look. "Oh no, did you—"

He pushed my hand away. "I'll do it myself. Later." A shadow passed over his face, and the warmth I'd seen in his eyes earlier this morning shut off. I got a hint of it then—what he was hiding from us—but I brushed it off as some kind of don't-touch-me-when-I'm-wounded guy thing.

Ben turned Crusoe's head to get a better look. "Who is he?"

The prisoner lay curled on his side, hands and feet bound. He was so filthy he looked like some ugly thing that had crawled out of the ocean and died.

"Someone who thinks we're in the South Pacific, apparently," Steph said. "I'm thinking keeping him tied up is a good idea."

"He must have been on your boat," Ben said, looking up at me. "He wasn't on ours."

"We had ten divers," I said. "This guy wasn't with us. And look at his clothes. He got here long before we did."

Ben shook his head. "No, he came from one of the boats. Doesn't make sense otherwise."

"Look at how frayed the edges of his pants are, and the sleeves," I said.

Ben examined the ragged hem. "Coulda just had a rough first day." He nodded at Steph. "Occam's razor."

Steph caught my confused expression. "When you have competing theories," she explained slowly, like I was five, "the one with the fewest assumptions is probably true. Simplest explanation here? He came from one of the boats."

"There were twenty people with us," Ben said. "I only knew half of them. We were from different schools."

Steph nudged the prisoner with her toe, clearly afraid he might bite, and picked up the gun. "But where did he get this?"

I reached out to take it from her before she blew my head off, but she pulled away, frowning. Then she squinted and fiddled around with the release on the side. The magazine fell onto the sand. "Gah! It's loaded!" She took a step back. "Okay, okay. Those are bullets. Real bullets."

"You know what this means?" Ben said.

I looked from the unconscious guy trussed up on the sand to our limited supply of water. "Our time on the island just got way more complicated?"

"No," Ben said, weighing the gun in his palm. "We have something other than palm trees and scuba tanks now."

It took me a moment to put everything together. "You think you can kill that thing with a handgun?"

"Of course not. But maybe we could use it to *set off* some kind of trap, or . . ." He turned the pistol over and examined it, eyeing the weapon like someone would examine a harmless piece of wood. It was obvious he'd never touched a gun before.

I put my hand on top of his. "Don't do that. There's still one in the chamber."

When I got nothing from him but a confused look, I carefully took the pistol from him and pulled the slide back. Ben's eyes widened as the last round fell into the sand.

"We should store this somewhere safe."

We all looked down the beach at the same time, to where Felix had fallen asleep in the shade of some driftwood, completely unaware of what had happened. Mom was right. An earthquake could hit and that boy would sleep through it.

I walked the gun to the boat, glad Ben was happy. But after two seconds with its cold weight in my hand, I wanted to throw it into the ocean. And not just because I'm haunted by the dream image of Ben gutshot on the beach. So here's confession number whatever: The gun reminded me of you, and not in a good way. That part of you I don't like, that part of me that won't forgive you for what you did that night, that stupid, stupid night that took you away from me, from Felix, and Mom, and landed you in a crappy prison. Pistols and bowie knives and punches that knock a guy out cold. Forever.

Sorry that hurts, but I promised you the truth. About you, and about me.

I stashed the gun under a seat compartment and washed my hands with sand and water, as if I were scrubbing off the memory of it from my skin. I should've thrown it into the ocean. Mom would have. She hates all the combat stuff now—the antique weapons and your martial arts posters and nunchucks and brass knuckles, all of which you won't find when you come home. The night you went away, after Felix drifted off, Mom boxed it all up and left it on the curb for garbage day.

So it's time for another confession. I almost rescued your death collection for you. I wanted to sneak it back inside our apartment and hide the box somewhere she wouldn't look. But I kept waffling about it. Lay on my bed watching videos on my phone until I drifted off, and when the roar of the garbage truck woke me in the morning, it was too late.

I threw on clothes and ran down our apartment stairs to save it. Really, I did. Or maybe I walked. Maybe I just wanted to see it disappear. I can't remember anymore, three years later, what I did. Anyway, you won't find it when you come home.

YOU PROBABLY KNOW ALL the species of fear, sitting in your tiny cell, surrounded by a reef full of dangerous creatures. So you know the kind of fear that makes your bladder soft, your bowels loose. The kind that reminds you that underneath all your thoughts and dreams and plans for the future, you're still walking around in a meat suit.

This kind of fear and me, we weren't friends.

Standing there in the wet sand, the sun hot on my scorched face, I looked for ripples in the water. Swells. Telltale humps under the waves. That thing tunneling its way back and forth along the coast of our mysterious island, tonguing the ocean currents for traces of us, my sweat, the blood from a tiny cut, a hint of my saliva.

And Dad, I couldn't even spit into my mask. My arms, my legs, they were parts that would go first. Pieces of me sputtering out like the edges of Easter fireworks, disappearing into the dark. Strange thoughts bubbled up. The Sense rose in me. I'd never felt so vulnerable, not even when I was floating in the dark that first night dive with you.

A long time ago Yiayia showed me an old black-and-white picture of her from the 1930s she kept tucked away in a box of letters. Her mother was in the picture too. They stood on a small fishing boat, both smiling, wearing old-fashioned swimsuits, their hair tied up in scarves. The cliffs of Kalymnos rose in the background, immense and jagged. She must've been fifteen at the time.

She told me that after her fourteenth birthday, she and her mother spent almost every day free diving. She told me what that was like; so little between your skin and the big blue, no neoprene or tank or regulator, plunging deep to find the sponges that would keep the entire family housed and fed all year. Her eyes seemed so young as she spoke, all the time between her old age and that perfect moment in the picture gone, somebody else's messed-up, off-track life. She was glad she had Mom and me. Still, a big piece of her wanted to go back to that moment in time when neither of us existed and it was just her, her mother, and the sea.

Yiayia and I drank mountain tea and talked about the big blue for hours—diving in the cold waters off Kalymnos where she grew up, then the warm waters of the Keys when her father moved the family just after the war ended, where she learned to judge her depth by the colors as they slowly seeped out of the reef. Red coral dimmed as she passed the twenty-foot mark. Orange seeped out of the fans when she'd passed forty. And when she couldn't see yellow anymore, she knew she was close to her limit. The greens and blues and purples, they stayed with her all the way to the glorious bottom, to eighty feet—where the other free divers didn't dare to go—all on a single breath. She told me that's why blue was her favorite color: it was one of the few things in life that never gave up on her.

As I listened, I imagined myself with her, back when she was young and no one called her Yiayia. When she was just Litsa, diving for sponges. We were creatures of the sea, nothing between us and the ocean. We belonged in a way I've never belonged above.

You always thought my love of the ocean came from you, Dad, from our time fishing and the first snorkeling trips. But she was first.

So I stood on the beach on this strange island that didn't make sense, the sun a hot coal on my skin, lips cracked like a dried-out flower petal, and focused on that image of Litsa and me, diving into the deep. A fantasy. Like I said, dreams and fantasies and reality all blend together here. That memory feels as real to me as my memories of you.

Unafraid, I slipped on my fins and my mask and walked into the surf.

The sand shifted underneath as I kicked my fins against the soft brush of current. Sunlight filtered down and illuminated the world below, patterning over the sand and embedded tiny shells, the moving tufts of seaweed. I could see for a hundred feet. You would've loved taking out a group of divers in this kind of water.

I counted. No more than ten minutes, I reminded myself. Before it could smell me.

My skin felt thinner the farther out I went in my search for lobster or anything slow. It was *my* day, I told myself, a good day for fishing in the deep. My grandmother swam a few feet ahead, her long dark hair trailing behind her.

Finally, when I was about to turn around and head back to shore, I spotted the crab. A nice one a little ways ahead and forty feet down. Its spindly legs stuck out from under a shelf, and I thought about how they'd look with steam coming off them. My stomach pinched with hunger.

Ten minutes were almost up, and if I turned around right

then, I would've made it back in time. But the taste of cooked meat rose up in my head, making me light-headed. What was another minute? Steph's ten-minute rule was a stab in the dark anyway.

I took a deep breath and imagined I was diving off Kalymnos. And I went deep, the red bleeding slowly from the coral, then the orange seeping out of the fish as the bottom rose up to meet me. I would stay down for the two-minute burn if I needed to, Litsa there beside me, young and strong and powerful.

Counting out the seconds, I descended to the rock where the food hid, a black, craggy mass the size of a car and covered with bright coral. I hovered above, eyeing the last leg that stuck out from underneath the shelf. The tip of its pincher moved, dragging in the sand. Litsa swam in circles like a mermaid a few feet away, her black hair twisting and floating in the sea.

Go on now, Child. You can do it.

I pushed off the rock and grabbed dinner.

The crab convulsed in my hand. A sudden shock of pain. I'd grabbed it in the wrong spot, and its pinchers took a slice of flesh from my thumb. Thoughtless, clumsy. An amateur's crab fishing mistake.

A tiny cloud of blood formed and floated past my mask. My heart picked up a beat. Thirty seconds into my free dive and there was already blood in the water. I pressed my thumb against it until it hurt, tried to will my heart to slow.

My grandmother didn't seem fazed, starting for the surface, asking me to follow with crab in hand. I started to swim up and passed the edge of the rock.

And stopped.

The light above me dimmed, as if a cloud had moved in front

of the sun. A flash of movement in the distant deep. Gray. Huge. And moving my way.

I sank down below the edge of the rock shelf, searching for a place to hide. Reef rock—that was my only option.

I told myself to stay calm and I kept the count to ease my fear. Forty-five . . . forty-six . . . forty-seven, gripping the crab hard, as if fear had turned to electricity, making my hands spasm and clench. It struggled, scrabbled, the sound of its scrape rolling through the water. I pinned it against the coral. And I counted.

Fifty, fifty-one, fifty-two . . .

Pushing myself up a few inches, I peered over the edge. A steely shape, forming and growing in the hazy distance. Absolutely nothing, I told myself. A school of snapper or smelt. Not the thing. Something else.

The gray shape grew, swimming straight for my hump of coral. I went still, like those rabbits in the book you made me read when I was twelve, and I watched it come, suddenly thinking about rabbits and how they're born to be prey.

The gray shape wasn't a school of anything.

An oversized dolphin. That's what I told myself. The shape shifted direction, and when I saw it from tip to tail, my heart flipped like a fish on dry land. Pale belly. Darker gray on the sides. Dorsal fin. It changed directions toward me, and I ducked lower, hugging the rock as if I could melt into it. It swam over the rock and me.

Sixty-one, sixty-two, sixty-three . . .

The burn would come soon, deep in my lungs. The huge tiger shark sliced through the water above me, circling. It turned its face to me, and I pressed myself into the rock.

The rounded head tapered to a snout as long as my arm. Its

mouth hung open as if tasting the water. It swiveled its head side to side, dumbly searching. Sharp teeth. A hundred of them. The seconds ticked away.

Seventy-five, seventy-six, seventy-seven . . .

My body's cry for oxygen was coming too soon, because I hadn't been practicing like I said I had.

I waited for the shark to turn away. I shoved my body between a lump of brain coral and an orange sea fan—becoming just another part of the reef. Except for the blood coming out my hand. Litsa swam in circles a few feet away, counting out the seconds. *You're fine*, her eyes said.

She could make it to two minutes. So could I.

Seventy-eight, seventy-nine, eighty . . .

The shark swam so close I saw its tiny scales, the remora on the underside of the white belly. The push of its wake swept over my skin, paralyzing. I thought of offering it the crab, a sacrifice to the sea god.

Fire burned inside my chest. I made myself stay. Closed my eyes and turned my face to the black rock. Pretended it was gone. Imagined my hand reaching out for the sponges down deep. My grandmother was no longer beside me. *I* was my grandmother, and I was fifteen and strong and free and hunting.

I opened my eyes just as the shark turned, its body curving, and swam back the way it had arrived, and away.

Ninety-one, ninety-two, ninety-three . . .

Black spots formed in my vision, my lungs burning away like tissue paper. My racing heart had betrayed me, taken all the oxygen from my blood. I got ready to shoot to the surface. Just a few more seconds to be safe.

Fifty feet away, the shark stopped. Struggled. It was tangled up in something, body jerking like it had been thrown into a pot of boiling oil. A phosphorescent green glow pierced the haze. My eyes widened.

No.

Not here.

Not now.

I pushed off the rock and raced for the surface. The green glow pulsed in the deep, and the shark twisted against the filaments that held it.

Not far now, the surface, shining above me.

One hundred two, one hundred three, one hundred four . . .

The black spots had become growing dark masses, the green glow nudging the corner of my eye, along with two strange white shapes my brain couldn't make out. Like huge rectangles, floating, bobbing. Boats. A small silver shape. The images faded, blacked out.

My eyes. They were dying, screaming for oxygen along with my brain.

I broke through the surface and gasped a lungful of air.

Something struggled in my hand. The crab. I'd held on somehow, a current of fear turning my grip into an iron clamp. It had sliced me again and I hadn't noticed.

I swam for shore, not daring to look back. Someone had set off a firebomb in my veins. Then I heard screams behind me. An explosion. And I didn't look. The crab struggled, slowing me down. I thought of dropping it. Then I imagined Felix's face when I told him there'd be nothing for dinner.

The land bobbed into focus ahead, suddenly bright, as if the sun had turned on like a light. And then I was remembering again, that Sense this had already happened in a thousand different ways, and in some of those memories, I didn't make it to shore.

That last thirty seconds . . . I'm not sure how to explain it, but I *became* the waves, became the burn in my muscles and the Sense building within me. Reason gone. I was nothing but the taste of salt water and the gasp of breath and the burn of effort, the rough shell of the crab in my hand. It's strange, the tricks your mind plays to get you through. The mind is a little kid shut in a room with toys and horrors, and it still has to play, no matter what.

The beast was gone. Had never existed. You showed up, swimming beside me. Litsa freestyled a few feet behind. We were all coming back from the perfect dive, my grandmother at fifteen, and you before you'd killed someone. An ice chest waited for us on shore. There would be water. Oranges and pineapple. Yellow snapper on ice. Your portable grill. And we would watch the night fall over the island, like we used to when we were together, and eat our fill and stare at stars and laugh at your ridiculously unfunny jokes.

I reached the shore. Crawled up onto the wet sand and collapsed face-first. The ocean swelled and faded behind me. Cool, drenched sand on my skin, I thanked Yiayia for staying with me. I thanked you. Both you and she disappeared in a puff of light and air.

I was alone again.

I lay gasping on the sand, too weak to do anything but breathe and hold on to our angry dinner, and a realization drifted to my mind, up from the place where I keep things I thought I'd forgotten, like the capital of Maine, the order of the planets, the atomic number of helium. And I laughed into the sand. Because my mind was assembling all the pieces I'd glimpsed out there in the ocean. A soda can, floating in the water as if some yahoo had thrown it at the shark. And the white hulls of two charters, side by side.

I staggered back to camp, the crab clenched in my fist, my legs shaking and my stomach queasy. Steph had put aside her home-made net and dragged the canopy from the *Last Chance* farther up onto the beach. She kneeled next to a pile of metal odds and ends, lashing together rods, making her sun shelter. It seemed such an odd thing to do—making us a shelter—when the world was splitting in half.

Ben sat against the boulder, the notebook in his lap, a couple of crude sketches crossed out. Felix was dragging a piece of drift-wood, heading to a spot down the beach where he'd laid out several others in a row. It looked like the beginnings of a giant *S*.

His face broke into a smile as I approached, although when he got a good look at my expression, it faded.

I dropped the crab next to the fire.

"Hey, you got a big one!" Felix said, leaning over the crab and poking it with a stick. It snapped at him.

I pulled him back and showed him my hand. "You wanna lose a finger?"

A few feet away, Steph put down her screwdriver, her expression unreadable. "Yeah, so if you get a cut like that, Felix, just keep it clean with seawater, okay? And we've got a tube of Neosporin in the charter." She glanced at my hand and went back to her work. "Don't use it all, Sia."

Ben limped over and picked up the crab. "Sorry, Felix, but this one's dinner."

His face fell and he turned away to the ocean, wincing. "Bye, Frankie."

Ben threw the crab on the coals. It struggled, its powerful claws fighting across the sizzling glow.

"You have to give some of Frankie to the guy," Felix said.

I followed Felix's gaze and my breath stuttered.

Our prisoner was awake. Blood from the wound Ben had given him stained the collar of his dingy white shirt. And his hands and feet were turning an unnatural blue. I'd tied the rope too tight.

I grabbed another line from the *Last Chance* and kneeled in front of him to tie a better version of your handcuff knot before taking off the old one. When I finished and stood, he looked up me at curiously and flexed his fingers.

"Better?" I asked.

He didn't respond, his gaze returning to the crab that smoked and turned brilliant on the coals.

"Did he say anything while I was gone?" I asked Ben.

Ben shook his head. "Nothing that makes sense. He keeps giving us his rank and serial number. He thinks he's a soldier or something."

"What is it?" I asked.

Ben squinted at me. "What is what?"

"His rank and serial number."

"Why? He made it up."

I didn't tell them what I'd seen, what I thought. I still had something to figure out. Occam's razor. Occam's razor told Ben the guy was from the science trip, wrecked here when we were, just getting out of the ocean on a different shore, and out of his mind with grief after watching all his friends die. That explanation had the fewest assumptions. But I'd formed a theory as I walked the crab over to the others. Weird and irrational, but a theory.

I kneeled in front of the prisoner. From a distance, the half-grown beard made him look like a man, but up close, he looked as young as Ben and Steph and me. A little acne over the cheeks and the bridge of his nose.

"How old are you?" I asked.

The question seemed to throw him. He swallowed, his Adam's apple moving up and down. "Seaman First-Class Graham Fitch, serial number twenty-eight—"

"Yeah, yeah, I get it. But you gotta know none of what's going on here is normal, right?"

Graham didn't answer.

"Have you seen the show?" I asked.

Smoke blew over both of us and he blinked, his eyes watering.

"Ben and I saw it last night. A ship out there." I nodded toward the sea, toward the west where the sun was making its way down. "Explosions. The ship sinking."

Steph got up from her rock, her face a mask of confusion. "Why didn't you tell me about this?"

"Because Ben doesn't know what it means," I said, "and he's been trying to work it out. But I've figured it out."

Ben side-eyed me. "No, you haven't." I got the feeling he liked to be the first one to decipher the math problem, the answer to the bonus question.

I turned back to the boy pretending to be a man. "Did you see it happening, over and over, like it was on a loop?"

Our prisoner's expression went dark, and young, like he couldn't keep his mask on any longer.

"Yes."

"And what do you think it means?"

"I got no idea."

His accent pegged him as a southerner. Maybe Texas. Alabama.

"One more question, Graham."

He looked up at me suspiciously.

"What year is it?"

Steph started to laugh behind me, and I raised a hand to shut her up.

"Not that it matters," Graham said, "but June. I think. Maybe July. And it's 1943."

I DIDN'T ASK SEAMAN Graham Fitch any more questions. Instead I pulled Ben and Steph down the beach to talk, and told Felix to tend the crab.

And I gave them my theory, nuts and all.

On this island, and in the waters surrounding it, time had become elastic, fluid. Time had become one big bowl of water sloshing about. It explained the light show the night before, that ship exploding again and again. It explained what I'd just seen out in the reef—our two charters, which should be either wrecked on the ocean floor or lying useless on the beach, somehow miraculously functional and floating side by side, just as they had been three days ago.

It was impossible.

But it was happening.

It was as if God had pressed rewind on the world, again and again, like a child replaying her favorite scene in a movie. And we got to see all that death played out again and again—a sick sort of *Groundhog Day* for sailors.

During my speech, Steph stared at her feet, concentrating. When I finished, she turned to Ben and said, "I think we should tie her up with Graham."

Ben ignored her. He scratched at his beard shadow. "It would explain the birds," he said.

"Would you stop it with the stupid birds?" Steph said.

"What about them?" I asked.

"The terns," he said, nodding to the flock congregating a little ways down the beach. "There are four of them. Always four, every day. In the same spot."

Steph threw up her hands in frustration. "So? It's a flock. And they like that spot."

He gave Steph a harsh look and moved close to me and pointed. "The one with the black spot on his wing, see that one?"

The terns made their way up from the surf and wandered into dry sand. The one with the black spot on its wing pecked something at its feet, the breeze from the surf ruffling its feathers.

"Keep your eye that one, Sia," Ben said, still pointing. "He's about to let go of that dead fiddler crab and attack the bird next to him, the one with the missing toe." He put his hand on my arm. "Watch," he finished in a soft, awed voice.

I waited and watched my feathered friend from my first day here anticipating his turn for grub. And I couldn't stop thinking about how good it felt to have Ben's hand on my arm, how calm I felt with him next to me.

Ben leaned in and whispered. "Three . . . two . . . one . . ."

Sure enough, the tern with the black spot attacked the one next to it. The other tern hopped a few steps, opened its beak, and let out an angry squawk.

"There, you see that?" He smiled at Steph triumphantly.

Steph looked from me to him, confused. "So you're psychic now?"

"No. It happens exactly that way a couple of times a day."

She stared blankly at him, and he let out a heavy sigh, his eyes closed.

"They hunt in the surf for exactly four and a half minutes—I've counted—and then they go up there on the sand, circle that dead fiddler, and the fight breaks out between those two. Then the one with the missing toe flies off above the palm forest."

Steph turned to stand next to us as we all watched and waited. I could feel her holding her breath. Then it played out exactly as Ben said. The tern with the missing toe took off and flew above the tops of the palms. The others stayed on the beach, fighting over the fiddler crab.

"See?" Ben said.

Steph shook her head and walked away, like she did that first night after I'd brought up her cousin. I waited for her to admit we were onto something, that we were right. Instead she turned, rubbing her arms, suddenly cold. She glanced at the ocean and then up and down the beach. Looking for rescue again.

"Can we eat now?" she asked. Not waiting for an answer, she rotated to walk toward the fire.

I shook my head, watching her clomp her way through the sand to the fire circle. She walked like a city girl, like the world was supposed to be smoothed out for her. A sudden image hit me, of Ben and Steph making out by his locker, and I felt a little sick.

"I really can't see you two together," I said.

"Why?"

I swallowed a few petty reasons before I settled on one. "She's so closed-minded."

"She's practical."

"She's useless."

"She's making us a shelter. I would call that useful."

"It'll probably fall apart and kill us all."

"She's actually the president of the engineering club."

I avoided his stare by examining my cuticles. Just out of earshot, Steph kneeled next to Felix, who was drawing in the sand. Trying to keep his mind off the crab dying in the fire behind them. She said something the wind whipped away before I could hear. Felix responded with his big belly laugh, something I hadn't heard in so long.

"Oh yeah," Ben said, nodding in Steph's direction. "I see your point. Completely evil."

"Now you're making fun of me."

"Just because she doesn't like you doesn't mean she's a terrible person." He nudged me with an elbow. "Maybe you should give her a chance to get to know you. And you realize you can't really blame her for not wanting to listen to our theories. Time loops aren't supposed to be real. She's freaking out."

I looked out into the water, where I'd seen the past come together with the now, watched the waves beat at the shore over and over. "She's not the only one."

I haven't had a chance to write for a few days, because Ben has been hogging my notebook. He's filled several pages with diagrams that look like traps. They all suck. Mine weren't any better, but I still didn't like him crossing them out. If you were here, we'd already be cooking bits of that thing over the campfire.

You may have your faults, but at least you know how to end something.

Sorry. I didn't mean to sound like that. I guess I'm just tired. And like I said, I don't have an eraser.

We needed supplies—food, mostly—so I decided to go

exploring. Alone. Ben didn't like the idea. Next thing I know, Steph signed up.

At sunrise, Ben dropped a couple of water bottles into Steph's makeshift net—which was only big enough to serve as a bag at this point—and took off his shirt to make a cloth handle—which I appreciated for several reasons—and slipped the whole thing over my shoulder. I caught his eyes lingering over what I'd chosen to wear for the expedition. Since I was nice enough to let pale-as-a-delicate-lily Steph wear my rash guard for the day, I wore nothing but the string bikini. Steph had fashioned part of a beach towel into a headdress to protect her face. The rest of the towel was tied around her waist to shield her pale legs.

She looked ridiculous. And I didn't. Which was, I have to admit, gratifying.

"Keep your eye out for anything we can use in the trap," Ben said.

"We heard you the first six times," Steph said, tying her ragged beach towel tighter around her waist.

Graham, who sat against a boulder, tied hands resting in his lap, cracked a smile. I frowned at him and he tried to hide it, checking out the knots around his wrists as if he'd just noticed they were there.

"You sure I can't come?" Felix asked, his voice full of pleading. "I'm good at finding stuff." He was right. At least half the converters had been built from his finds.

"You need to stay here and take care of Ben," I told him. "He needs help fetching things."

"You could untie the guy," Felix said. "He can help."

Graham raised an eyebrow at me.

"Not yet," I said.

"Your brother's right," Graham said. "I can help."

I ignored Graham and kneeled in front of Felix. "We'll talk about it when I get back, okay?"

Felix nodded sullenly, and I wiped some dirt from his cheek. Then Felix threw his arms around my waist and hugged me so tight I felt my throat constrict. "You're gonna find Mom. I just know it," he said before he let me go.

Steph and I set off down the beach into the brightening dawn.

Our first hour was spent in blessed silence. The sun rose steadily before us, a ball of molten glass, hot and red, spreading out over the water. The glow turned orange, then faded until the strip of beach ahead lit up bright white, like an endless path to nowhere. The surf to our left crashed and surged. To the right, the palm forest loomed. Its darkness looked cool, and I wanted to feel it on my skin, press the bottoms of my feet into something other than sand.

But the thought of going back into that place, into the root cellar smell, made my insides twist. Though it wasn't really the smell that got to me. It was that odd, intense déjà vu washing over me in a sickening wave. I know it sounds strange, but the Sense, it courses under the skin sometimes. Curdling me from the inside out.

We rounded a bend and discovered a small cove the size of a basketball court. My heart leapt, because at first I thought I'd found a place too shallow for that thing to hunt me. I could fish in peace, bring up everything we needed to survive. Lobster. Crab. Sea urchin. A whole sushi buffet.

As we got closer, a second look at the color of the water—a dusky blue—proved I was wrong. It was deep enough.

I could almost hear the island laughing at us, its throat full of broken glass, promising us a safe haven before taking it away.

When Steph finally spoke, I was so focused on the nooks and crannies of the rocks, wondering how much time I'd have to search, that I'd almost forgotten she was there.

"Okay, I'm game."

I turned, startled. Steph walked briskly alongside me, squinting into the sun, her towel hat flapping in the stiff breeze coming off the crashing surf.

"Game for what?" I asked.

"Let's say you and Ben are right." She held up a hand to stop me before I could interrupt. "Just for argument's sake. The weird time loop thing. How did it happen?"

"You believe us?"

"No."

"Then why even ask?"

"Look, if you two are so sure, then you should have a theory or something."

I thought about it for a few wave cycles, walking closer to the water so that sea-foam brushed over the tops of my feet. Steph stepped away from it. Made of sugar, you would say. Afraid to melt. The water surged, swirled, and turned into chaos before it rushed the shore again.

"Okay then," I said. "Time, which should be going forward, is all mixed-up because of solar flares and . . . changes in the earth's magnetic field."

"Mixed-up?"

"You know, time soup."

"Your seven-year-old brother would come up with something better than that."

I hate to admit it, but her comment actually bothered me. "You got a better idea?"

Steph's sigh was so dramatic I heard it over the waves. "It's like a . . ." She paused. "Like a Klein bottle."

"A what?" I asked before I could stop myself.

"A bottle where the outside and the inside are the same. Not time soup. A Klein bottle."

"There's no such thing," I said.

"You could google it."

"I could google mermaids too," I said. "If I had a *phone*."

"It's a real thing. Trust me. At least that's what Ben was saying last night. Not that I didn't already know about them."

Steph left it at that, leaving me to stew in the silence.

"You tossed around a bunch of theories with Ben about time loops because you don't believe any of it?" I asked. "That makes a lot of sense."

"I like to hear Ben talk," she said. "He's so pretty."

"You do remember you're not together anymore, right?"

She stopped walking. So did I.

"No, we're not together," Steph said. "But he's my friend. And that means I talk some sense into him when he's on the wrong track."

"You mean . . ."

"He's wasting his time."

"With . . ."

She paused long enough for her gaze to become razor sharp. "Some things will never work, no matter how much effort you put into them."

"Are we still talking about our trap?"

The small smile touched the corner of her mouth as she turned away to continue walking. "We need to focus on signaling the Coast Guard, not killing a squid. Thing. Whatever it is. That's all I meant."

A bit of you rose in me then.

"Waste of time, huh?"

"Yeah," she called over her shoulder.

I grabbed her arm and pulled her around. She stumbled, her expression startled.

"What the—"

"I'm not going to bother trying to defend myself and who I am, because that's a colossal *waste* of time. And it doesn't really matter. But you can't ignore what Ben and I saw two nights ago. Or what I saw yesterday morning, out in the water. Or the . . ." I trailed off as sudden déjà vu slid under my skin.

A collection of images.

A memory.

Steph and me brawling it out on the beach, pulling at each other's hair, old-school girl fight. The sunlight glinted like teeth on the water, blinding me. My knee in her stomach. A mouth full of sand. Her nails down my cheeks.

My hand dropped from her shoulder. I touched my face where the marks would have been. I blinked into the sunlight and the beach lurched. The images faded.

"Whatever, Sia," Steph said, stepping back from me, and the look in her eyes made me think she felt it too. Saw it even. "Make up whatever theories you want."

I stood still, staring at her, my stomach reeling as she backed away from me.

"You know what we do?" Steph said. "I say we finish the SOS message on the beach—your little brother is a genius, by the way. I don't know why the rest of us didn't think of it—and then the Coast Guard comes. We won't need the net. We won't need that useless plan you and Ben keep talking about. Because there's no Klein bottle. No time loop. And we're going to get off this island. Ben and I are going to go back to our world, and you'll go somewhere else."

I was about to argue with her, but something over her shoulder stopped me. In the forest, just beyond the shadows. Movement—a flash of it, like someone slipping behind a trunk. And with it came a sudden tumble of images in my mind and an overwhelming nausea.

Steph turned to follow my gaze. "What are you looking at?"

I blinked, waiting for the flash of movement again, but it didn't come. Then I noticed a dark circle, an inky hole punched into the forest. Perfectly round and nestled within something green.

I made my way across the sand and stepped into the shadows between the trees. The relief from the sun was instant, a cool salve to my skin. The sand gave way to crisp palm fronds under my feet that crunched in the stillness.

I blinked as my eyes adjusted to the shadows. The fist-sized hole was ringed with dark, thick metal and directed at me, peeking from under a heap of fallen fronds and a ratty-looking cloth tarp. The boxy shape underneath the tarp was as big as a small car.

I walked around it, searching the shadows in the nearby trees for a hint of motion. The feeling I was being watched welled up again, like it had that first day. A pinprick of fear piercing my mind, bringing up a bead of blood.

"Hello?" I called into the forest.

"Sia, there's nobody here," Steph said, her attention on the tarp. She stepped to the side and pulled. It fell in a heap at her feet, revealing the shape underneath.

"What. The heck. Is that?"

I put my hand over my mouth. I'd seen something like this before. And it made no sense that it was here, on an island twenty miles from mainland Florida.

You and me, walking through a field behind a museum. At age five, the name of the place went right over my head, but I remembered the sunshine, the mowed grass, and the glint of brass plaques. We stopped in the shadow of a huge machine. You let me climb up onto its wheel, throw my arm around the long black tube, and hang from it. I remember hooking my ankles around the sun-warmed metal and dangling upside down, you laughing. Then the park attendant started yelling. I don't remember his name, or the argument that followed, just his angry face, and yours. And I remember what you called it.

"It's a howitzer," I said.

"A what?"

"I'm guessing they used it to blow boats out of the water. It's a little different than the one I saw before, though."

I ran my hand down the metal tube until it thickened and attached to the cart. The gun was at least seven feet long.

I searched around the base of its two wheels, which came up to my chest and had sunk an inch deep into the sandy earth.

"Why would anyone put this here?" Steph asked.

"Maybe some weird anarchist or something?" I moved the dead fronds next to the wheels, looking for ammunition, careful not to blow us both up.

"I thought all of those guys were in South Texas."

I thought about Graham's strange delusion, his belief that it was 1943 . . .

I kneeled and crawled underneath. Nothing but more fronds.

I lifted a few and a glint of dark metal caught my eye. Long, thin, and sharp. I scooted out and handed it to Steph, who took it gingerly with two fingers, her expression pinched.

"That's a bayonet," she said.

"Yep." I nodded toward it. "Ben's going to want that."

She threw it beside the wheel of the howitzer. "I don't think we should encourage him."

I picked it back up. "It's a tool, which means it's useful."

Steph stood with her arms crossed in front of her chest, staring at the gun. Then she chuckled.

"What?"

"Ben. He's absolutely gonna love this."

I ran my fingers over the numbers near the base of the cannon. You'd love it too, if you were here.

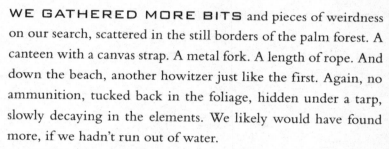

WE GATHERED MORE BITS and pieces of weirdness on our search, scattered in the still borders of the palm forest. A canteen with a canvas strap. A metal fork. A length of rope. And down the beach, another howitzer just like the first. Again, no ammunition, tucked back in the foliage, hidden under a tarp, slowly decaying in the elements. We likely would have found more, if we hadn't run out of water.

When I kneeled by the second gun, investigating, I noticed a few vines had climbed up the wheels, twining their fingers in between the spokes. An image of the *Andrews* flashed in my mind, how the red scale grew on its skin. How nature takes everything back into itself, makes it beautiful again. I touched the gun's cold metal. Is that what death would do to me? Transform me? What would I look like when nature took me back into herself?

That's when a weird prickling ran up my neck, down both arms, and stopped my breathing. The beach. Visible through the thick hashed trunks. White sand and blue water. It was supposed to be empty. And suddenly it wasn't.

I stood, my back to Steph, who was rooting around in the undergrowth for supplies just out of sight. I rubbed my face. Blinked a few times. My eyes were lying to me. They had to be.

There on the beach, bathed in full sunlight, were three guys dragging a dinghy out of the surf.

I dropped my bag and rushed into the glow. Rescue. Finally. I was so caught up in that swell of hope, my brain barely processed the rest of the details. That there were two more soldiers standing just a little farther down the beach, leaning against a large wooden crate. That they were all dressed the same, like Graham but cleaner. That two of them had canvas belts holding holstered guns. And then there was the shimmer. Like a mirage on a Florida highway, the details wavering just a hair.

Once my feet touched the hot sand, the scent of gasoline from the boat engine hit me. One man turned to the other and spoke, but the crash of the surf swallowed their words. Another turned and looked directly at me. I could swear he was Graham's twin. I had enough time to see the shock register in his face before all of them disappeared.

I skidded to a halt, the prickle of heat over my skin replaced with salt spray. Both ends of the beach were empty. No dingy. No guys. But I would swear on your life that they were there, as much as I was there.

The soft push of feet in the sand came from behind. "Sia, did you actually leave me alone in there? Real nice."

I didn't answer, staring at the surf and rubbing my eyes. My bag shifted, and something heavy dropped to the bottom.

"Found another canteen. This one has a better strap." Steph stood beside me and fell quiet for a second. "Thank you so much, Steph. That's a good find. Gee, you're welcome, Sia."

I turned to look at her. "What?"

Her annoyed expression shifted into concern. "Are you okay?"

On our way back to camp, I didn't tell Steph what I'd seen. When Ben's form materialized in the distance, I wondered if he was *really* there, or if that was the real Felix at the water's edge, throwing pebbles into the surf. I helped Ben unload the bag of supplies while Steph went into great detail about the howitzer, like she'd been the one to figure out what it was.

Ben pulled out the bayonet. "What are we supposed to do with this? That thing's barely going to feel it."

Steph patted him on the shoulder. "I don't know. Open clams with it."

Ben put the bayonet down and turned to me to say something. Then he stopped and gave me an appraising look. "You okay?"

I nodded, absently scratching at my forearms, which had been itching since we'd started back. I thought of those anatomy books you had in your office, the ones that had the different organ systems drawn on layers of plastic film, each one perfectly aligned to make a complete body. Some force had shifted one of my pages, I was sure of it. My insides felt wrong, out of whack.

"I'm going out hunting again," I said, my eyes on the waves.

Everyone was hungry, so no one argued when I grabbed the snorkel gear and waded into the surf. Once my head ducked under the waves, the image of the five men on the beach dimmed and my body felt better. I came up and fed everyone. Again.

I dried out under the shelter and listened to your voice in my head until the sun sank low in the sky, wondering what you would think of everything I'd seen over the last few days. Wondered if you'd be able to make sense of any of it.

All those tiny pinpricks of light were out early tonight, before twilight had faded. That and some forks of lightning far out to sea, each a brilliant vein in the sky.

As I watched the show, that camping trip we took when I

was nine, when the thunderstorm washed out the road, played in my head over and over on a loop. I remember us huddling together beneath the overhang of that old barn you found. We couldn't see the stars through the clouds, so you had me counting imaginary dolphins. One, two, three, you'd say. Watch them, Sia, leaping over the limbo stick. Four, five, six. That lightning's just fireworks. Watch the dolphins.

You smelled like fire smoke and the sort of sweat you get from being outdoors all day, doing good, honest work. Even now, I imagine that scent and I feel safe.

One, two, three. I counted the stars slowly brightening above our island. Drew lines between them. I imagined those lines were pathways. I would walk them like tightropes to get back to you. Time was elastic here. Anything was possible.

Ben didn't seem to care that night was coming on, instead sketching in the journal, coming up with spiked traps made from felled palm trees. Steph, being the *practical* one, had told Ben she wasn't going to help him one bit. Instead, she helped Felix with his SOS message, each letter as big as a two-story house. Graham lay a few feet away, tied up in the far recess of the sun shelter, stinking up the place.

I started to get up to join Ben down by the water. Lie beside him and draw my own plan on a fresh page. I'd been forming a monster trap in my head, which included dropping an empty howitzer on it. At the very least it would make Ben laugh.

"You're not what I expected."

Graham's voice made me jump. I turned to find him watching me. "What did you expect?"

He shrugged, looked out to the ocean again with that long,

farm-boy look, as if he were predicting the weather or planning the harvest. "You going to untie me?" he asked.

Texas. It was more obvious now. The western half. The long drawl, a guy in no hurry to get the words out. Like they'd been baking inside him.

"I could help," he said. "Scout for food."

"You could hit me over the head with a rock and steal all our stuff."

A smile. The first one I'd seen from him in two days.

"I won't hurt you," he said.

I nodded west, toward the water and the buoy marking the wreck. "Tell me what happened out there. How you got here."

"Does it matter?"

"It might help me figure out what's going on. How we can get home."

He sighed and looked at the heavens. "Graham Fitch, serial number—"

"Enough."

He smiled again. "Okay, okay. I'll lay off. Just havin' some fun." His attention went down the beach, to where the surf made the sand dark. I wasn't sure if he was checking out our boat, which he could raid for supplies, or if he was looking at the white buoy way out there, bobbing in the waves. Or planning to kill "the enemy" with a rock, Piggy-style.

"All right," he said, and rolled his shoulders like dust had collected in the joints.

"All right what?" I asked.

"All right, I'll tell you."

He took a big breath, as if preparing for a speech.

"I enlisted in the Navy at fourteen. Lied on my application and said I was seventeen."

"I didn't mean for you to go that far back, Graham."

"Just wait, Baby Doll. Be patient."

He leaned back and put his tied hands behind his head. Like a teenager hanging out, watching the waves. And it was then I got the feeling he was used to all this. All his life, something had always been in his way, causing bruises. So a day or twelve or thirty on a deserted island guarded by some horrific sea monster from hell didn't faze him that much.

"So I had to be seventeen to join, but I thought, hey, three years don't matter, especially when you're big like me. Back in Lubbock, wasn't that hard to fool the paper pushers, not after Pearl Harbor."

"Pearl Harbor. You're serious."

"They needed bodies. Cannon fodder. All I had to do was get past the dentist and I was Seaman First-Class Graham Fitch." He turned his head to meet my eyes. "Teeth don't lie. So I looked that dentist in the eye and I say, 'You really think I didn't see you letting those two guys before me pass? I go to school with them. They're both sixteen. You really gonna stop me? Won't you get in trouble if I tell?"

I sat with my mouth open. All this time and not a word. And suddenly he wants to spill his whole history.

"After basic, which was great—what with all the food, which there wasn't much of at home with all seven of us fighting for whatever Momma could scrape up from the church or the ladies club or whatever charity was doing good deeds that week—well, the food was good. Three squares a day. After basic, I got myself on the USS *Andrews*."

I leaned forward, a chill running through me. The image of that ship wrecked at the bottom of the ocean flashed in my mind. The huge tear on the side.

"First real home I ever had, that ship." He nodded to the white buoy. "Loved that girl. We all did. After a few years, I became a gunner's mate, a loader on a five-inch thirty-eight-caliber gun mount. I can see that doesn't mean squat to you, but it's a big deal, gunner's mate. Saw action too, lot of it. Ryuku Islands. Philippines." He sat up and with bound hands raised the cuff of his pants, exposing a nasty red scar on his ankle. "Got that when a kamikaze winged us and set the aft section on fire."

"Stop stalling. What happened out there?"

The light that had been in his eyes through his whole story dimmed. He broke eye contact. Fear, maybe. Guilt. I couldn't make it out.

I rose, grabbed the bottle of water from the opposite corner of the shelter, and handed it to him. "Two sips."

He paused before uncapping it. I decided to play along.

"It's not 1943 anymore, Seaman First-Class Graham Fitch. The war's been over for seventy-plus years. You won't be breaking some code or betraying your country if you tell us the truth." I waited and got silence. "If we don't get off this island, we're going to die."

He shook his head. "I can't tell you. They said no matter what, keep quiet about this. It's treason to talk about it."

"It's not. It's called living. Past next week. Just tell me this—do you know a way to get off the island?"

"No."

My heart fell.

"Do you know why we're here?"

He nodded.

I was about to pull out the big guns, the heaviest guilt trip I could muster, jam a crowbar right in the crack of his resolve, when a rustle came from the palm forest. And with it came the faintest scent of a clogged drain.

THE SHARP SOUND of breaking wood startled me, jolted me upright.

I watched the edge of the palm trees, which started thirty or so feet from our shelter. Between the trunks, the shadows lay thick and deep. The feel of that place rose in my mind, the unnatural stillness sweating through the vines and palms that drifted up from the thick mat of rot and dead insects that lay underfoot.

Crack. Something moving beyond the shadows. I put my hand on Graham's shoulder. *Stay quiet.* A rustle, a brittle sound, like the forest was saying *shh* and the dead things in there were singing to us in a chorus.

I checked over my shoulder for Felix and found his slim form bent over the bottom of the giant *O* he'd built in the sand, adding rocks to the edges of his SOS message.

"Untie me," Graham said, his focus on the forest.

I stood. "Why?" I whispered. "What is it?"

He held his hands out. "Untie me. Now," he said, his eyes pleading. I shook my head, and the pleading look turned to fear.

A whisper of palm leaves. *Snap.* A dry swish of dead underbrush swept aside. Closer now.

I'm sure you would've left him tied up. Because Graham Fitch was dangerous. Unpredictable. He'd tried to rob us. Maybe kill us. You'd say to yourself, him or Felix? Easy choice.

I didn't think about any of that. I bent down and fumbled with the ropes at his ankles.

Crunch. The wind blew through the trees toward us. The scent of a bitter sea came with it, a caustic smell, like bile and low tide.

I'd trussed him up well in your fancy handcuff knot. My fingers strained on a tight loop until it finally gave way.

"Hurry!" Graham said, holding his hands out, kicking his feet until the ropes slipped off. I stood, my eyes on the jungle. A glimpse of a yellow stripe moving in the shadows.

At first, I thought it was a colorful bird. I squinted, and no, it was too big. I had this weird jolt of panic, a feeling that whatever it was had *smelled* us, and that's why it had come.

Graham was up, pulling at my arm. "C'mon!"

But I didn't move. Yellow stripe. Yellow stripe on black. Not an animal. The stripe moved again in the shadows, moving away from us. And I caught the unmistakable shape of a person attached to that stripe. A person walking the edge of the forest, all in black.

A wet suit.

Mr. Marshall's wet suit.

And I was running. Toward the forest, aiming for the inky gaps between the trunks. Shouts followed me. Graham, his warnings lost on the strong wind coming off the ocean.

Mr. Marshall was alive, and he had been on the island with us all this time.

I crashed into the palm forest and tripped over a root, landing face-first in the rotting undergrowth. I scrambled up, tasting blood but not feeling a thing. My voice echoed in the stillness and shadows.

"Mr. Marshall!"

Two cuts on my hand and tree bark imbedded in both knees. Reckless, you would say. Running into the forest like that. I'd have to use our precious tube of Neosporin. But I didn't care, because Mr. Marshall was alive somehow. And you of all people understand what drove me to run after him, ignoring the warning signs.

As I moved deeper into the palm trees, the temperature of this place finally registered, fifteen degrees cooler than the beach. Like I'd walked into an air-conditioned cottage after being roasted in the sun all day. My arms broke out in goose flesh.

Five minutes of threading my way through the trunks and peering into the shadows for the yellow stripe and I still didn't get it. How still the air was. The unnatural quiet. The shimmer of sunlight caught high up in the canopy. Fluttering of green. Patches of blue sky.

As I made my way into the trees, I felt like a coward for avoiding the forest for so long, sweating it out on the beach. The ache of the ocean swell had left my ears for the first time in three days. The drain cleaner scent was gone. I didn't even recognize that it was the wrong time of day, that it had been twilight when I'd entered.

"Marshall?" I called out. God, he was alive. He must've been only stunned. He'd had his reg in when they found him, and it had still been in when they surfaced. He'd been breathing air the whole time and we didn't know it. In a coma, perhaps. And Mom was no EMT, so she'd missed the faint pulse.

"Mr. Marshall?" I yelled, but the sound moved strangely between the palm trunks, as if the distance swallowed it up faster than it should. I had this feeling that no matter how much I screamed, they wouldn't hear me on the beach. But I was too excited to think about what that meant.

I stepped over roots, around boles of palms, pushed through a weedy undergrowth that showed up in patches. The place shifted, smelled old, like the corners of that abandoned fishing shack I used to play in as a kid.

"Mr. Marshall? It's Sia. From the *Last Chance*. Remember?"

Poor guy, under the tarp all that time, probably moving around and moaning when we were asleep, and none of us noticed. Poor Mr. Marshall, I remember thinking. He must've thought we'd buried him alive. Then the boat capsized, and the shock of hitting the water woke him up, and . . .

I kept that in my head for a while, spinning theories. As I moved deeper into the thickening shadows, the Sense hit me again, the one that had followed me around the beach, into the water, down into the reef and back again. The thin tendrils of thought sliding up out of the deep, telling me this had happened before. Or some version of it.

A prickling on my scalp. A crawling sensation on my legs. The excitement that had driven me inside the forest disappeared, and I stopped and scanned the area, checking above and behind.

I called his name again. The sound came back to me like a cave echo. The hair on the back of my neck stood. Something wrong in the palm forest. The Sense hit deep, screaming inside me. All of this had already happened. And we'd been right to sleep on the beach.

Too deep, too dark, too cold. Get out and go home.

The yellow stripe appeared, small in the distance, moving between two trunks. Gone behind a thick clump of trees, like a tropical bird.

"Mr. Marshall?"

Palms fronds rustled high in the canopy, shutting out the sunlit world. The crawling sensation on my legs intensified. A thousand ants slipping under my skin.

The yellow stripe appeared again, emerging from a cluster of hashed trunks. Walking now. Toward me, his dark form slowly materializing. I waved wildly and smiled, my heart swelling with hope. Marshall. Another person. An actual adult to help us get home. Fix the boat. Find a way to avoid that thing that attacked us, and we'll sail right . . .

I stepped forward to close the distance, ready to throw an arm around his neck and welcome him back to the land of the living. Closer now, I could make out his pale face in the shadows. His thinning hair, thinner now.

I stopped walking. Mr. Marshall wasn't smiling. And he moved sluggishly, as if he couldn't do more than that. Maybe injured. Or confused. The smile fell off my face. The prickling ants crawled to my scalp.

When he'd covered half the distance, I still hadn't figured it out. And I thought, Why'd he keep on the wet suit? In this heat, you'd sweat like crazy, even in the forest. And rash up. And there he was, walking toward me, slowly growing larger and more distinct, zipped up to the throat in black neoprene.

I took a step back. His pale face. His arms swinging at his sides like they no longer belonged to him.

I took a few more steps back.

It was a trick of the shadows, I told myself. The way cameras catch your friend's eyes and make them look strange. No, Mr. Marshall was fine. He would help us fix the boat.

"Is that you, Mr. Marshall?" My voice came back to me, and this time I was inside a glass coffin. My breath close and warm on my face.

My body knew it then, that this too was wrong. But the rest of me . . . I had almost killed him, and he was sick now and I would help him remember. Give him water. Bring him back to his wife.

He passed through a ray of sunlight that had broken through the canopy. His eyes were off. Milky. Patches of his bare feet were raw and tinged with pink, like the inside of a blister.

I stepped back, and a root caught my ankle. I went down.

For half a second, the dim forest disappeared. I was inside the *Andrews* again, when I'd gotten lost and found that dark compartment. Shut your eyes, I thought. Pretend this isn't happening. But I didn't, and what I saw in his face forced me back over the roots and onto my feet.

And I ran. I crashed through the trees, the last sight of him staying with me. Mr. Marshall staring like that lifeless eye I saw in the water when the boat went down, huge and unblinking, watching me through the flames.

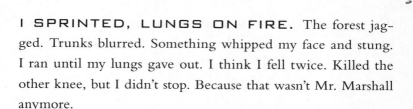

I SPRINTED, LUNGS ON FIRE. The forest jagged. Trunks blurred. Something whipped my face and stung. I ran until my lungs gave out. I think I fell twice. Killed the other knee, but I didn't stop. Because that wasn't Mr. Marshall anymore.

A burst of sunlight flooded the world. The heated air hit my skin as I exploded from the invisible boundary I now realized had been holding me in.

I skidded to a stop at the water's edge. Ready to dive in, to get away from what followed me. Instead I turned my back to the swell and crash, feet planted in the wet sand, and watched the darkness between the palm trees for a flash of yellow.

Don't go into the water.

Don't go into the trees.

As I stood there, panting in the surf, a lesson came to me from one of your favorite stories, the one you made me read over eighth-grade summer—our last summer. Odysseus choosing Scylla or Charybdis. The six-headed monster or the whirlpool.

The sea-foam brushed over the tops of my feet as the ocean surged, its heart beating out a rhythm. That's where the six-headed monster roamed, out there in the waves. And the thing in the forest, that was the whirlpool. No escape. And I didn't know what was on the other end. That left me and Ben and Felix and

Steph owners of this narrow strip of beach between, trying not to step too far one direction or the other.

Like a child's game, I thought. Stepping around cracks in the sidewalk.

After my heart slowed, I took stock of where I was. This part of the island didn't look familiar. Big black boulders as high as my chest lay scattered in the surf. The waves broke around them, sending a spray of foam over their jagged crowns. A few additional boulders dotted the long expanse of sand leading into the palms, maybe a ton each, as if spilled from a giant's pocket on his way over the island.

I checked both ends of the beach to figure out where I was. And that's when I noticed the strangest thing.

The sun. When I'd gone into the palm forest, it had been hovering just above the horizon, ready to plunge into the ocean.

I held up my hand and squinted. Two fingers. That's what lay between the sun and the water. The sun had gone *up*, not down as it should have. Twilight was gone, along with the stars. It was day.

I licked my dry lips. Imagined the water bottle back at camp, and the need for it hit me hard. Sweet water. I couldn't wrap my mind around the sun reversing itself. But a drink, a bite of food—that was real.

So I started walking. Staying in the surf, as far as I could from the horrible place I'd just left. I imagined the converters, hoped Ben, Steph, and Felix hadn't drunk everything inside.

Every few heartbeats, I checked the forest. During that long trek, Marshall's face popped into my mind again and again, and each time the image felt like a slap. The eyes, the way his skin sagged. I didn't want to see him again. The real Marshall was dead. I didn't know what I'd met in there.

Soon sweat coated every inch of my body, and the humidity wouldn't let it dry. My bikini was soaked. I walked until the sun touched the water. Until it sputtered like a hot coal in a pond. My mind drifted. The thirst filled my throat with sandpaper. I thought about Mom, about whether she'd made it to shore. If she was hiding somewhere in the trees.

Dusk had fallen when I saw it. A dark stripe lying near the surf. Trash, I thought. I grabbed it just before a wave tried to take it. When I flipped it over, my pulse leapt.

A watch. A Casio G-Shock. Black.

My mother's watch.

I checked both ends of the beach, shouting "Mom!" into the trees, into the water, into the sky.

The only answer was the crash of the waves.

I examined the watch again. Casio G-Shocks like that were common. What were the odds it was actually hers? And if she made it to the island, why would she take it off and leave it here?

You once told me the big things wear us down, but the small things break us. I didn't get it then. I do now. The watch. That tiny glimmer of hope, and then here comes logic to stamp it out.

I don't know how else to explain what happened next, but I . . . cracked. There I was, making my way down the beach, alone. Then you appeared beside me. As real as can be. Carrying an ice chest full of pineapple and bottles of water.

I was about to throw my arms around your neck when another voice came from behind me.

"*Pamé.*"

Yiayia. When she was young. *Let's go*, she'd said. And the sand disappeared, replaced by docks and a thick crowd all around me. Epiphany in Tarpon Springs, to celebrate the new year. The bishop was about to throw the crucifix into the water, and all the boys would dive in to see who could get there first.

Then the crowds melted, and the bishop, and next all of Tarpon Springs, until suddenly I was swimming, free diving, following Litsa into the deep.

I kicked my way down, where the world becomes dark blue and endless, and both of us shed everything that weighed us down on the shore. Dresses, shoes, polite conversation. All of it floated off as we made our way into the reef, following the glittering gold crucifix as it plummeted into the deep.

Forty feet. Sixty. Eighty feet and then a hundred. Farther than any free diver had ever gone. And the bottom suddenly there, like magic, appearing out of the murk. Sandy, dotted, and crusted with fat sponges.

We opened our bags and filled them. The crucifix first. Then the sponges. I remember thinking we'd make a killing at market. Buy food for a month. Me and Litsa, saving everyone. On the way up, Mr. Marshall appeared, in his rich-man's scuba gear, following us back to shore.

Somewhere in the fantasy my face felt hot, and I came out of the water dream suddenly. Or maybe it was real? I don't know, but I'd lost track of time, and I wasn't sure if I'd been walking in circles.

The waves moved strangely, the forest too. Even now, I don't know what happened to me that day. The stress, dehydration, exhaustion. Maybe the Sense taking me in and out of myself, pulling apart all my layers and reordering them.

"Pamé," I said to myself, walking toward that last sliver of sun. "Let's go."

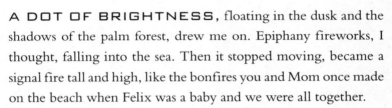

A DOT OF BRIGHTNESS, floating in the dusk and the shadows of the palm forest, drew me on. Epiphany fireworks, I thought, falling into the sea. Then it stopped moving, became a signal fire tall and high, like the bonfires you and Mom once made on the beach when Felix was a baby and we were all together.

By the time I got close enough to be seen, my legs shook and my joints hurt. Felix's small form materialized out of the dusk, running toward me. Yiayia squeezed my arm once and disappeared. You gave me a two-finger salute, turned, and walked into the waves.

I stood alone on the beach for a few breaths, and then fifty pounds barreled right into me and almost knocked me over. I caught Felix and held him tight.

"You're okay you're okay you're okay," he said in one rushed breath, laughing and pulling away to dance a little bit before throwing himself at me again.

"Yes, Felix. I'm back."

When we got to the warm circle of light, Ben looked up from something he was whittling with an expression both intense and a little sad. When he saw me, the shock in his eyes made me stop mid-step. He stood with difficulty and made his way toward me.

I started to ask for water, my only thought. Before I could, Ben drew me into a tight hug.

"Thank God," he whispered into my hair. "We thought you were dead."

I glanced at Felix, who was smiling at me. Then I closed my eyes and leaned into Ben's shoulder, the relief of being held for the first time in . . . I guess since I saw you last . . . almost taking my legs out from under me.

He pulled away and motioned for Felix to bring the water bottle. It was a quarter full. He told me to drink it all. At first the sweet taste of it was all I could think about. Not the lack of questions from Steph, who sat outside the ring of light, her face in shadow. Not the way Felix clung to me, afraid if he let go, he'd lose me forever.

I took two deep swallows and sighed. Water, sweet water. How awesome it was. Drinking water was better than falling asleep in a bed with clean sheets in an air-conditioned room. More relaxing than the sensation of a cool cotton T-shirt against my hot skin after a day in the sun, or the smell of the ocean in the morning, when I drove to the marina before sunrise with the windows down. Sweeter than my favorite song, the one we sang together when I was little, and more beautiful than everything ever in my life, water is so much better . . .

Then I saw Graham.

Our prisoner sat against a boulder, hands and feet again tied. The bruises around his mouth distorted his face so much I barely recognized him. Above his right eye, a two-inch gash angled down to his temple. Even in the flickering firelight and heavy dusk, I could see how deep it went. One of his eyelids had swelled until he couldn't open it.

Steph wouldn't look at me. Instead she stared listlessly out to sea, her fishing net beside her, which was enormous now and weighted on the ends with shells and stones. The firelight showed the bruise under her eye.

"What the . . ." I looked from Steph to Ben, who tilted his head toward Steph and gave me a meaningful look. Graham glared at me through his good eye, and I couldn't tell if he was mad or afraid.

"I told you to run the other way," Graham said, mumbling through his bruised mouth. "And you went all hell-bent into the forest after it."

"Oh, he speaks," Steph said.

"Enough, Steph," Ben said, his voice low.

She looked at me as if hoping for an ally, a "Can you believe him?" look.

"What happened to Graham's face?" I asked.

Steph ignored my question and began fiddling with a thin piece of driftwood. "What happened to you?" she said, and for a second, it sounded like she actually cared.

"I went in after . . . I saw something. But I came right back." The sun appeared in my mind. Rising, sinking. Didn't I come right back? I rubbed my eyes, trying to square the circle. It was all so hazy now.

Ben gave me a puzzled look. "Sia, you've been gone for three days."

"That's not possible." I rubbed my face again, my head full of sand fleas and seaweed. Was it possible? I tried to remember, but my head started to ache with the effort. "No, I've been gone for less than a day."

Steph and Ben exchanged a glance. Felix clung to my hand, watching me with wide eyes.

I patted Felix and kneeled down in front of Graham to assess the damage. He flinched back from me.

"He was a danger," Steph said.

"He was *talking* to us," Ben said. "Walking toward us and talking."

"He was tricking us." Steph pointed at Graham with an accusing finger. "About some imaginary thing he saw in the palm trees. He was tricking us to set him free."

"He was *warning* us," Ben said, settling himself with a grimace by the fire. "You didn't even give him a chance."

Steph went back to playing with the stick. "I'm not going to take a chance with Felix. I'm just not." But she sounded like she was trying to convince herself, rather than us, that she'd done the right thing.

Graham let out a humorless laugh that ended in a cough and set his good eye on me. "Soon as you ran off, the redhead flipped her wig. Smashed me over and over with a rock as big as the professor's ego over here—"

Ben's voice snapped out of the darkness so loud I stepped back in surprise. "Call me that one more time and—"

"And what? You ain't gonna do nothin'. That's the redhead's job."

Ben got up and started toward him, his hands clenching into fists. One step and he'd already put too much weight on his bad leg. He stopped, his face twisting with pain.

"Eager little beaver, she is," Graham said, and then turned his eyes on Ben again. "And I don't know why you snap your cap every time I say that anyway. I've known plenty of mama's boys like you that didn't mind. And I like 'em well enough. Knew one who was a real gas, guy who slept in the bunk next to me, always screaming out in his sleep when he had his nightmares. It was real entertainin'."

The shift in Ben's expression, along with the sudden quiet around the fire, seemed to be exactly what Graham wanted. "Guess school can't teach you everything after all," he finished, looking genuinely pleased with himself, as pleased as a man can look with one of his eyelids completely swollen. "So like I was sayin', sweet little dollface here took this rock and she smashed me. When I was down, she kept going until the professor"—he nodded toward Ben—"got her off me."

"I'm starting to regret that," Ben said.

Graham tongued the inside of his mouth, and then his lip. "In the service, we got a name for ones like her."

"You've got a name for everything," Ben said.

Just as I was realizing what kind of names a guy from 1943 might have called Ben, Steph spoke up again. "I was defending myself. He was free. He was going to hurt us. And Felix."

I started to tell her off, but that was when I noticed Felix sitting just outside the ring of light, arms wrapped around his knees, shoulders hunched. It's the way he sat in the visitation room at the prison while we waited for you, surrounded by strangers with harsh voices. I hadn't noticed it when I'd first come into the fire's glow, but fresh ink covered his calves and half of his thighs. He must've found Mom's pen in the toolbox. Intricate drawings of boats and hamburgers and clownfish and coral, all over his skin. At least three days' worth of drawings. Keeping himself busy. And calm.

He didn't need to hear about what I'd found out there.

I kissed him on top of his head. "I'll be right back."

He turned his innocent eyes up at me and nodded.

I gestured to Ben to follow me away from the others and ignored Steph's poison look. As we left, I caught Felix's only comment to Steph, small but determined: "It wasn't right, what you did." He sounded so grown-up. Three days without me and he'd aged a year.

When there was enough blackness between us and the fire, when I was sure the sound of the surf would drown out my words, I turned to face Ben. The moonlight caught the white of his shirt, his bandage, but his expression was lost to me.

"You were gone a long time," he said.

"No, I wasn't."

"What did you see out there?" He nodded to the trees.

I looked to the palms, and then to the ocean, its enormous black body roiling in the darkness, under the moonlight. A faint green glow caught my eyes about a hundred yards beyond the breakers. A patch of phosphorescence lighting up the black water. It brightened for a few seconds, then dimmed, sank until the world became dark again. The sight of that thing haunting our coastline took the last of my energy from me.

"We're gonna die here," I said. "And then we're not. That's what I saw."

WHEN I FINISHED MY STORY, Ben didn't say any-thing. I stood beside him, bare feet in the wave fingers and wet sand, and watched a wisp of a cloud slide over the full moon, which hung low over the island like a bright eye.

"It's not possible," Ben finally said.

"How is it that, after everything we've seen, you can't bend your mind around *this*?"

He sighed and rubbed his face. Somehow, the idea of Marshall roaming the palm forest bothered him more than anything else. A creature attacking our boat, the weird time loop we saw on the horizon—he accepted it. But a dead guy walking? Apparently, that was one degree of weird too much.

"When people die, that's it. They move on." Ben made the motion of a bird flying up, his gesture caught in the moon eye. "What's left behind isn't *them*. It's an echo."

"I know, but—"

"A memory. People don't get up from the table they're lying on. Or walk. Or look at you." As he made his list, his voice became more and more adamant. He wasn't just talking about Marshall. He was talking about the family business.

"I guess on this island, the normal rules don't apply."

He shifted in the sand and stumbled. I slipped my arm around his waist to steady him. He looped his arm around my shoulders.

At first, I thought he needed a moment, that the pain had thrown him off balance. But he didn't take his arm away. We stood there for a while, the cool ocean breeze pushing against our faces. Voices drifted from the fire down the beach, too low to make out.

He shook his head. "You know, I've had three days to think about you being dead."

"I still can't believe I was gone three days. Sorry I wasn't here to catch dinner."

"You think that's the reason I missed you?"

Something in his tone stopped me, made my heart flutter. Adrenaline, the kind I feel when I jump into the water after too long on land. That sweet pulse of anticipation that hits me when I'm airborne and about to break the surface.

He took my silence for confusion. "You're really slow, Sia. Like, glacier slow." There was a smile in his voice. It was contagious.

"I am. It's true. Why don't you spell it out for me?"

He let go of my shoulders. I thought I'd said the wrong thing. Something homeschooled and awkward. Then he turned me to face him. The moonlight lit up the waves and the angle of his jaw. His warm brown eyes. The pulse inside my chest told me that for once, I hadn't said anything wrong.

A small voice to my left made me jump. "T?"

I let go of Ben.

"Yes, Felix. Hi. Felix, yeah, what's up?"

"I—I wanted to make sure." He closed the distance and reached for my hand, his small face turned up toward mine.

"Make sure of what?"

"That you were still here."

Felix led me back to the fire. I glanced at Ben on the way, who limped alongside us, his face a stoic mask. Suddenly I was glad Felix had interrupted us. I don't know what Ben was going to say. Or do. Kiss me, or tell me we were all going to die. Or that he'd gotten back together with Steph. I wasn't sure I was ready for that news—or a kiss, for that matter. Not in this place, when the world was falling apart.

We got back to the fire, and I checked on Graham, fully taking in the damage to his face. I reached out and touched the edge of the gash above his eye. He winced.

"They put anything on that while I was gone?"

Graham blinked with his good eye, the right side of his mouth turning up into a half smile, the other side too stiff to move. "Yeah, Ben took care of it. Put some kinda paste, yeah, like it would help or something."

"So you *do* know his name."

He shrugged. "I like getting a rise outta him."

"Why?"

He considered that for a moment. "You know what they never told me about being a prisoner of war?"

"You're not a—"

"How boring it is."

Strange how his words hit me. I saw you again, rising out of the sand like a ghost, taking your seat next to Graham. Your hands tied, your face a mess of bruises. And you looked into my eyes and I knew what you'd done. Started a fight in gen pop because you were bored. To add texture to the day. Then you melted into the sand, and it was just the five of us again.

We sat quietly until the moon dipped below the line of palms. My stomach growled. Four days on the island—no, six, was it six? Maybe it'd been ten—and already Felix's cheeks had hollowed. Steph's legs looked thinner. The small pile of fish bones by the fire said Steph had caught something with her net. From the size of the bones, it didn't look like much.

Felix huddled up against me; I could feel his ribs through his shirt. He'd always been skinny, but this . . . You'd have gone crazy, trying to get something to eat for him. You would've cut off your arm and given it to him.

That thought made me a little sick, and I scanned the black ocean for boat lights. The whole moving mass of water had become nothing but darkness and sound. The signal fire, was it even worth it? Was anyone out there at all? That Sense I'd felt earlier hit me hard in the brain pan.

All of us, lost forever.

Something brushed over my skin. A familiar feeling now, as if someone stood too close, breathing on my neck. Near the water a silhouette appeared, then a second. As soon as I realized who it was, my heart made its way up my chest and into my mouth. My mother. There on the beach, watching the waves.

I almost got up. Then I saw the second figure turn away from the surf. A girl with dark hair, wearing my rash guard. Mom was talking, and crying, the girl listening.

I was listening.

That was me, down there on the beach, standing next to Mom. Which meant what I was seeing wasn't real. Or maybe it meant that I wasn't real.

The other Sia turned to look toward our fire, and we locked eyes for one heart-wrenching second. Then both figures melted away.

I buried my face on Felix's tiny shoulder.

"What do you think Dad is doing now?" he asked.

Felix's voice was so small, his question so earnest, I felt something deep and painful gather in my chest.

"It's dinnertime. He's eating with all of his friends."

Felix watched the moon, which still hung low above the palm forest, fat and white, shedding a pure light over the beach. "Does he have a window in his cell?"

Out of the corner of my eye, I caught Ben glance my way.

"Yeah, a little one by his cot. After dinner he'll lie on it and watch the sky."

"Like we used to when we went camping?"

"You remember that? You were so little then."

He didn't bristle at the word *little* this time. "Yeah, I remember I helped him catch that fish and he made a fire and he cooked it. That was fun."

I hugged him a little tighter. "And Mom fell asleep in the hammock, and you put a lizard on her and she freaked out."

He giggled. "Did I do that?"

"It was awesome. I laughed so hard I almost peed my pants."

He giggled some more and fell silent. The wave song pushed its way in around us, circling the fire and filling the air, an endless tune of swell and fade. I listened to it, lost in the completeness of it, until I felt Felix's body shaking. When his voice came out again, it was thick with tears. "I don't like it here."

"It's all right." It wasn't, but I didn't know what else to say.

"I want Mom," he said through a sob.

I let him settle his head on my lap and stroked his hair as his small body shook. I held him there on the beach in the middle of nowhere and let him cry. And I cried too, for you in your cell with your view of the moon, and let the tears blur the fire until it was nothing but color, and pretended it was your fire, and all of us were together, camping on the beach.

I'M SURE YOU'VE GOT a daily schedule in your cell-block. This is mine:

> Gather driftwood.
> Tend the fire.
> Continue building the world's biggest SOS message.
> Give Graham his rations. Fight with Steph about it.
> Search the reef for crab and lobster while Steph fishes on shore and catches almost nothing.
> Find just enough to keep us from eating our own fingers.
> Race back to shore before I'm eaten alive.

And the sun goes up and the sun goes down, but we're stuck here on an endless loop, like that exploding cruiser on the horizon. Ben has put away his diagrams and sketches, and he watches it every night. The last movie in the world, he says, and I sit with him, mostly to keep him company. Felix calls them island fireworks. Steph and Graham refuse to even look.

Ben and I don't talk about the night I came back from the dead, about what he almost said. Or did. But when we watch the island lights, I lean against his chest, and he wraps his arm around my waist. Like we're together, even though we're not. I'm pretty sure if I didn't have Ben, I would absolutely lose my mind.

Because something on the island has changed. I have this feeling I'm inside a car, and someone's just put their foot on the gas pedal. And every day, I watch the dead—the ones who died that day the creature attacked us, the ones who should be lying peacefully in Davy Jones's locker—wander out of the surf and walk right onto the beach.

The first time it happened, I was alone, a mile from camp, scouting a new dive spot just past the section of the beach where the big boulders start. These rise up taller than you, pushing themselves from the crashing surf, lying in random patterns scattered across the white sands.

Up in the dunes, my back to the waves, sitting on my heels in the sand as I adjusted a strap on my mask, the brace of the wind against my rash guard lulled me into a false sense of security. The sand was a rough cat's tongue on my shins, the bottoms of my feet. I was thinking about all the delicious things clustered at the base of those boulders. My mesh bag would split, there'd be so much. If the ocean let me. If I had time.

I didn't realize he was there at first. The soft push of footsteps in the sand had become a familiar sound. Like surf crash and the cries of the herons near our camp. When any of us moved about the shelter, or around the fire, there it was, the muffled push of heels, toes, the balls of our feet. None of the surfaces here stay still. Not the ocean. Not the beach.

I started to turn, expecting Steph or Felix. Coming down to make sure I was okay.

The breeze shifted before I finished my rotation. The salt scent disappeared. What replaced it was the smell of a clogged drain.

I didn't even look. I just ran.

I threw myself behind a boulder. Held my breath. Peeked around the edge.

A teenage boy stood with his back to me, about a car's length away, feet planted in the sand. The kind of stance I would see on the basketball court. Just a guy waiting for a teammate to pass him the ball.

He wore a pair of baggy nylon shorts with a blue stripe up the side. His T-shirt had a logo emblazoned on the back. *Camp Tahona*. His clothes dripped with seawater, and his skin gleamed pale in the sunlight. I had an urge to call to him. I tamped it down my throat and put my hand over my mouth.

He turned, and I froze.

Underneath one of his dark brows was a ragged hole. Even from this distance I could see that the other eye had a milky cast, like Marshall's. The image of him making his way across the sea floor, fish feeding on him as he traveled to us from the wrecked *Ruby Pelican*, filled my mind.

I wanted to stop watching. Turn away. I had interrupted a private moment somehow. Like I had wandered into an undertaker's office and I didn't belong. Ben's family would know what to do; I didn't. And I was afraid if I turned away, when I looked again he would be standing a few feet away, peering down at me.

The dead boy walked across the sand toward the jungle, like he had a mission in there.

My heart started to slow. He hadn't seen me. He wasn't here for me. I stepped out from the shadow of my boulder and watched him make his way into the shadows.

We're all connected, I thought.

I didn't know where those words came from. Maybe they came from Mom, or Yiayia. Or you. But I had this feeling—that the boy had a destination. I thought again of what I'd seen when I was perched on top of the palm tree, a line of shimmer between that thing and the dark patch in the middle of the island.

Connected.

I stepped into the fringes of the palms, about to follow him inside, to see where he would lead me. Then the smell of the shadows—the underside of a rock—hit me. The fear of that place, mixed with my hunger, was enough to turn me back to the ocean.

The five of us don't talk about the dead. Felix pretends he doesn't see them. And the rest of us—the ones still alive on this island, the ones who don't belong—we have the same argument over and over, about what will happen if we touch one, whether they can think, whether they're zombies, ghosts, or something else. Problem is, none of us want to test our theories. Our prisoner keeps his trap shut about what they are and where they go. And we live with it, with them, because what else can we do?

The only good times—other than my stolen time with Ben—come at night, when we gather around the fire and conjure weird theories about time funnels and sea monsters. Steph talks about the Coast Guard and I let myself believe for a little bit.

When that talk dries up, Ben recites the script of a movie—he has a freaky memory for things like that. So far, we've made it through every Star Wars film ever made, even the bad ones, and *The Godfather*, because Ben takes requests. I've caught Graham staring at him with a kind of fascination, and Felix sits next to Ben like he's finally gotten the big brother he always wanted.

When Ben is through, or walks in that painful-to-watch gait toward the surf to clean his leg, Felix snuggles next to me and asks me to talk. I try to tell him *Peter Pan* and *Transformers*, but all he wants are bedtime stories about you. So I tell him all the good things I can remember, until we fall asleep next to the lowering fire, under a million stars.

A few mornings after the dead boy wandered into the jungle, I woke to the sound of a gunshot.

I jerked upright; so did Graham, who slept a few feet away. Steph stood and peered toward the beach, confused.

Even Felix sat up and rubbed his eyes. "What was that?"

The sun had barely begun its climb, and the world smelled of seaweed and salt. It was hard to see anything in the gray morning light. The sea was dark.

Another gunshot sounded, from down the beach. Graham jolted. And this time my eyes picked out the green glow. And a silhouette standing at the edge of the farthest boulder, the one I told Felix to avoid because of the deep water on the other side.

Ben.

I was up and running, kicking up sand, Steph only a few steps behind. I think Felix yelled out behind me, but I didn't stop. The world jagged in my vision. Ben had somehow made his way across the gaps to the last rock, where he'd positioned himself at the edge that jutted out into the water. A familiar green glow lit up the surface not far away. Ben pointed the gun toward that glow.

I didn't have time to wonder why. I just yelled his name. The wind took it from me. He fired again. The kickback of the weapon made him stumble this time, and he almost slipped over the rocky edge, into the waves.

I thought he hadn't heard me, but when I came to a halt and started to climb, his voice cut through the wave song. "Don't come up."

"Have you gone insane? Get down from there!"

He pointed into the waves again and shot. The green glow moved another foot toward him.

"You're too close to the water! It'll pull you in."

"I'm gonna kill it." Two more shots, dead center.

I clambered up the rocks, leapt from the one to the next, wondering how he'd managed. His leg must have been in agony. By the time I reached him he'd fired again. Two tentacles slid over the surface of the rock toward his feet. I grabbed him from behind and both of us went down. I almost fell off the side. The gun tumbled from his hand, clattered across the boulder, and disappeared over the edge.

I pulled him up and helped him across the gap to the second boulder, then to the first. A few minutes later we were both lying on the sand, a few feet back from the water, our chests heaving. The green glow floated out from the rock and dimmed.

Steph's voice came from behind us, soft and questioning. "Ben?" Felix stood next to her, his eyes wide.

Ben sat up, wincing as he did. "Steph, just take Felix back to camp. I don't want to talk to you right now."

"But—"

"Just do it!"

Steph put an arm around Felix, her expression confused and hurt, and they left. But he didn't ask me to leave.

"You want to tell me why you just wasted all the ammunition in our only weapon while shooting into the water?" I asked him.

"I just wanted to do something."

"Well, that certainly was something."

His gaze drifted away from the ocean, as if he couldn't bear to look at it.

"I'm glad it's gone."

At first, I thought he meant the creature, and I was about to tell him it wasn't gone. His bullets had done nothing but piss it off. But then a creeping sensation ran over my skin. A memory, something that hadn't happened yet. Ben, on the boulder, with the gun in his hand. Different this time.

The gun. He was glad the gun was gone.

I sat next to him, stunned into silence, trying to figure out what that meant.

"Steph doesn't understand, but you need to," Ben finally said. "We're about to have one less mouth to feed."

I shook my head, and I think I said something. No. You're not going anywhere. Stay with me. God knows what I said. But I already understood. I understood why he'd climbed up on the rock, why he'd emptied the cartridge into the ocean.

He unwrapped the bandage around his leg. I had seen him down by the water, rinsing his wound and changing the dressing, at least four times a day. He never took it off in front of us. I hadn't seen the wound since that first day.

When the last piece of cloth fell away, the smell of rot hit me so hard I almost gagged.

The gaping red trench ringed his thigh, an inch deep. I made myself lean closer, trying to breathe through my mouth. Pus, a lot of it. Red lines spread from it, as if searching, probing.

Ben leaned back on his hands and grimaced. "I've taken enough biology to know I'm going to die of infection in about a week."

"You don't know that. Maybe we could find a natural remedy in the palm—"

His hand on my arm quieted me. "There's nothing we can do. We don't have an axe."

I felt sick at the thought. An axe. What had happened to us?

"I'm not sure I could live through that anyway." He rubbed a hand over his face and chuckled humorlessly. "And the gun was there, and I kept having these strange . . . dreams, memories. I don't know what to call them."

"Yeah, I've had them too."

He closed his eyes and rubbed the line that had appeared on his forehead. Trying to rub something out.

"In this dream, the gun is nothing but trouble." He looked out into the waves again.

Nothing but trouble. I blinked and digested that. His expression told me everything. He didn't have a doctor, or an axe, or a bottle of penicillin. But he had a gun to end it now, before the pain got too bad.

A salt breeze picked up. We sat together and watched the waves roll in, and I thought about what it would be like to lose this person I'd just met. I couldn't. I wanted to know him when he wasn't here, in this horrible place. Hang out with him over burgers and fries. Go to a B movie with him and talk about it until dawn. Bring him to meet you, if he'd come. I think he would.

He turned to me then, and all that emotion he kept so controlled unraveled right there in his eyes. "I'm not afraid of death," he said. "No one in my family is. So that's not what I'm afraid of."

"What are you afraid of?"

He didn't answer at first, his gaze back on the water. "It's different than I expected."

"What is?"

"The way it feels to know it's coming." He met my eyes again, and there was no peace there. "I thought I'd have another seventy years."

"I guess none of us know if we've got that long. I guess—"

"Sia, I'm gonna end up wandering around the palm forest. With all the others. Because that's what's wrong with this place. Nothing *ends* here. Not really."

His voice faltered on the last word. Part of me broke with it.

That was it, what terrified him. Not that he was dying too soon, or that he didn't get a chance to have kids or fall in love. He was afraid of going on forever.

We sat together quietly and watched the fairy terns plunge down into the surf, their feathers catching the breeze and the salt spray.

Ben squeezed my hand and I rested my head on his shoulder.

When he brushed the top of my arm with his fingers, I thought, yeah, this is a guy who would walk through the gates with me, sign his name in the prison log, and call you sir. In another life maybe.

We stayed there, leaning against one another, until the sun fell past the horizon and dove into the sea.

The next morning, when the sun finally climbed high enough to cast shadows, I fished in a spot far down the beach. I found only one lobster, a small one. I was halfway out of the surf when the Sense rose up, and I knew I wasn't alone. Something was coming out of the waves. Something behind me.

I dove sideways, the lobster bucking in my hand. I'd caught

only a glimpse, but it was a girl this time, one of the dead. She hadn't seen me. And what would she do when she did? I didn't want to find out.

I turned, twisting underwater to face the threat. White foam slid in the chaos above my head. My knees digging into the sand, I surfaced slowly, holding my breath. My eyes broke the water-line, and I stopped to watch her make her way to shore.

Later I would piece together the details. That she wore a Maroon 5 T-shirt. That her blond ponytail hung over one shoul-der, trailing water down her front. That she was one of the divers who backed out at the last minute because the seas were rough. But I couldn't wrap my mind around how she ended up here, when she'd never even gotten close to the wreck that started all this. All I could see while hiding in the waves, the lobster scrab-bling at my hand and the salt water burning my tongue, was that half of her right arm was missing.

I held my breath for the next minute and a half, hoping the ocean's roar masked me. The bright white of my rash guard. My long black hair swarming around me, pulled by the waves like a flag, waving, *Here I am! Come and get me.*

She moved slowly, staggering only an arm's length away. A wave knocked her over more than once. The girl struggled to her feet every time, her face turned toward the palm forest. Hiding there in the surf, I surfaced twice to get a breath, forgetting about my ten-minute rule.

She finally passed me and staggered her way onto dry sand, heading toward the trees like she had someplace she needed to go. I then stood, still in waist-deep water, a piece of driftwood nudging me in the back every time the waves rolled in.

I would follow her. Into the palm forest. Find out where

she went. A strange flash of a dream lit my mind, like a grainy five seconds of a film. The Sense again, giving me memories of something I'd never experienced. A clearing ringed by palms, the girl heading to the center where the shadows from the trees pooled, forming what looked like a pond, or a small lake, or a—

A sting on the back of my calf made me jump. Something had brushed me, as hot as the lit end of a cigarette. I turned and backpedaled toward the beach, scrambling across the soft sand. A breaker hit me full in the face, blurring my vision. But I could see them. Clear ropes, as thick as cables, rising from the chaos of the waves. Trembling in the sunlight, as if tasting it. I watched as it reached toward me, wrapped around the driftwood instead, and dragged it below the surface.

A second later I was out of the water and stumbling onto dry beach, hugging the lobster to my chest.

It took a long time for me to stop shaking. So close.

And then another memory came, not of the strange clearing and the shadows that pooled like water. This one was of the girl with the blond ponytail helping me build a signal fire. Putting a bandage on Felix's leg while he cried. Helping me make water converters.

Zoe; that was her name. She lasted one week on the island before the accident. She'd gone out to fish for lobster, and she hadn't come back.

I sat back in the dry sand and cried, my brain trembling, ready to split apart. Something sharp cut into me. A part of me realized it was the lobster. The rest of me didn't care.

A dream, that's what Zoe was. But I cried for her anyway, and the others I now remembered, if only for a moment.

As I made the long trek back down the beach toward camp,

I felt all wrung out. My lobster had gone quiet. I had held him too tightly.

Thirst hit me hard, as it always did after a long swim, like it used to right after my swimming lessons with my grandmother. The clouds moving over the island, out to sea, were swollen with rain. But somehow, I knew it wouldn't come. The storm always blew past, our hopes for rainwater dashed.

This place is alive, Dad, and has a will of its own: the palm forest, the sand, even the passionless stare of the sky—huge, end-less, the kind I'd always loved but now hated. Too big. Too remote. And I remember thinking, It won't give us what we want. No, those clouds will blow by like the others.

When I got back, Steph was gone, and Ben and Felix were down in the wrecked charter, trying once again to get the radio working. Useless activity, but you know how Felix is happier when he's busy. And I didn't want Felix to see me until I had shaken off my encounter with the dead girl, and that thing.

I threw our tiny breakfast onto the fire. Graham was a couple of feet closer to it than usual, sweating, his face buried in his bound hands. I searched the beach for a flash of red hair. She did this on purpose. Dragged him close to dry him out, kill him before I came back from the free dive. Zoe's image came into my head again. All the others we'd lost. I wondered again how she'd ended up here if she'd never left the dock.

"C'mon." I reached under Graham's armpits and pulled. "Let's get you under the sun shelter and out of the heat."

He pushed with his legs to help me—awkwardly, since they were tied together—and I got him away from the fire and under the patchwork construction of boat pieces that had become our home. I settled him, trying to ignore how filthy he'd become.

Our time here felt so much longer than a few weeks. Maybe we'd been here years, and I just couldn't remember.

I set him up against a pile of wet suits we used for pillows and gave him his ration of water. He swallowed, watching me the entire time. The smell from the neoprene was comforting—to me, at least—and I sat next to the pile and drank my ration and watched the waves roll in.

"Why are you so nice to me?" Graham asked.

"Haven't heard you talk in a week. I'm honored."

"I didn't expect it, you know."

"Yeah, well, Merry Christmas."

Something about my comment sent him back into silence, and I figured our fragile peace was over. But then he rolled onto his side, toward me, and that surly side I'd seen so much of melted. "Is it already Christmas?"

"No, of course not," but as I said it, suddenly I wasn't sure. Had we been on the island for weeks, or had it been months? Could it be December? I rubbed my temples, feeling that strange stretched feeling that had been dogging me for hours.

He lay on his back again and stared at the ceiling of the shelter. "Best Christmas I ever had was on that ship out there." He pointed to the water without looking at it.

"You're kidding."

"Nope."

"Did you have a tree?"

"We didn't need one. We were happy because we had something else."

I waited for him to tell me what it was. He didn't.

I sat there beside Graham and thought about what that something else was. For me, I mean. Last Christmas, with your being in prison bringing in a big fat goose egg into our accounts, we couldn't afford anything beyond Felix's presents. And yours (Mom insisted). But I didn't want to share that kind of family stuff with a guy who had, not that long ago, held a gun to my head.

"My bunkmate, he always liked Christmas," Graham said, his gaze far away.

"You mean the one with the dreams you found so 'entertaining'?"

Graham looked at his hands. "Yep."

"I get the feeling something bad happened to your friend."

"He wasn't a friend."

"Then why are we talking about him?"

We sat for a long while, not speaking. Hot sand, the swell of surf, and his farm boy face taking in the horizon. I got the feeling he was about to spill something important, maybe some clue to why we were here, and why we couldn't leave.

"Even if we find a way off the island, I'm not sure I can go home."

"Why not?"

His expression took on a heavier cast, but he didn't answer. Instead he smiled at me, as if trying too hard to forget something. "If you didn't go home, and if you could live anywhere in the world, where would you go?"

"Fiji."

"Where on God's green earth is that?"

"About a six-hour flight from Australia. White beaches, beautiful reefs. My family and I, we're moving there, when Dad gets home."

"Why would anyone move to Fiji?"

"Dive charters. Big business over there." I took another sip of liquid happiness. "My family and I, we'll be set up for life, taking out a bunch of fat wallets to see pretty fish. Felix gets to grow up in paradise. And I get to spend every day underwater."

"And that makes you happy?"

"A lot of things make me happy."

"But diving, that's it for you?"

"Everything makes sense when you're breathing through a regulator."

My response stumped him, and he went quiet for a while, focused on the *Last Chance*, where Ben and Felix still fiddled with the dead radio. Then he looked down the beach, toward the spot where Steph gathered driftwood, a small figure scavenging in the distance.

His gaze came back to the wet suits. "That equipment you got on the boat, the tanks, you can stay underwater a long time with that?"

"Why?"

"Humor me."

I shrugged. "Maybe ten hours of bottom time in all those tanks. I don't know. Depends how deep you go."

He pressed his lips together as if deciding whether or not the next words were worth it. "I know where we can get more food."

I stopped with my water bottle halfway to my mouth.

"A lot of it," he said. "Canned food. We could eat for months."

I stared at him, stunned. "All this time, you've had a stash of food and—"

"No, no, not like that."

"—and you didn't tell us?"

"Will you shut up and listen? I couldn't get to it. But with the diving equipment, maybe we could."

I looked out to the crashing surf and beyond, where the sea stretched out blue and long to the horizon. "Do you mean the USS *Andrews*? Two hundred yards offshore, past that thing, we'd never—"

"No, Sia, not out there." He nodded to the palm forest.

"You're kidding me."

"It's in the middle of the island."

"There's no water in the forest. I looked."

"You didn't explore as much as I did, then. And before you say anything, it's not fresh water, so you can't drink it."

Food! I imagined what might be in those cans, and my mouth watered. Thought about eating, really *eating*, and my hands went up to my own ribs. I could feel them through the rash guard. And Felix looked even worse.

"And there's something else." He looked toward the *Last Chance*, where Ben labored over the radio. "Antibiotics. Real ones."

I actually hugged him, despite the BO that hung about him like a fog. We could save Ben's life, which at the moment was more exciting than the food. All I knew was for once, the island wasn't a thinking, self-aware monster hell-bent on our destruction. It was just an island, and we were just shipwrecked survivors. And it was about to give us what we needed.

He huffed an awkward laugh, and I let him go before he could push me away.

I stood, ready to grab a mesh bag and fill up. "How do we find this place?"

His expression darkened and he broke eye contact, looking toward the fringe of the forest.

And that's when the dream rose in my mind again, the girl who'd come out of the surf with one arm missing, making her way through the palm forest into that clearing ringed with palms. Not a dream. A memory. And I remember following her, something I've never done. In that memory, I hid behind a trunk and watched her step into the pool of shadows, until she disappeared, until the earth swallowed her completely.

He finally met my eyes again. "We follow the—"

I cut him off, the dream a sharp piece of glass in my mind. "We follow the dead. That's where they all go."

THE SINKHOLE'S MOUTH yawned open to the sky, its dark surface still, like a pond. From edge to edge, it was about the size of a four-bedroom house. The hole plunged into the earth for at least a hundred feet—or so Graham said, though he still refused to tell me how he knew. And I couldn't shake the feeling I'd been here before.

I leaned over the edge to stare into the shadowy water. Even with the sun dead center above me, I could only see twenty feet before the murk stole the details.

"Don't know why it happened," Graham said, squatting down next to the water and peering in, "but one day the lab was normal—here, above ground—and the next, I go off to the ship, and while I'm gone, the lab just disappeared into the ground, like something had sucked it under. The whole thing flooded. Everyone inside died." He rubbed his cheek and looked out into the palms. "I think."

"What's a lab doing here?"

"That's classified."

"Unclassify it."

"Sorry, Baby Doll."

I peered into the water. "The dead all come here?"

Graham nodded, his face turning a shade paler.

My stomach squeezed as I leaned over the water to peer in. All

I could see on the oily surface was my own gaunt face reflected. My braid fell over my shoulder, and when the tip touched the water, I drew back, suddenly afraid something would reach up and grab it like a rope and pull me down.

"Do you know *why* they're attracted to this place?" I asked.

Graham shook his head. "That's beyond my paygrade, sweetheart." He looked up at the crowns of the trees, the patch of blue sky. "All of this is."

The footsteps said Steph had arrived, but her steps were short and her breathing labored. She had one of the tanks from the *Last Chance* over her shoulder, and she set it down next to the others. The small duffel I'd given her to carry was still over her shoulder, and I nodded to it. She handed it over without a word. Then she gave Graham a look you would recognize, an "I've-got-a-shiv-up-my-sleeve" side-eye, the kind you get across the yard when you've done someone wrong.

Ben emerged limping from the palm forest, two regulators slung over his shoulder. Felix followed, one mask in his hands, the other perched on his head like he was ready for a snorkeling excursion. I'd brought the rest of the things I needed, and the fins lay at my feet, as well as the mesh bag I'd rescued from the head.

Steph put the tank down with a grunt. "This is a bad idea."

"No one asked you," Ben said as he dropped the two regs.

"I'm so hungry," Felix said, sitting down next to me and peering into the sinkhole. "Do you think there's pizza down there?"

"It's full of water, Felix."

"Maybe it's in a can. Canned pizza." And he giggled and said it again through the giggles. Graham and I laughed. Steph frowned at us.

"We can't trust Graham," Steph said. "He was going to kill us."

Felix stared at Graham's profile, curious but not afraid. "You weren't going to kill us, were you, Graham?"

"Nope."

"Just trying to scare us, right?"

"Yep."

"Like at Halloween. A trick."

"Right."

Felix looked at Steph triumphantly, and Graham's smile faded. "I was just hungry. I wouldn't have pulled the trigger unless you were armed and pointing something at me."

"Comforting," Steph said.

His expression went a shade darker. "If I'd wanted to kill you, you'd be dead."

Steph turned away and crossed her arms, contemplating the canopy of palm fronds moving in the wind that ringed us and the sinkhole. Then she turned again to peer into the dark water, a ripple of fear passing across her features. "You sure what we need is actually down there?"

"Yeah, I'm sure. A big mishmash of supplies, things we brought with us on the *Andrews*, things we took from the enemy. Why would I lie? I don't want to go down there any more than you do."

Ben limped to a flat rock near the edge of the water and sat, grimacing as his leg bent. Red streaks now spread out from the edges of the bandage, and everyone knew, even Felix, that Ben was dying. He told me that morning he'd been wrong, that he had only a few days, not a week.

I walked to him and felt his forehead with the back of my

hand . . . burning up with fever. I looked into that sinkhole one more time. Dark. Murky. God knows what's in there, I thought.

"Bad idea letting him off the leash," Steph said, nodding to Graham.

"Graham knows the layout of the place," I said. "Besides, I could use a dive buddy. Might get into trouble."

Steph pointed at Graham accusingly. "*He's* trouble. He said he's never been diving before."

"He's willing and you're not."

"I don't know how."

"That's not stopping Graham, now, is it?"

Steph glanced from Ben's face to mine, and then settled her scrutiny on Graham. "Suit yourself, Sia. But I learned a long time ago not to trust people like him. I bet a thousand bucks he's gonna kill you down there, load up on food, and come back up with a bazooka. Then we're all dead, and he can eat for friggin' weeks."

All of us fell silent, and I turned back to the sinkhole. On impulse, I dipped in a finger and tasted it. Salt, like Graham said. Which meant this body of water somehow led to the open ocean. Could be an aquifer, all the water bubbling through the little pores of limestone, although Mom and I had been to dozens of these islands near Key Largo while scouting out new dive sites, and we'd never come across any sinkholes or limestone anything. Of course, at that point, I wasn't sure we were anywhere near Florida anymore.

As I stood and got to work, fitting the regulator on the tank, showing Graham how to do the same, another thought came to me, that the sinkhole was connected to the ocean by caves. My hand stilled halfway through tightening the strap on the BC.

"What is it?" Graham asked. He had been watching me and mimicking my every move, putting together his gear.

"Nothing," I lied. Caves tunneling under the island, leading out to sea. That thing could smell us in the water, so we were in a special kind of trouble. I doubted we could find the storeroom Graham had told us about in less than ten minutes. But I didn't tell Graham what I suspected. This was a reckless first dive as it was—into a deep, dark hole with poor visibility. No one did something like this on a first day. But today would get even more dangerous if he panicked.

I finished slipping on my gear and sat near the edge, watching Graham fumble his way into the BC. He stumbled as he adjusted the strap, the weight of the tank throwing him off. As he picked up his fins and made his way gracelessly to me, I couldn't help but laugh. I had been laughing more today, ever since he told me about this place. Hope bubbling up from a deep place, which felt fantastic after two weeks of despair. Or was it three weeks? A year? I wasn't sure.

"You making fun of me?" he asked.

I nodded.

"Yeah," he said, and he sounded defeated. "Like I said, water's not my thing."

"You joined the *Navy*."

"That's how I found out."

I peered into the sinkhole again. "Before we go in, I'm gonna give you one more chance to tell me what's going on down there."

"Told you. It's a lab."

"Who created the lab? The United States?"

"Can't say."

"What were they doing, or studying?"

"Can't tell you that."

"Was it dangerous?"

He paused, thought about it, like a man probing a wound in his mouth with his tongue. "Yes."

"Why?"

"I can't tell you that."

Steph made a disgusted sound. Ben was too focused on the pain, which seemed to come in flashes, to notice the conversation. And Felix, sitting there, rubbing his empty belly and staring at me, his big sister, as if I was going out for takeout and would come back with a grocery bag full of sushi and Subway sandwiches.

I turned to Graham. "You're going to help me find food and medicine, and you're not going to do anything to screw this up. I don't care how scary it is down there."

"Yes, ma'am."

"Don't call me ma'am."

"Roger that."

"Get in."

"Yes, ma'am."

In Clear Springs Lake, just outside of Dallas, there's a dive spot you've never tried called the Silo. It's sixty feet down and has a circular catwalk on the bottom so students can kneel on it and practice their skills, like knot tying and mask clearing. But it's silty and black and cold, kind of like diving in a well. Dark as death, as oblivion. You find the catwalk railing by touch. Shine a light on your instruments and you see number soup. Tie knots blind. If you drop your mask, you'll never find it. The fire department trains there for rescue dives, and they all hate it.

Just after you went away, Felix, Mom, and I missed our weekly visit with you because we were at that lake. Mom and I lied and told you we'd had the flu. She didn't want you to know she'd called up her old boyfriend and begged for work—anything—so she could pay the bills. Steve hired her out of pity, and all of us headed to Texas. He even sent her a hundred dollars through Western Union so we'd have gas and food money. It was a two-day drive, and Mom drove straight through.

When we pulled up to the lake and stepped out of the car—which was running on fumes—Steve didn't say hello or hug anyone. He just handed Mom an envelope of money. She burst into tears. And took it. Hugged him for a long time while I took Felix down to the lake to look for turtles.

That was the trip when Mom and I started to fight. A lot. She wanted me to sit in the advanced course with the paying students, read the textbook, and get a 100 on everything. I wanted to play my guitar in the tent and do the easy dives when I felt like it. I'd never gone deeper than forty feet before, and I wasn't ready.

In the end, Mom won, like she always does. She took the guitar she'd bought me six months before, the one she'd been so excited about me learning to play, and locked it in the trunk. Then she told me to sit at the picnic tables by the lake with all the adults. I took knowledge tests and learned how to search and rescue, tie knots, navigate blind, and all the things I can now do in my sleep. I had no idea she was grooming me to be your replacement.

On day two, we dove the Silo, all the way to the dark and muddy bottom. We'd been warned, but when I hit that first thermocline—the cold seeping into my wet suit and the black-ness thickening into a hood over my eyes—I sucked down my air like a sprinter. At the bottom, my ears filled with the sounds of my own breath, and I shined my light through the silt to find Mom. The beam made it three inches and petered out. In the Silo, unless you're holding someone's hand, everyone's on their own.

One of the guys with us panicked, although I didn't know that until we'd finished our dive and Mom and I debriefed in our tent. Too much for him, even after all the warnings about disorientation and darkness and cold. Mom had to hold on to his leg to keep him from bolting to the surface and popping a lung, or worse. But I didn't see any of that. At the bottom of the Silo, all I knew was what I could feel: the blackness, the cold, and something hitting me in in the stomach and in the face . . . an elbow, a fin, a who-knows-what, because you can't see crap.

After I'd finished tying a bowline and checking out colors on a color chart—I couldn't see anything, so what was the point—I felt around the dark for another diver, hooked arms, and surfaced. Topside, the seven of us floated on the warm surface layer of the lake, and everyone talked at once, lots of swearing and "I'll never do that again." But I didn't say any of those things. And not because Mom was watching me for my reaction, to see if I had the stomach to do what had to be done—dive when it wasn't fun, lie about my age, and help her run the charter. No, I didn't say those things.

Because I *wanted* to go back.

That's what I've been afraid to tell you, Dad; why I didn't rat out Mom when we saw you again, about her old boyfriend and the weekend trip to Texas.

I wanted to go back down to the bottom of the Silo, which I'm pretty sure is not normal. And not in a "being different is good" way. More of a dysfunctional, "I'm-going-to-end-up dead" way.

The feeling, the thrill of fear, the whole world eaten up and gone, it did something for me. No yesterday. No tomorrow. Just my instincts and breath and the glorious challenge of it all.

So here's my third confession. At midnight, I snuck out of the tent, put on my gear, and swam out into the ink-dark lake. Then I sank to the bottom of the Silo, six stories down, and tied knots in the dark. Sheep shank, bowline, clove hitch. Without gloves first, then again with them on, because my fingers were so cold I couldn't feel them. And for the first time since they locked you away, all of me was in one spot. Not thinking about you, or how I would manipulate the parole board at your hearing with my sad, sad story, or Mom and how she needed me to grow up and keep the charter business from failing. I wasn't thinking about the crappy apartment we'd moved to after you left, how the lack of heat made it hard to sleep because we couldn't pay the electric bill, how we kept our food in an ice chest because the fridge didn't work. All of that was gone. In the Silo, I was new, just born, tying knots in the dark.

So when Graham told me where we'd have to go, to the bottom of the weird sinkhole on a haunted island in God knows where, planet Earth, yes, I was afraid.

But I'd be lying if I said I didn't like it.

All that stuff I wrote about how scared I was to fish for lobster, with the *thing* out there, sniffing the water for me—I wasn't telling you the whole story. Truth is, this island has done something to me, molecule by molecule, making me, I don't know, more *me*. I didn't tell Ben, or Steph, or Graham. I kept it from Felix, who would just copy what I do and end up dead. I never once told anyone, throughout all the horrible things that happened to me on the island, that I needed the fear some- how, regular, like a daily coffee. But I'm telling you now, Dad, because . . . I don't know why. Because I wanted you to know.

Graham and I slipped into the sinkhole, and I went over the basics. How to purge the air from a BC so you sink. How to add it so you rise. How to release your buckles if you catch on something. How to buddy breathe if you run out of air. It was the quickest scuba lesson I'd ever given.

He floated beside me, looking down at his BC like someone had just put an alien suit on him and asked him to fly.

I pointed to the two lift bags I'd attached to a clip on the front of my gear. "If we have the time, we'll send some food to the top with this."

He eyed the equipment. "How does it work?"

"Kind of a reverse parachute. I fill it with air from my reg- ulator and the whole package floats to the surface. Can you tie good knots?"

"Every knot in the Navy manual, plus some you've never heard of, sweetheart."

I took in the cocky expression. Good. Where we were going, he would need that.

"Are you ready?" I asked.

"Always."

"I think the answer is, 'I was born ready.'"

He nodded. "That sounds about right."

I smiled and put in my reg. That smile was cheap to give and cost me nothing. Chances were high we were dealing with caves, not an aquifer. I was expecting the phosphorescence to light up the sinkhole. The Sense said it was coming, that the beast liked it here. That it *belonged* here. And I'd feel that beautiful fear turn to a hammer, until that monster swept up, wrapped its silky filaments around our ankles, and pulled us down.

The dive knife strapped to my thigh gave me comfort. For fishing line, not coral. You used to tell the dive students that, back in the Keys when you had a career and a life, when my only job was to help people fill out the waivers. Leave Mother Nature alone, use the knife to deal with what mankind gives you. A bad way to go, tangled up in fishing line until your air runs out.

Today I was breaking my rule, ready to shove it into what Mother Nature gave us. It would cut through filaments as easily as fishing line. As long as there weren't too many of them, as long as they didn't pin my arms by my side, as long that thing didn't pull me into its body, wriggling like a fish . . .

I fit my regulator into my mouth, the equivalent of five cups of coffee pulsing through me. Graham did the same. I gave him a thumbs-down. He blinked at me with a blank expression. He'd already forgotten my crash course in hand signals. I flipped on my dive light, purged my BC, and sank. He'd figure it out.

As soon as we left the air and sunlight, I felt better. The world of bubbles and neoprene, compressed air and breath, rock and silt, and the hollowed-out bodies of ships—it all rushed back, my days with you and Mom on the charter, exploring the coast one breath at a time. Descent. Weightless, we drifted into the dim water of the sinkhole. I hooked my arm through Graham's to keep us tethered. Below my fins lay darkness, endless velvety black.

I focused on our goal. Five stomachs. One bad leg. We had problems and problems had solutions. And those lay somewhere below.

At forty feet, the natural light disappeared, blocked out by the heavy silt layer above us. The world became a dark closet, a universe without stars or moons or anything but two beams of light.

We kept our descent slow. As we dropped, the air in my BC compressed and we accelerated. I tapped in a few puffs. Reached over to do the same for Graham.

Fifty feet.

Fifty-five.

Breathing and plummeting in slow motion into the dark.

A quick sweep of the sinkhole's walls gave me nothing but rock. Brown. Gray. Ordinary. No green glow in the abyss below, thank God.

Sixty feet.

Sixty-five.

It was too dark to see Graham's face, but his hand tightened on my arm.

Seventy feet.

Seventy-five.

Eighty.

Past the point where my grandmother could free dive, when she'd stop her descent and change directions.

Graham's grip hurt. Nobody did a dive like this their first time. Would he bolt for the surface, like that guy in the Silo? If he did, Steph would get her wish. One less survivor to feed. I pulled him an inch closer.

Eight-five feet.

Ninety.

And then in the depths below us, my beam caught a glimpse of silver.

THE LAB. The glint of silver grew distinct. A railing. It came up fast, to my left, and I hooked an arm around it before I passed.

We dangled there for a few seconds as I put a little air into both our BCs. Once we were weightless again, I checked my gauge.

Ninety-five feet. I pointed my beam down, and the sinkhole kept going, until my light couldn't reach any farther. A wave of relief passed through me. Most of the dead would plummet right past the railing and keep going. I had no intention of ever finding out how deep that sinkhole went.

I'd looked at dive tables often enough to picture the rows of numbers. At ninety-five feet, we had twenty minutes to get what we needed and get out. If we overstayed our welcome, we couldn't skip the decompression stop, which would become a problem if Graham kept sucking on his tank like he was.

We needed to get going, but Graham's fingers clamped my wrist so hard I couldn't feel my hand. Terror, panic. I'd been there before, before I developed a taste for places like this. The animal self doesn't like all that water above, all the blackness.

I turned him to face me, shone my light at an angle so he could see my eyes. Calm and steady, I was telling him. Then I shined the light on my hand and made the okay sign I'd taught him. Not a statement. A question.

Are you okay?

I kept my light on his hands and waited, letting precious seconds tick away. Each moment in the open was one more chance for that thing to smell us, slip through its caves and find us hanging there like ripe fruit on a tree. His grip on my wrist shook.

Too dark. Too cold.

If he bolted, would I go after him? Would I stay here and find the food on my own?

After a full minute of us floating at the railing, he made the okay sign. My body relaxed. I hadn't wanted to make that choice.

I swam in a circle with my light. Metal dangled off the walls of the sinkhole, glints of silver through the silt. Remnants of something manmade ringing us, as if we were floating in some sort of cored-out engine and its parts were all out of whack. One more sweep of my light and my brain finally made sense of it.

I was looking at the floors of a building built *inside* a machine, but something had cut clean through the center, the way Mom cuts through the center of a pineapple, turning and coring until it has a nice clean tunnel. That's what it looked like, a cored-out pineapple, riddled with hallways and gears.

I floated at the railing, stunned. What could do this? Whatever it was, I didn't want the machine to turn on when we were down here. The image of me in a blender came to mind.

Cup of coffee number six, injected directly into my veins.

Without warning, the Sense rose up from nowhere and blindsided me. Images flashed in front of my eyes, a montage of light and shape and memory. Graham and me rising with bags full of food. Graham and me tangled in the filaments of a something we couldn't see. Metal falling on us, trapping us, until we ran out of air. A string of flashes. In some memories we lived. In some we died.

Lost in the show in my head, I sucked down air like a new

diver. I held my breath and made myself ration it. And without explanation, the Sense left me, descended back into the deep.

Graham had finally shaken off the last of his fear, or swallowed it, and his dive light danced over the metal curves and angles like a bright little fish. The beam stilled on an opening to our right, two floors down. He pushed off the railing and swam toward it, and I followed.

Under a catwalk that dangled drunkenly off a few metal bolts stood a door, yawning open on one hinge. Graham slipped halfway through before I grabbed his ankle. He turned, and I held up my coil of bright orange line.

Keep it in sight, I was telling him. *Don't go anywhere that you can't see this.*

I secured my line to a bolt on the outside and led the way, unspooling our lifeline as we swam into the yawning opening of the cored-out lab. Machine. Whatever it was.

Beyond the doorway was a flooded hallway, the kind you'd see in a hospital, with white, institutional walls. Six doors down the hallway stopped and became a T junction. I ran my light over the walls, stopping on a sign.

In Japanese.

My heart thudded as I realized what that meant.

I then puzzled at the lettering through my bubbles.

A tap on my ankle made me jump. Graham pointed down the hall and then at his stomach and his wrist.

Let's get going.

Another sweep revealed three doors on the left, two on the right. And a body at the T junction, lying on its side. I knew I'd encounter one eventually. Thankfully, it faced away from me. I didn't want to see the empty stare.

Graham glided past me, kicking up a cloud of silt. I grabbed his ankle again. When he turned, I pointed at the silt cloud, which now completely obscured the hallway behind us.

He looked at the cloud, and then at me. I pulled out my slate and wrote a message with my golf pencil—*Fins off floor*—and shoved it in his face.

He blew out a cloud of bubbles and held his hands out as if to say, "Ladies first."

That's all I needed—underwater sarcasm.

We continued on with me in the lead, two floating lights in the dark hallway. I checked my watch. Five minutes had elapsed. Fifteen minutes left.

Graham stopped swimming and shined his light at an open doorway on his right. When he turned to me, he made a few garbled hand gestures that I interpreted as *Stay here.*

I shook my head.

He made the sign again. I poked my light inside and found it to be the size of a walk-in closet. No way he could get lost in there.

I nodded and he slipped through the doorway, soon returning with a small white case marked with *US Navy* on the front. He pointed to it, then his leg. My heart swelled with relief. Medical supplies. Antibiotic, in a sealed case. Thank God. I punched Graham on the shoulder and he nodded, blowing out a cloud of bubbles. We gave ourselves a few seconds to celebrate before I stuffed the case inside my BC and tightened my straps.

Graham led the way and I unspooled our orange line, foot by foot. Left turn. Right turn. Past another body, this one wearing a white lab coat, who I gave a wide berth. Halfway down a corridor, where we had to skirt a pile of debris where the ceiling had caved in, Graham pointed his light at a doorway that led to an empty room. We swam inside and he passed by me to grab the handle of a door I hadn't noticed. With a yank and a cloud of silt, it swung open. Another dark room. I dragged my light over the walls and . . .

Sweet mother of God.

Cans.

Stacked in neat rows five high. Potatoes, beans, pudding—pudding!—peanut butter, fruit cocktail, and—oh yes—mandarin oranges. My mouth watered, and my regulator mouthpiece slicked. Spam. Tea. Canned biscuits. More Spam.

Five shelves on each side of the room. Each one with at least a hundred cans and tins, some in Japanese, some in English.

A bubbling, gurgling sound came from Graham. He was laughing.

I floated there in the darkness, scanning the shelves. Green beans, apples, meat and vegetable stew. My body shook with need. I slung an arm over Graham's shoulder and squeezed, laughing into the water with him.

I filled my bag with food, on the most glorious shopping trip in history. Graham worked on the other side of the room, his fins splayed on the floor. Stuffing his sack like a thief who'd just set off the house alarm.

Graham finished when I did. The excess weight of cans in the bag over his shoulder dragged him down, and every kick created an enormous, blinding silt cloud that would soon fill the room. I grabbed his vest and yanked him until he stilled. Pulsed a shot of air into his BC and secured the food on his back. But it was hard to be mad at him. He had forty things to remember, and he just couldn't process it all. I'd give him lessons on the beach, and he'd be more controlled next time we came down here for supplies. And we'd both operate better with full bellies.

Once I'd cut the orange line and tied it to a shelf so we could find this place again, we slipped through the doorway and into the hall to make our way out of the maze. My light hit the silt cloud and bounced back to me. The muck Graham had kicked up was so thick that if I extended my arm, my hand disappeared.

I tapped Graham and flashed the signal in front of his mask, two index fingers together.

Stay close.

He nodded.

I wasn't worried then. We had the line and eight minutes to spare. Mom and me, we'd done this kind of dive a dozen times in the *Spiegel Grove* and the *Duane*. Mom and I did the hallways of the *Vandenberg* for my seventeenth birthday. Piece of seaweed cake. As long as the thing hunting the coastline wasn't waiting for us in the sinkhole, we were home free.

We started our exit, swimming through silt soup, my finger hooked around the line. I pushed thoughts of the green glow out of my mind and imagined the luau we would have on the beach. Laughed into the water again. My heart thumped and my whole body celebrated.

At the first turn, the silt thickened. I couldn't read my gauges unless I held them a few inches from my eyes. Mom's training had prepared me for this too, and my heart was all kinds of calm. No green glow. No problem. I loosely hooked my finger around the line, linked my arm through Graham's, and kept moving.

And then the line went slack.

Ten cups of coffee in my bloodstream now. All at once.

I stopped, bringing Graham to a halt. Picked up the line and pointed to it. No reaction. He couldn't see me. I reached for my slate to write him a message, to tell him the horrible truth. Then I let my hand fall to my side.

He didn't need to know. Not yet. Trapped underwater. Lost in a maze. The truth would only make him burn through his air faster.

I finned my way through the soup, careful not to pull the line. Maybe it would still lead us out into the clear water of the sinkhole. The knots you taught me were perfect, so it hadn't slipped free of the bolt. Which meant the bolt came off the wall. And the bolt would weigh down the end and lead us out. I rationalized my panic away, telling myself we were fine. Piece of seaweed cake . . .

Halfway down the hall, the end of the line appeared out of the murk, right in front of me, floating like sea grass. I grabbed it to get a better look, the thunder of breath in my ears speeding up, mocking me. The knot had come loose from the bolt.

My knot had failed.

I couldn't hide the truth anymore, so I tapped Graham and held the frayed end a few inches from his mask. A startled gurgle came back to me.

I had the sudden urge to stop and write Felix a note on my slate, to tell him I was sorry. That I loved him. But what was the point? Ben and Steph could never come down to find what was left of us and bring our bodies home. So I kept us moving, straight ahead, into the brown haze.

Halfway down the hall, something brushed by my leg. Startled, I flashed my light on it. A hand, floating there, attached to an arm. Which was attached to a body that faded into the cloud of silt.

The fingers twitched.

I pushed it away, a scream caught behind my regulator. Oh God. I couldn't see, and I didn't know where I was, and maybe those things were everywhere.

After a few more kicks and me barely controlling a hyperventilation attack, we reached the T junction. I directed the beam of my light left. Then right. My adrenaline flush had gone to low tide, and my body remembered hunger. My head swam, a hazy confusion filled my mind. I grabbed Graham's arm and squeezed twice, pointed one direction, then the other, and pointed at him.

Which way?

He floated for a few breaths, searching both directions with his light, his beam bouncing back at us like the high beams of a car in a fog bank. He didn't remember either.

Flipping a mental coin, I dragged him to the left, my arm a clamp on his. I wasn't letting go, not for anything. If I let go, it would be too easy to lose him in this mess, like I'd lost Marshall.

We swam side by side, my breath a constant Darth Vader in my head. My body weightless and trembling with cold and adrenaline. I counted my kicks to estimate the distance.

Five. Ten. Fifteen.

And then we crossed some kind of threshold I couldn't see. My mind stretched, popped like a rubber band. My body pulled apart and came back together, my stomach took a journey on a tightrope between two buildings. A muffled, watery cry next to me said Graham felt the same thing. And miraculously, the silt disappeared.

I floated to a stop, staring all along my light beam at perfectly clear water. How had the cloud disappeared so quickly? Had we hit a strong crosscurrent? But that feeling, my mind flipping over like a fish on a deck, just like that first day I swam too far away from the island . . .

A sweep with my dive light revealed gray walls lined with bolts. A long room. A large wooden crate dominated the end. Metal barrels stacked two high. The door on the opposite wall had a wheel on it, the kind you'd find in a . . .

I stopped breathing.

We weren't in the lab anymore.

I scanned the walls. A glint of glass drew me, and I swam to it, past the barrels, past the wooden crate that towered above us. I reached the porthole and pressed my mask against it with an audible *thunk*. More water on the other side. A lot of it. And faint light.

Sunlight.

Open ocean.

Something brushed my waist and I startled, turning. Graham grabbed my slate and wrote something. I yanked it from his hand and shone my light across the message. But it couldn't be. He'd written one word.

Andrews.

I SHOOK MY HEAD. Graham went into a complex pan-
tomime that involved pointing at the barrels, then pointing at
his mask, and a lot of nodding and gurgling and pointing out the
porthole. The gist of it—he'd been here before. He recognized
the room.

Andrews.

The USS *Andrews*, where he'd served before a torpedo sent
the ship to the bottom of the ocean. Which means that Graham
and I were now somehow two hundred yards off shore, ninety-
five feet down, in the bowels of a shipwreck. We'd entered a
sinkhole in the middle of the island and been magically trans-
ported a mile away.

My mind was still reeling from the weird rubber band effect,
that stretching and popping that happened as we crossed the
boundary that brought us here. The ceiling, the floor, they spun
once, then righted themselves.

Coffee cup number twelve. Even for me, it was too much.

A flash of something out the porthole. A dim phosphorescent glow. There and then gone. I choked on my regulator. Of
course that thing was here. Where it *belonged*. Where it was born.
Senseless thoughts, bubbling up and stirring me into a panic.

I pointed the way we came, hoping it wasn't a one-way trip.
He nodded, we secured our stores of food securely on our backs,

linked arms, and swam, praying that thing wouldn't smell us down here and follow us back to the other side.

As I hit the invisible boundary, my stomach turned inside out. My legs stretched, my arms twisted, my brain smoothed flat as if by a steamroller. I dry heaved into my regulator. A rush of bubbles came from beside me, but I barely registered the sound.

We were in a brown world again. I kicked and pulled Graham tight against my side, but he weighed me down like a dead body. I stopped swimming and almost dropped my light.

I slid the beam over his face and saw his half-slitted eyes, his fins kicking weakly. A flush of relief flooded over me. Graham was alive.

Somewhere amidst the detritus floating in my mind I remembered the turn we'd made, the wrong way. Now we were heading the right way, toward the sinkhole, a straight shot down the hall.

Swimming, swimming, just keep swimming, I told myself. That dippy cartoon fish singing in my head. The Sense returned, rising up from the deep, full of splinters and teeth. Us, lying against the lab wall, choking on the last bits of oxygen. Us, knocking over a barrel in the *Andrews*, and the blast pulling us apart. Us, dragged over the edge of the catwalk and into the dark. And I kept swimming, swimming, just kept swimming, the images breaking and shattering and replicating in a hundred different variations.

A dim glow penetrated the darkness. A hazy rectangle. Five more kicks, and it became a doorway. The world opened up, and we were in the sinkhole again.

I closed my eyes and floated a moment, so relieved that my body felt light, my blood felt new.

When I checked on Graham, my relief disappeared. He pushed his fins so weakly through the water I thought he'd passed out. I pulled him to the catwalk and set his hand on the railing. He grabbed it and floated there, trying to put the pieces of himself together.

I checked my gauge: 300 PSI. I calculated the air I had left, checked my dive watch, and my breath stuttered. Twenty-nine minutes had passed. Too long filling bags. Too long swimming in the wrong direction.

Nine minutes past our safe point.

We needed to get to fifteen feet, then stay there for at least fifteen minutes if we wanted to, as you used to say, live past Sunday. If I breathed shallow, maybe I'd make the full fifteen before the air ran out.

I passed my light over Graham, who floated motionless, the only sign of life his death grip on the railing. One look at his gauge and the blood drained from my arms. He was redlining. And I felt so stupid. He was a guy, which meant he ran through his air faster than I did. More body. Bigger lungs. Of course he was out.

Only a few minutes left. We'd have to share.

I ran the numbers again. There wouldn't be enough for both of us, not if we stopped to decompress for fifteen minutes. And if we didn't make it, neither would the food.

My hands shook, but I managed to connect the lift bag to the cans. I firmly stuffed the medical kit in, filled the bag with air, and sent the whole thing flying up to the surface.

As I watched it disappear, I thought about what you would do, what you wouldn't do. I considered going with the food. Graham was so out of it he wouldn't realize I was gone. And even if he did, he wouldn't find me in the dark. Wouldn't panic and grab the regulator from me and take my air. No, I would go to the surface and leave him behind. I would be there for Felix. A necessary sacrifice. Felix needed me.

All of that scheming made its way through my brain in a breath. Two more seconds, and the shock of what I'd just considered ran through me like an electrical current.

I started to take Graham's bag, and he pushed me away, yanking the rope from my hands and threading the end through the loop on the lift bag. His mind was back, the rubber band pop of his brain a memory, and these final bits of him wanted to show me how good he was at tying knots. Could I? Could I leave him there in the dark?

I took my regulator out of my mouth and filled the second lift bag with some of my precious air instead of using the little he had. A decision. Now I didn't have enough either.

Together we watched the mesh bag of cans slowly rise. We both kept our eyes on it until it disappeared into the darkness above us.

I turned him to face me, put my mask against his. It felt right to do this. Because we're all in this together, and we don't leave anyone behind.

The two of us at the bottom of the world, just out of the blender, floating together. Ben had his antibiotics. Felix had more food than he could eat in a month. And Steph, well, I guess she'd be along for the ride.

We started our ascent, and Graham jerked in the water. I shined my light on his mask. His eyes were wide. He tried to talk and got out a burble. He'd forgotten the signal for *out of air*, but his panic said everything.

I handed him my regulator and counted to five while he breathed. Then I gave his shoulder a quick squeeze and took it back. We swam up slowly, sharing air as we rose to the surface.

Time clicked through my head. Seconds, minutes, hours, years. Backward, forward. Somewhere in the kaleidoscope in my head, I laughed into my regulator, like I had when we'd found the food. But this time I was laughing at myself. I had miscalculated so many things—tied a bad knot, turned the wrong way. And what killed me in the end was forgetting an itty-bitty detail—I'd left no tank hanging at fifteen feet in case something went wrong. After over a thousand dives, I had forgotten to rig a safety stop. I laughed again as the flash of possible futures coalesced into one. We were about to die.

Graham had no idea. He probably thought we were in the home stretch. When we got to the surface, I wouldn't have time to explain what was happening to him, but Ben would. He was kind, and he would lay him down on the edge of the sinkhole and tell him why he couldn't breathe, why blood was bubbling out of his lungs. And I would have just enough energy to say goodbye to Felix before the nitrogen bubbles in my brain and heart shut the light out forever.

I passed Graham my reg for a breath and checked my depth. Thirty feet. The needle on my air gauge sat in the red line. As the surface inched closer, light filtered down through the layers of silt.

And then a dark shadow appeared above us, descending. I stopped kicking, my eyes wide, taking in this new threat. We couldn't head back down. Impossible. The shape grew.

A diver. Growing, growing. Small, a woman with a tank on her back. Steph. Steph had come for us?

The diver closed in. No. Not Steph. Black hair streamed out behind her as she fell in slow motion, and for a moment I thought I was dead and my grandmother was coming for us, her fifteen-year-old self descending from heaven to hold our hands and take us to the next world.

The diver closed in and slowed with precision, her fingers pulsing a few puffs of air into her BC. She stopped, floating a few feet away, and held her hand out flat, palm down, a signal I knew.

Stay here at this level.

She flashed her hand three times.

Fifteen minutes.

I blinked into the gloom. It couldn't be. But it was.

Mom slipped her BC and tank off her back and handed it to me. Our safety stop. I didn't know how, but she was there.

I was laughing into my regulator as Graham drank in the air from the new tank, as my mother slipped her hand behind my neck and pressed her mask to mine.

ONCE WE GOT TOPSIDE, we held on to each other for a long time, me and Felix and Mom, huddled in the soft mud by the sinkhole. Mom laughed and cried and held on to me in a way so desperate, I knew the last few weeks for her had been no easier than mine. Or maybe it had been months. Perhaps years? And even without you there, I felt the lines that tied my family together draw tight. One perfect moment.

"How did you find us?" I asked her.

"We heard gunshots a couple of miles away from our camp. It seemed to come from the center of the island, so we plotted a course and here we are."

I glanced at Ben over her shoulder, and he met my eye briefly before he looked away. My body felt wrung out. I was shivering from exposure and stress and hunger. Mom felt so warm I could fall asleep on her, the way I used to when I was little, when we'd come back from a day at the beach and doze off watching TV, my face pressed into her neck.

Graham sat nearby on a mass of roots, his wet suit peeled down to his waist, watching us. When I caught his eyes, the gratitude there was so intense I had to look away. I thought he hadn't understood the choice I made down below, but it was clear he did.

The clink of cans being sorted drew me out of the huddle.

It came from the other side of the sinkhole, just inside the ring of palm trees. I turned, expecting Ben. Or Steph. But the figure with his back to me, examining each can and making two piles, wore a familiar stonewashed purple wife beater.

Phil.

Steph stood next to Ben off to the side, an open medical kit in front of her, and a syringe in her hands. But she wasn't injecting Ben with anything. She was watching Phil quietly, a wary look in her eyes.

Phil turned to me. He'd lost at least fifteen pounds, his usual round cheeks concave, the hollows under his eyes dark. His gray, thinning hair was out of the ponytail and hung loose around his shoulders. It looked greasy, as if he hadn't been in the water since he'd arrived on the island.

Phil held up a can and raised his eyebrow. "Either of you geniuses think to get a can opener when you were down there?"

"Well, hello to you too, Phil," I said.

He glanced at me and went back to sorting, and I got this feeling he thought the whole pile of cans belonged to him. "That's Captain to you, girlie," he said over his shoulder.

"You're not on a boat anymore, *Phil.*"

Mom put a hand on my shoulder and squeezed. When I turned to look at her, she gave me the barest of head shakes. I tried to read the look in her eyes, and as usual I couldn't. But I got the gist. My usual Captain Phil baiting was no longer a good idea.

Phil turned again and pointed at Graham. "Who's this yahoo?"

Graham answered before I could. "Seaman Fitch, sir." He started to stand, and I put a hand on his shoulder.

"He's not that kind of captain, Graham. You don't have to salute him."

Phil laughed and the sound of it bounced around the palm forest, up into the canopy of fronds. A flock of birds took flight far above.

"Phil!" my mother said in a stage whisper, fear rising up in her eyes. She glanced around at the ring of trees.

I had a thousand questions for Mom: how she survived the explosion, where she'd been all this time. But all I could manage was, "What happened?"

She touched my cheek, gave me a small smile, and pulled Felix in close to her side. "It's a long story." She scanned the palms that surrounded the sinkhole, her eyes troubled. "Let's get to the beach first." She smiled at Felix and rubbed his back. "And get a meal into you."

I nodded. She didn't have to say it. They'd seen strange things in the forest as well, perhaps Marshall. My stomach flipped when I considered who else might be out there. Candy, the girls from the roof. Whatever was left of Teague. I still didn't know what would happen if we encountered one of them again. The way my mother hurried told me perhaps she and Phil had had a few close encounters of a more revealing nature.

A tap on my shoulder made me jump. It was Steph, her hands full of medical supplies. "We don't know which one is antibiotic."

I poked around the collection, finding a few clear vials, along with something that looked like tubes of superglue topped with needles. "Mom?"

Mom examined all of it and handed Steph the vial. "This one." As Steph turned away, I saw Mom glance at Phil over her shoulder and pocket the tubes. Something in her eyes told me to ask later, when he was out of earshot.

We left the empty tanks by the sinkhole and headed into the forest. Mom kept Felix by her side, constantly scanning the trees and looking behind her. By the time we'd made it back to the beach, I was thoroughly spooked. Other than the day that thing attacked the boat, and the day they took you off in handcuffs, I've never seen her so scared.

That night we ate a feast, using my dive knife to pry open the cans. At first, I ate without warming anything up—peaches— and the juice was so good and sweet I couldn't help but close my eyes. Oh, the sheer pleasure of food, food, delicious food. Steph laughed and talked between bites. I saw another side of her come out, the girl from the mainland. Funny, pretty, charismatic. The side of her Ben fell for. I caught him glancing at her every so often. And then he would look into his can and take another bite. It almost took the taste out of my food, seeing that. Then Felix would stuff his mouth and grin at me, and I'd forget all about my crush. Or whatever it was.

Phil had arranged the rest of the food in two piles on either side of him, and he sat between them like a grocery king on his makeshift throne. He'd make a big show about passing out US rations to us, making recommendations, pretending he could read the Japanese tins. As if it had been him, not me and Graham, who'd almost died bringing them this feast. Graham had become absolutely ridiculous since meeting the *captain*, nodding in thanks and calling him sir, until I was sick of both of them.

Felix wolfed down a can of apple pudding so fast he almost

threw up. After that, Mom sat next to him and portioned out his food, with a small, motherly smile I hadn't seen on her in so long. My first day of freshman year, when she dropped me off near the front entrance, she had the same look—her hope and love and pride all wrapped up in one moment.

Phil stopped eating and sniffed the air. His gaze finally settled on Ben.

"Good God, man, is that your leg I smell?"

Ben gave him a sharp side-eye and took another bite from his can. Without a word, I helped Ben change his bandage, which did smell like death.

When I walked by Phil with the bandage, he made an exaggerated gagging sound. "I woulda dumped you in the drink by now," he said. "Let the tide take you out."

"Sit upwind if it bothers you," I said, and Mom shot me another warning look.

I sat back next to Ben.

"Thanks," he said, rubbing the top of his thigh just above the bandage and wincing. "It feels better already. I think."

"Give it a day."

Steph leaned over and looked at the red streaks spreading down his leg. "I gave him a quarter of the vial. I hope it's enough."

I nodded. "We'll give him another shot tomorrow." Steph met my eyes, and it was strange to see something other than anger or fear there, as if I'd just met her and she wasn't so bad after all. And then I realized why. For the first time since we'd been on the island, Steph and I had agreed on something.

When all of us had stuffed ourselves sick, we lay on our backs in the sand. A sense of well-being flowed through me, a good humor that came from having a full belly. My limbs hummed with fresh calories. I was uncomfortably full and already planning my next meal. Lobster marinated in the juice from the mandarin oranges and a drizzle of butter, all wrapped in a palm leaf, then cooked on the coals nice and slow. I didn't need to go out into the ocean anymore, take the risk, but as I sat by the fire, listening to it swell and fade in the darkness, I wanted to go. Like I said, Dad, I'm pretty sure something's seriously wrong with me.

Felix fell asleep on Mom's lap, a half-eaten can of apples in his hand. She carried him a few feet away and settled him in a hollow in the sand. The rest of us sat around the fire and fell quiet. I stared into the flames.

When Mom returned, she was lost in thought, a warm glow drawing the angles of her face, the flickering light shining in her eyes. Her hand lay next to mine in the sand, her pinkie finger overlapping the edge of mine. Still trying to convince herself I was real, I guess.

"Have you guys been on the other side of the island the whole time?" I asked.

She nodded.

"So how did you and Captain Phil find each other?" Ben asked.

She and Phil looked at each other, and Phil broke eye contact first. "Another time," Mom said. "I'm pretty tired." Then she cleared her throat and put a hand on my shoulder. "Tasia, let's go down to the charter. I want to see what's there."

Phil sat up a bit next to the cans. "No need to do that, ladies. We got all day tomorrow to sort through things."

Steph and Ben looked from Phil to me, then to Mom. We could all feel the weird vibe. Phil didn't want to let Mom out of his sight.

Mom held up a hand. "I need a moment with my daughter." Her voice broke in a way I'd never heard before, not even when you went away to prison, not when she cried on her ex-boyfriend's shoulder at the edge of that lake in Texas. And I realized she was acting, putting on a show for Phil.

Phil sat back, the expression in his eyes settling into something dismissive. She was a silly, emotional woman, the look said, and he didn't want to be around to watch the sloppy reunion talk. He waved us toward the surf and went back to contemplating the piles of cans surrounding him.

Mom and I walked through the soft sand, the ocean pulsing in the background. Both of us had gone quiet, like we'd just finished a four-tank day. Since you went away, most of our relationship exists in this silence, her head always in the next morning's dive and next week's money, and mine wondering when we'll ever have a break to be something other than boss and employee. But down here on the beach, surrounded by darkness and wave song and salt spray, the silence felt different. The words were all there under the surface, and she was desperate to tell me something.

The charter formed in the darkness, listing starboard. Its white paint glowed faintly in the moonlight. High tide had arrived, and the sea-foam brushed its keel, bringing swell and pulse and the scent of brine. She stopped and looked back toward the fire for a good ten seconds, which I thought strange. Counting silhouettes, I finally realized. To make sure Phil hadn't followed us.

She pulled out something from her pocket and leaned in close. "I need you to hide these somewhere Phil can't find them." She opened her palm. The needle-topped tubes glinted in the moonlight.

"I know Phil is a jerk, but why do you need to hide medicine from him?"

She shook her head. "Ben and Steph have the only vial of antibiotic. This"—she pushed the tubes into my hand—"is morphine."

I squinted at them. I still wasn't following her. "It's a painkiller. It could come in handy for Ben. Why would—"

"There's enough in these syrettes to keep Phil high for two straight weeks. You know what Phil's like when he's drunk. Imagine him with morphine in his system." She went quiet, a dusky figure looking out over the dark ocean. "There was another survivor."

"What happened?"

Phil's voice rolled through the darkness. "What are you girls doing?"

She put her arms around me, and I smelled salt in her hair and stress sweat. "Another time."

She squeezed once and let go.

When Mom and I got back, Felix was still sleeping peacefully under the shelter. Steph sat close to Ben, next to the fire, braiding her long red hair over one shoulder. Phil still sat between the piles of cans and tins, his elbows resting on his knees, watching Graham intensely. Graham fingered the tattered hem of his pants, which were so far from white now they'd pass for khaki. He scratched his pale beard absently, as if deciding something. I got the feeling I'd interrupted an important conversation.

I settled myself a few feet away from the fire. Steph and I made eye contact, and I noticed she'd sat as far away from Phil as possible. Smart girl.

After a few loaded seconds, Graham wiped his palms on his pant legs and nodded, as if answering a voice in his head.

"It all started when we anchored off of this island," he said.

Now that *Captain Phil* had asked the question, it was time to tell us everything.

"Who's we?" Phil asked.

"The USS *Andrews*." Graham nodded west into the darkness. "The one that's out there now, lying at the bottom of the ocean. I'd been on that ship for two years, me and four hundred other guys, and we'd been everywhere, seen things you can't imagine."

"Let's skip the history lesson, son," Phil said, and Graham straightened up.

"So we'd just finished a few weeks of hell near the Ryuku Islands, getting worked over by every Japanese destroyer in the South Pacific, when we were called away. No explanation. I wasn't someone who got to know things, and none of us enlisted had a clue. We just changed directions. A few days later we met up with a small supply ship and some white coats got on board, and—"

"White coats?" Steph asked.

"Scientist types. Snobby and talking in low voices all the time, shutting up when anyone passed them in the halls, which was all the time, we were squeezed into the *Andrews* so tight. Anyway, we docked off this here island."

"Where is here?" Phil asked.

"The Solomons."

Mom and Phil exchanged a shocked look. Graham kept talking. "The *Vermont* had bombed the tar out of it a week before and taken control." Graham grabbed the can of apples Felix had left unfinished. "Took out the whole place." He hooked a piece of fruit with one finger, popped it into his mouth, and chewed thoughtfully. "Me and some others, we were sent to shore with the white coats to be mules. You know, carry stuff."

"I thought you were a gunner's mate," I said. "Why did they have you doing grunt work?"

He paused before he answered, as if considering whether or not he should lie. Then he sighed. "I was in the brig. They used us for grunt work sometimes."

"What did you do?" Steph asked, and I was reminded again of that night by the fire, her and Ben asking about you.

He put the can down. "My bunkmate, well, I let it slip how old I was, that I wasn't even fifteen when I enlisted and had lied about it. He blabbed to the captain."

"Why would they throw you in the brig for *that*?" Steph asked.

"Even if the Navy wants to keep you, they can't, legally. You lie on your application, it's like lying to Uncle Sam, right to his face. They'll strip you of all your medals. When we got stateside, they were going to court martial me."

He shrugged as if it didn't matter, then went on about how many crates they hauled through the jungle, how they stacked them up in a clearing. Steph's suspicious expression had melted away, and Ben and Mom watched Graham talk, slow and steady in his Texas drawl. All I could think was that this guy had lost more than anyone I knew, except for you. It's why he didn't want to go home—ever.

When he finished the can I handed him another, and he took it, avoiding my eyes as he pried it open.

"Back then the coconuts weren't blighted yet—that happened after the accident—so we gathered them up for later, to share with the kitchen so we'd have something to drink other than armored heifer. And the white coats took us to this little nub of a building smack dab in the middle of this island. I thought it was nothing but an arsenal or storage area or something. But then they told us to leave the coconuts outside." He chewed thoughtfully, still trying to make sense of things. "And then we got in an elevator."

He took another bite of apples, the firelight playing over his face, his eyes full of memories. Phil looked fascinated, his elbow on his knee and his fist propping up his chin. All I felt was dread. Because part of me felt I'd heard this before, and the memory was just on the tip of my brain.

"Twenty stories down. That's how deep that elevator went." He nodded at me. "You seen how deep it goes. And strange, fancy machinery on every floor, like the whole thing isn't really a building, more like a machine with offices and hallways honeycombed in its gears and pieces." He shook his head and put the can down. "I never been claustrophobic before, but it's weird, being inside something like that."

Mom's eyes were wide, as if she'd just heard whale sharks could walk on land. "What does—or did—the machine do?"

"I never found out, but the white coats, they'd bring out a prisoner, and they'd ask him questions and point at stuff, and the guy would shake his head and frown and be quiet. And then the MPs would threaten him with a gun, and then the person would talk. Same thing, every day. Always took shouting and threats to make him ease up."

"Was that your job?" I asked. "To beat him?"

Graham shook his head. "No, just had to carry stuff for the white coats. Keep my gun handy. Look over their shoulders in case something happened. Like I said, they didn't tell me squat.

All I knew was it was useful to the war effort. So I did what they told me. Just another way to serve my country that doesn't want me to, I guess."

His expression darkened, as if he wasn't so sure about whether that had ever been a good idea. "So one day, they call us in from the *Andrews*, and when we get down into the lab, one of the scientists they'd captured is slumped by the wall, all beat up to hell, worse than what Baby Doll did to me"—he nodded once at Steph, whose face flushed—"and the white coats are standing by a big crate the size of a car. They tell us we gotta put it on the ship. So we picked up that big boy—took five of us—and got it out of there. Got it on our little skiff to take it out to where the *Andrews* was anchored, and . . ."

He trailed off.

"And then what?"

"We got a hundred yards offshore, and I felt something weird happen. This feeling, never felt anything like it." His gaze shifted to me. "Till today. You felt it, Sia."

My hand automatically went to my stomach.

"A kind of stretching, like your stomach's become saltwater taffy and some kid's pulling it apart. And my brain felt crushed. All of us felt it. One of the other guys in the brig with me, he spewed over the side. And then the feeling went away, and we were fine. We hauled that box up on the *Andrews* and put it in the hold. The white coats radioed to have us come back for another. Halfway through what they were saying . . ." He trailed off again and picked up a stick, dug his fingernails into the cracks on the side, worrying it. "The enemy found us."

Graham dropped the stick and rubbed his face. I got the feeling the memory was too much for him.

"Big Japanese destroyer. *Boom. Boom. Boom.* Everything shaking and tilting. A lot of guys screaming. Burning. Jumping off into the water or blown to bits. And the captain called for us to abandon ship." He rubbed his eyes with the heels of his hands and then stared into the middle distance. "And I did. Swam toward the island. And when I crawled up onto the shore and looked back, no one was left. I don't know where they went. Maybe all of them drowned. All of them. Everyone I knew." His voice broke on the last bit, and he cleared his throat.

"I'm sorry, Graham."

When he met my eyes, he didn't look angry or bitter, just had a sort of raw sadness in his young farm boy face. He threw his stick into the fire and straightened his shoulders, letting out a big, old man sigh.

"I made my way to the middle of the island, to find somebody and radio for help. But the building was gone, and there was the sinkhole in its place." He smiled at me, a humorless smile. "The whole time I been shipwrecked here, I always wondered where it went." He looked out into the ocean. "Now I know. Leads back to her."

The affection in his voice was so thick, I knew he meant the wreck. The *Andrews*. It might not be much, but for him, even in the brig, it was home.

"Took me this long to wrap my mind around things," Graham said. "And now I know whatever was in that crate caused this. I think it was a piece of the machine the white coats were poking around in. And maybe the scientist they'd been grilling found a way to mess us up. 'Yeah,' he'd say, 'this is how you take it apart, this is how it works. Yes, this is the right piece to take with you.' And all along, he was just sabotaging us." He stared into the fire. "One thing I learned out here in the South Pacific: the enemy might be afraid of losing control, but they ain't afraid of death."

Ben had been lying on his side in the sand, drawing in the grains with his finger. "Occam's razor," he said. Steph stared at her hands, lost in thought.

Phil shifted in his seat. "Occam's what?"

"He's asking for the simplest explanation," Steph said absently, half lost in thought. "The one with the fewest assumptions. Which means we need to think about the evidence. Make a list."

With nothing better to do, I thought about it, listing all the weirdness in my head.

"One: the light show we watch every night," I said.

"That was the *Andrews*," Ben said, "Sinking over and over, like it was on a loop. Went on for at least four hours."

"I've seen other things here," Mom said. "Things happening over and over on a loop."

Ben continued, ticking off the evidence on his fingers. "Two, we've got this weird machine in the middle of the island."

I nodded. "Looks weirder than anything I've ever seen in my life."

Everyone was nodding except for Felix, who just looked scared.

"And three," Ben said. "Graham here. Unless he's operating on some sort of delusion—"

"Whatever that means, I ain't operating under it," Graham said.

"So if he's telling the truth, he's from 1943."

We all went silent, thinking. Phil held a can covered in Japanese writing in his hands, turning it over and over and staring at his wrecked charter as if it had answers. I looked up at the sky, the stars so bright with no light pollution to block them out. The moon was gone, so the Milky Way spread out over us, thick, like a highway leading somewhere I would never go. Or maybe we were there already.

"Number four," I said. "I've had this weird feeling." I stopped. It felt strange to say it out loud. The Sense had become so personal to me, like an infected wound I didn't want to show anyone. "Felt it first when our charter boat anchored above the *Andrews*. And I've felt it all over the island. Like all this has happened before. Or some version of it."

No one looked at me, but all of them were nodding, even Steph. I wasn't alone in this.

Ben put his hand over his face and rubbed his eyes. "Do I even have to say it?"

"Yep," Phil said, "you gotta."

Ben took his hand off his face. "Time machine."

Steph started laughing. And not a polite laugh. No one tried to stop her or talk over her. We were all too tired to argue. I braced for the complaints, her whining, her stubborn insistence none of this was happening. That we were all irrational.

"No, Ben, it's worse than that," Steph said, wiping her eyes with the heel of her hand. "It's a *broken* time machine. And there's no one to shut it off."

IN THE MORNING, Felix and I walked down to the water to play with fiddler crabs. He squatted in the wet sand, his toes digging deep, looking for bubbles. Then when the tiny crab emerged, waving its little claws wildly at him, its legs all in a panic, Felix would scoop him up with a large clamshell and play with him.

We did this for hours while Steph laid out her big plan to the others. Turns out people who build things are really good at destroying them. I was relieved to let someone else be in charge for a while.

Felix played his game over and over, like I used to play with the little Captain Neptune figurines you brought back from the trinket shop near the beach, lining them up just to knock them down. Again and again. Strange how kids don't seem to get tired of their favorite game, as if they're on an endless loop, stuck seeking out the pleasure of the things they love.

Steph wandered over with a bottle of water and handed it to Felix. While he drank his ration, she crossed her arms, her gaze set on the horizon. For the first time since I'd met her, she looked calm.

"What are you so happy about?" I asked.

She shrugged and tossed her hair over her shoulder. "It's a machine. That's something I understand."

"You understand a time machine. Really." I took the water from Felix and drank my ration slowly. "I'm surprised you believed us."

Steph shrugged. "Occam's razor."

"Really? You got 'broken time machine' out of Occam's razor?"

"I can't believe I'm saying this, but yes. Fewest assumptions and all that."

"If you say so."

She took the bottle from me before I finished screwing on the cap. "So are you ready for the big finish?"

I held a hand out and looked at Felix. "I haven't told him yet."

"Told me what?" Felix said, looking up from the fiddler crab he had cupped in his hands.

Steph's face softened, and she put her arm around Felix. "Don't worry, little dude. We got this." As Steph turned to leave, for once I was grateful she hadn't ended up at the bottom of the ocean. We needed a little unearned confidence right now, just to make it through.

Felix and I sat in the sand, the waves reaching out long white fingers to brush the tops of our feet, and talked about the time machine. I saw no point in lying to him about it, although I left out my suspicion that the monster and the machine were somehow one. Connected. Fueling each other. I know just about as much as you do about the theory of time travel, so I wasn't about to put my crazy ideas out there.

I pulled a clean page from the journal out of my sleeve, then drew two dots on either end. "You see these dots? One is our time, the one you and me and Mom and Dad come from. The other one is Graham's time, over seventy years ago." I folded the paper so the dots came together. "This is what the machine did at first—it folded space-time. At least that's what Ben says."

"Can't we just press a button and make everything go back?"

"The machine broke, and now we have this." I wadded the paper up into a ball. "Lots of little time crumples."

Felix wouldn't look at the paper anymore, instead squinting into the sun that reflected off the waves. I threw it into the sea and watched it flatten and expand in the water, until a wave swept it under.

I reached over and brushed Felix's hair out of his eyes. It was longer than I'd ever seen it, a tangle on his forehead and lying in a curve on the back of his neck. He didn't seem to notice what I was doing, his gaze set somewhere on the horizon.

"Is that why I have the dreams?" he asked.

A chill went down my arms. "What did you see?"

"Lots of things." He looked down at his feet, digging little trenches in the sand with his toes. "Some scary. Some good. Sometimes I'm not asleep when I have them."

"I have those too."

"They make my head hurt."

"Me too."

"If we stay here, will we ever grow old, or will I stay little forever?"

"You mean like Peter Pan?"

He smiled, the first real smile since I'd tried to explain what was going on. "Yeah, like Peter Pan."

"No, I don't think it works that way," I said, although I really had no idea.

"Maybe that's why there are people walking in the forest," he said.

"Why do you say that?"

He turned to me, his intelligent eyes shining in the sunlight. "If time is broken, then you can't really die." He looked back over the ocean. "I guess that's good. I don't want to die. I don't want you or Mom to die."

I put an arm around him. "It's good to not die."

His eyebrows came together. "But I don't want to wander around like that in the palm forest either, not talking." He looked up at me, fear in his eyes. "Are they zombies? Will they eat us?"

"No, that's just a silly story. Dead people don't eat."

"Why are we afraid of them?"

I didn't know the answer to that. I just was. My insides recoiled when I got close.

I squeezed his shoulder. "We're going to be fine. Nobody's going to die or wander around in the palm forest." I nodded toward where the others were still huddled, next to the blackened remains of the signal fire. Steph hadn't bothered to relight it, finally accepting the Coast Guard wasn't out there. "Mom and Phil and I are going to fix everything. They're working out the details now."

"What are you going to do?" Felix asked.

"Blow up the time machine. Easy peasy."

Felix turned to me and his eyes went wide. "No, I don't want you to do that."

"Graham says the barrels down in the *Andrews* are depth charges, and—"

He shook his head, putting his hands over his ears. "No, no, no."

I raised my voice. "And everything will go back to normal. The Coast Guard will find us."

"No, no, no, no."

"Felix, it's okay."

He looked up at me, his eyes filled with tears. "I saw it. Out there." He pointed to the white buoy, the one that marked the wreck. "It blows up and you don't come back." He started rocking and crying. "You don't come back."

The waves of the now-rising tide washed around us, soaking me to the waist, and I pulled him up to sit in the dry sand. Shushed him until he got quiet. "Felix, in your dreams, did I come back sometimes?"

His rocking slowed. After a few seconds, he nodded.

I didn't know to explain it to him, that all of this had happened before, a thousand times, in a thousand different ways. There were a thousand other Felixes and Sias and Moms and Bens out there, living this over and over. I didn't know which one we were. But if I had to be any of them, I would be the Sia to get us all home. Turn a thousand Felixes back into one. Pick up the pieces of myself that had been scattered through some weird multiverse and patch me back together until I felt whole again.

I rubbed Felix's back. "I want you to think about the good dream, the one that brought me back to you. Really hard."

He looked up at me, his eyes swollen with tears, and nodded.

"Good. Now think about it over and over. Stay in that spot for me. I think it will help us. Can you do that?"

He nodded, the panic faded, and he wiped his tears with the back of his hand, a little hope flaring in his eyes.

I'd wanted him to be calm, so you understand why I said what I said. You would know. You remember what you did when they took you away. When the deputy was about to usher you out of the courtroom in your cuffs, and Mom held so tight to the edge of the wooden bench her knuckles were white, and Felix grabbed hold of your leg and wouldn't let go. Crying and saying "Daddy" over and over again. And I saw the struggle in your eyes, saw the moment you decided which way to go. "Felix, I'll be home for dinner," you said. And Felix looked up at you and nodded, so trusting, believing you'd be home for dinner, and he let go, took Mom's hand, and waved bye-bye. How much I hated you at that moment. Because I was old enough to understand that when people panic, they lie to the ones who rely on them, who need them.

And there I was, sitting next to Felix on the beach, telling him Mom and I would be okay if he just thought about it real hard, like a kid clapping his hands to prove fairies are real.

I hugged him tight, my face buried in his bony little shoulder.

"It's alright, T," he said, patting me on the knee. "Everything's gonna be alright."

The next day, we moved bombs.

Down in the machine, in that honeycomb of water and blackness, Phil and I swam past the people who died when the place flooded. They lay in the hallways. Floated near the ceiling. And they *moved*. Reached for you when you nudged one out of the way, in slow motion, like a jellyfish's filament reacting dumbly to fish that strayed too close.

Even you, with your steel cage heart, would flip out diving in a place like that.

We moved the depth charges one by one. Graham said they won't explode unless they hit the two-hundred-foot mark. So at ninety-five feet, we're safe. I kept telling myself that. *We're safe.*

Me and Phil, rolling two-hundred-pound barrels full of explosives through a flooded pitch-black labyrinth. Sure, that's *safe.* And then there's the creature that attacked our charter. No way something that big can get in here, I whispered to myself. And then I remembered Marshall, and how he died.

As we made our way through the hallways, I spun theories about the creature and what it really was. Some part of me knew, although it felt like a childhood memory, all fuzzy around the edges and half-forgotten. I couldn't shake the feeling that the monster and the machine were a part of each other somehow.

Phil and I got four bombs out and into the hallways before we redlined and had to head up to the world of light and air. As we made a slow ascent, I was feeling pretty good about our plan to blow—as Graham put it—the whole tomato. Ben and Steph, who'd both taken some electrical engineering summer course at some fancy university, would show us how to rig them to explode. And boom goes the machine, and pop goes the bubble.

I kicked my way up, fantasizing. What it would be like to step on board a Coast Guard vessel. Take a shower. Wear something other than a bathing suit. Stand at the bow of our rescue ship and lean into the wind, Key Largo growing on the horizon. And then I'd drive my truck—God, I miss that beat-up truck—to Pine Key Prison and give you the biggest hug in the history of hugs. Yeah, I thought, everything's going our way now. Finally.

When I broke the surface of the sinkhole, the clearing was quiet. Everyone stood under the shade of the tall palms, huddled around a piece of paper. They all turned at once to look at Phil and me. If a stare could have weight, theirs weighed a ton. They'd decided something. I could already tell I wasn't going to like it.

While the others moved to the edge of the sinkhole to help, Graham stayed next to the pile of scuba tanks, watching the perimeter of the trees, waiting for shadows to change and something to emerge. Only the rustle of palm leaves high up in the canopy broke the stillness.

I swam to the edge. Mom grabbed my forearm to pull me onto the slick mud bank. While she helped unbuckle my gear, Phil slid out of his BC and dropped it, splashing a dark streak across Steph's ankles. She glared at him.

"No sign of the calamari," he said. Then he nodded to the equipment, which sat in a heap in the dappled sunlight. "Get that for me, will you, sweetheart?"

Steph hauled his stuff over the boulders. "Why do I have to clean your gear?"

"You want to dive in the hole?"

She glared over her shoulder again and began breaking down the BC. "Have Graham do it."

"He's watching the woods." He turned to Graham. "Seaman Fitch, you see any roadkill walking around?"

Graham gave him a sharp military head shake and continued his vigil.

"We got four bombs over the threshold," I said, stripping my wet suit down to my waist and shimmying out of it. "Five more to go. You guys decide where to put them yet?"

Mom studied her fingernails. "I've checked the tanks, and we have enough to move the rest. So that's good," she said, her voice unusually flat. And she hadn't answered my question.

Ben took my wet suit from me and hobbled over to a boulder to lay it out to dry.

"You're moving better," I said.

He looked past me, into the dark water. Distracted. The others fell quiet, and I again got the sense that they were about to drop something big—bomb number ten—right on my head.

Phil stripped his wet suit down to his pale waist and rubbed the sparse dark hair on his chest. "Well, ladies. Time to drain the weasel." He paused like a stand-up comic waiting for a pity laugh. "I get nothin' for that?" He shrugged and wandered into the palms.

"Please tell me we're not bringing Captain Horrible to Fiji," I said to Mom.

She gave me a brief smile, her eyes lighting up for a moment. Then they clouded with worry again.

"Okay, guys," I said. "Spill."

Everyone except Felix exchanged a loaded look. My little brother didn't take his eyes off me, his expression a little excited, a little scared. I had a sudden urge to pick him up and run to the beach, where we would find something for him to do. A kid thing. But whatever they were hiding from me, Felix had already heard.

Ben settled himself against a boulder and motioned me over. He nodded to Mom, who unfolded a crude diagram.

I walked through the mud in bare feet and sat on the rock to get a better look. Xs on the drawing marked nine spots all over the hallways.

"As best we can tell," Mom said, "we have to put the bombs in all these Xs or we'll just knock the machine off kilter. We'll never get home."

"Could make things worse," Ben said.

I tried to overlay the diagram onto my mental image of the dark labyrinth. The place wasn't familiar. "You know that for sure?"

"If Graham's memory of the hallways is solid, then yes," Mom said.

Graham turned his head and gave her a little nod. Then he went back to watching the palm forest.

"And Steph has a good eye for this," Ben said. "How to make a structure collapse. Where the supports are." He exchanged a brief glance with his ex. She raised an eyebrow and turned away, focusing on Phil's gear.

"Place the bombs, wire them up, press the trigger," I said. "Boom. It doesn't seem that difficult. What am I missing?"

Ben met my eye, and for that less-than-a-second moment, I saw all of it—the whole scene they'd had while I was down below, how much he didn't want to have this conversation. He pointed to the X on the left side of the page again and dragged his fingertip down the sketch of a hallway. "Depth charge nine needs to go here, which is ten feet past a locked door. It's reinforced steel, so we can't knock our way through it."

"Can you pick the lock?" I asked.

"No. But there's a small opening above the door. Ventilation. We can get the flimsy grate with nothing more than a screwdriver."

"How big is it?" I asked.

"About one and half feet wide."

"How on earth is someone going to get through that?"

Ben pressed his lips together, holding his breath. Then he looked at Felix.

I didn't understand. My brain wouldn't put it together. Maybe I didn't want to understand. And I really don't want to tell you now.

My lungs picked that moment to quit working. No, not

enough air on the planet to fill me. I leaned against the boulder, put my hands on my knees.

Ben spoke, his voice low and full of regret. "I know you don't want to hear this—"

"No, I don't," I said, cutting him off. Then I looked up at Mom.

Mom didn't answer. Ben, who looked like he was about to be sick, shoved his hands into the pockets of his board shorts, his jaw tense.

"What kind of mother sends her kid into a place like that?"

Mom straightened up, as if to remind me who was taller. "What kind of mother?"

"Sia, calm down," Ben said.

I held my palm out to Ben to shut him up, my eyes on Mom. "Yeah, you heard me."

My words lit that short fuse in her. You know it well.

"What kind of mother? One who wants both of her kids to get out of here alive! You think this is easy for me? We can't stay here anymore, Tasia." She flung an arm toward the forest. "It's getting worse. I've seen it." She tapped her temple with one finger, her eyes wild with a memory. Something that hadn't happened yet. "We're gonna die if we don't fix this. All of us."

"I'll squeeze through," I said.

"You won't fit."

One more look at Felix and I was scrambling for ideas, no matter how insane. "We'll fix the charter. Patch the hole with . . . I don't know, Steph will come up with something. Make a sail. Once we get past the edge of the bubble we're in, the Coast Guard can find us."

Steph's face had gone a shade paler, if that was possible. "We'll never make it. That thing will drag us under. Kill us all."

I put my face in my hands. "This can't be the only way."

"It's all we've got," Ben said.

A tug on the sleeve of my rash guard made me turn. Felix. His head barely came up to my elbow. His face small, full of determination, looking up at me. "I'm a good swimmer. I'll use the orange ropes to get me in and out. Mom showed me a pony bottle that's nice and small. I can switch to it and slip right through the hole and open the door. Easy peasy. Mom and Phil will come with me. Mom let me use the scuba gear in the pool last month and—"

"You *what?*" I turned back to Mom.

She threw up her hands and shook her head, as if she'd gotten exactly what she'd expected from me. "He was four feet underwater," she said, raising her voice. "He was *fine.*"

"He has no business breathing compressed air. He's *seven.*"

"No, I'm not," Felix said. "I'm eight. Today's my birthday. You forgot."

Eight. His birthday. Was it?

Had we been on the island a month? Six months? A thousand years? When I spoke again, my head was spinning. "Eight, seven. You're just a little kid."

"Stop calling me that!"

"Come with me," Ben said, and his tone had none of his earlier patience. He walked into the palms, certain I would follow. I stood stock still a moment, stunned and wondering what the world had come to, that my mother wanted to send my kid brother into a bottomless sinkhole filled with dead bodies—dead*ish*—to navigate a labyrinth only the best divers in the world would chance. And then there was the calamari.

Ben stopped mid-limp between two massive palms. "C'mon. Your mom and your brother need to cool down."

Mom gave me an angry glare. Felix had his back to me. And Ben suddenly thought he was in charge.

I threw up my hands. "Fine. Whatever."

Once inside the perimeter of the palm forest, I stopped. The cool air inside felt good against my hot face, the scent of the place rose up like a root cellar. But the shadows, they slid over the dry bed of fronds and slithered up my legs. I was torn between wanting to run out into the sunlit clearing and needing to get away from Mom and her suicidal plan. My little brother down in the hole. In the silo. Tying knots in the dark. I just couldn't.

Ben limped over to a fallen tree, sat on the trunk, and stretched out his bad leg. I leaned against the smooth bark of a palm across from him.

"I'm not letting Felix go down there," I said.

"Why?"

"One, it's full of dead people."

"So's the island."

"Two, he could die."

"Naw, that's not what you're afraid of."

"Oh really?"

Ben angled his head to the spot on the trunk next to him, and gave me his best "C'mon now, don't be like that" look. I sat, still steaming.

"Your mom will be with him the whole time," he said. "He's just hitching a ride until they get to the grate. Then he lets go of her, swims through the hole, unlocks the door. Hitches a ride back up."

"He'll panic. When you're diving, panic gets people killed."

"He cries when things get bad, but he doesn't rabbit."

The thought of Felix crying while trying to breathe into a

regulator hit me like a five-foot breaker. "Felix should be playing on a jungle gym. Learning math. Not risking his life."

"Just being a kid, right?" Ben asked, an undercurrent I didn't like in his tone. My anger kicked up a notch.

"Every kid should have the chance to grow up without . . ." I trailed off.

"Without what?"

I didn't like the words that had popped into my head. "What did you mean when you said, 'That's not what you're afraid of'?"

Ben leaned on his knees and stared at his hands, which were loosely clasped in front of him. "You've got a screwed-up idea of how to make someone happy."

"You didn't answer my question."

Ben side-eyed me. "Neither did you."

"Okay, fine. I don't want him to go through what I have."

"Why?"

"What do you mean, *why*?" I asked.

"Because he'll be a better person if he never has pain? Is that what you think?"

"Yes." As soon as the word was out of my mouth, it sounded ridiculous.

"You turned out okay."

"No, I didn't."

"Yes, you did. You're kinda wonderful."

I was vaguely aware that Ben had taken my hand. My fingers were numb, the rubber band pop of the threshold down below still reverberating through my blood, but the warmth of his palm cut through. Wonderful. He said I was wonderful.

Reality flooded back. Felix. The Silo. I pulled my hand out of Ben's grasp and stood.

In the stillness of the forest, the memory came flooding back, that quiet mausoleum I visited with you forever ago, when you dragged me along to pay your respects to that dive buddy, the one who drowned cave diving in Montego Bay. The Widow Maker had taken another soul from the earth. And that place was nothing compared to where Felix was going.

"Sia, if you need to get something out, just say it. It's just you and me here."

I had my back to Ben, so he was little more than a deep voice. I kept my eyes on the hashed trunk, toed the crisp palm fronds beneath my feet. I remember standing next to you in that mausoleum, sure I'd never be reckless enough to dive the Widow Maker. Three years later, I was checking flights to Montego Bay, making a list of stuff I needed to make it through.

Then the confession started pouring from my mouth before I could rethink it—my midnight dive in the Silo. Like a breath I couldn't hold anymore.

Ben didn't seem impressed.

"A lot of people like a rush," Ben said. "Roller coasters. Mountain climbing. It's not that weird."

"Not that weird?"

"You're just being hard on yourself."

"One time, I was using a box cutter on an Amazon package and sliced my arm open. Had to get five stitches and couldn't dive for a week."

"Ouch."

"So, yeah, on day three, I get itchy. Climb up to the roof of our apartment building. Four stories up. Nothing but concrete below. And I stand on the edge. Hang my toes over. And not to kill myself or anything. Just to feel scared. To feel the bottom of my stomach drop."

The palm leaves in the canopy above rustled in the ocean breeze, filling the space between us. Ben's silence was worse than an insult, or a slap. I guess what he was thinking was so awful he couldn't say it.

I'd never told anyone that before. Not Mom. Not you.

So I stared into the shadows between the trunks and imagined the ocean at night, its whitecaps lit up with moonlight. Me, finning my way through the dark reef, a dive light in my hand. You, right beside me. That's what I wanted to be doing, back in Key Largo, while Felix stayed at home and watched cartoons.

Ben's voice came out of the dark, bringing me back. "If you're trying to scare me off, it's not working."

A crunch of dried fronds sounded behind me. Ben limped to the tree trunk and leaned against it, crossing his arms. "I can't talk to you with your back to me."

"You think you know what I'm afraid of?" I said. "You don't have a clue."

He took a deep breath and blew it out. "Felix is going to be okay."

"You can't guarantee that. And when he comes up"—I had to say *when*, not *if*, or I would lose it right then and there—"he *still* won't be okay."

"You're wrong."

"How do you know that?" I asked.

"Because he's got you and your mom. Because he's going to

go see his dad when he gets home. Because he has all of us to help him through. Just like you have all of us."

He took my hand again, and this time I let him.

"Except maybe Steph," I said.

Ben let out a little laugh. "True."

I leaned my forehead against his shoulder. The smell of his clean sweat overpowered the root cellar scent of the forest. I found it comforting. His hand came up to stroke the back of my hair. We stood there listening to the rustle of the palm leaves high in the canopy, the cry of the fairy terns as they flew over the island. And I knew he was right. I wasn't afraid of Felix dying. I mean, yeah, I was, but that's not why I was freaked.

I was afraid of Felix becoming me.

"You know," Ben said, his baritone a low rumble in my ear, "halfway through this conversation, I'd decided to kiss you—finally—and instead you ruined the moment by talking about your weird risk addiction."

My eyes popped open. "Kiss me?"

"Yeah, it's this thing people do when they like each other."

I pulled away and met his gaze. "Is this your way of getting me on board with . . ."

The warmth in his eyes dimmed. "You really think I'd do that?"

"No. I'm sorry. I don't know why I said that."

"I do."

"No, you don't."

"Not afraid of sharks, or a long drop from the roof of an apartment building. But this"—he touched my face—"scares you half to death."

I blushed and looked away, and when I met his eyes again, a small smile touched the edge of his mouth.

"Just think of me as a really tall cliff," he said.

I laughed and put my forehead against his chest. Closed my eyes.

"You're standing on the rocks," he said, the smile still in his voice. "The sunset is beautiful, and you're teetering *right* on the edge."

I pulled away from him to meet his eyes. "Just close my eyes and jump? Is that the idea?"

"Yeah, that's exactly what—"

Then I kissed him.

No details. My gift to you. But I'll tell you this much. It was the kind of kiss you get at the end of a pier. The ship's waiting. One of you is leaving. The engines roar to life, and you have so little time. A goodbye kiss, filled with "sorry" and "I wish" and "I wouldn't leave you if I had a choice." I imagine it's the kind of kiss you get when you're going off to war.

And for once, I loved the island. Adored it. Worshiped it. Most people get moments like these measured out in the lives of mayflies. A brief flutter and gone. But here in this broken place, that kiss happened a thousand times, in a thousand variations. And it keeps happening, in my head, splintering into perfect moments that fall through my fingers like broken glass.

Ben and me, holding on to each other like there's no tomorrow.

So I didn't screw it up, Dad, not this time. I didn't need high school after all to teach me what to be.

THE NIGHT BEFORE we were supposed to blow the machine, we had a feast on the beach. Steph built a roaring fire high and hot. Ben spent at least an hour retelling *Survivor* episodes to Felix and sending me an occasional warm look that made me blush all the way to my toes.

Mom and I stacked more driftwood, getting it ready for the signal fire we would light when the Bubble popped and the Coast Guard could see us. Despite my awesome mood, the unspoken words between Mom and me weighed as much as a barrel of explosives. Neither of us were ready to talk about our fight, so we stacked driftwood and told Felix stories about you and how you would be getting out of the pen soon. Six months wasn't too long to wait to have you home again.

We ran out of small talk, and Felix moved to sit beside me at the edge of the fire glow, watching the dark ocean crash on the beach. I put my arm around him and leaned back against a stack of wet suits I had been using as a pillow, my eyes half closed, the smell of neoprene lulling me into a partial sleep. Nothing wipes me out like a four-tank day.

Felix's voice was sudden, a harsh stage whisper. "There it is."

I snapped my eyes open, scanning our camp for this new threat. But he was pointing into the dark, toward the ocean. At first all I could see were the stars, the Milky Way stretching like a highway above our heads until it plunged into the black sea. Then I saw the glow that lit up the water about two hundred yards offshore, near the buoy that marked the USS *Andrews*. Green, phosphorescent.

"Do you think it knows we're here?" Felix asked, his eyes wide.

"Probably," Phil said from the other side of the fire. "I bet it can smell us on the wind, especially Ben."

Ben's voice came out of the dark. "Shut up, man." A moment later he was limping over to settle himself next to me. The three of us sat side by side and watched the creature rise to the surface, a patch of light in the distance that brightened as it did. Then it sank, its phosphorescence growing duller until it disappeared.

"You still think that thing came up from the Mariana Trench?" I asked Ben.

He shook his head. The creature rose again, then sank, its light fading, moving slowly toward the beach. I was horrified, but I couldn't look away.

"I have these dreams," Ben said, a brittle, frustrated edge to his voice. "More like memories. It's like there's a part of me that *knows* what it is, but I can't totally remember." He rubbed his face. "It's a really weird feeling. I want to remember, but I can't."

Felix's voice followed, small and curious. "I think it's an immortal jellyfish."

"There is no such thing," I said.

"Yes, there is. I learned about it in school. It's this sea creature that can't die unless something eats it. It grows up and gets bigger and bigger, and then it becomes a baby again. Over and over. It's *immortal*."

"Jellyfish don't have eyes," I said. "And they can't move like that thing does."

Felix went quiet while he thought about that. The creature rose again, this time farther away. A shiver hit me, along with a memory from that day on the charter. Teague holding on to me and the blood and the smell of fire and gasoline and—

Felix reached for my hand and threaded his fingers through mine. The images faded.

"T?" Felix's voice was small in the dark. Nervous. "When we blow everything up, the Coast Guard can find us, right?"

"That's what we think."

"But who's going to kill the monster? Won't it just follow us?"

Ben and I exchanged a glance. I didn't answer. The images of our charter taken apart by that thing, the heat of the fire and the smell of blood, rose again. But this time Teague falling over the side shifted and melted, until he became an image of Mom, and then Ben, and then men and women in uniform, dragged into the ocean.

The vision had come to me a dozen times while I slept, and I'd hoped it was nothing but a nightmare. Felix and me, standing on a deck of an unfamiliar ship, holding each other as that thing took everything apart, as it sent us all to the bottom of the sea. But like I told you before, dreams and fantasies and memories are all the same here. I have no idea what's real anymore.

When Ben's voice came out of the dark, it was heavy with dread he couldn't entirely cover. "One thing at a time, Felix. One thing at a time."

At the end of the night, after Felix had gone off to find Mom, I fell asleep next to Ben, his arm around my waist. Neither of us cared about the poison look Steph sent our way, or the curious glance from my mother, or the obnoxious smirk from Phil. Could have been our last night—I didn't know—and I wanted him with me.

Then in the early hours of the morning, the Sense rose up, like a creature coming from the deep, dark places of the ocean. Teeth and spines and bloodlust in its dumb shark eyes. Me on the beach, watching the *Andrews* explode. Felix standing on the ocean, waving to me desperately and crying. The island splitting open and the monster rising from within, swallowing us like a Leviathan. I woke in a cold sweat, and the splinters of my dreams set so deep in my head I couldn't shake them.

Ben's arm lay heavy around my waist. His breath warmed my neck. The dark world swelled with wave crash and the scent of seaweed. A silhouette stood down by the water. Mom, staring out to sea. Just beyond the breakers, a hundred yards offshore, a faint green glow lit up a patch of dark water.

I slipped out of Ben's arms and made my way down the beach to stand by her side. She acknowledged me with a brief nod. I gave her a small smile she couldn't see. My insides as tight as a drum, I stood next to Mom and watched the phosphorescence until it faded into darkness again, and my body relaxed. I hoped to God I would have the chance to blow that thing into hell where it belonged.

"I'm going down with Felix. Not you," Mom said.

"I know the hallways. I'll get in and out faster."

"Phil can go with me. Or Graham."

"It's okay. Let me do this."

"No!" she said, her tone so sharp I blinked in surprise. "No," she said again, this time softer, as if she'd regretted losing control. "Because I'm the kind of mother who wants at least one of her kids to be safe."

I stared out into the ocean, the way it rushed the land, disintegrating into white froth before pulling its arms back into itself, gathering power. My mother stood with shoulders set. But then her shoulders slumped, and she put her hands over her mouth as if trying to hold back a cry.

"I'm sorry," she said, and her voice stuttered over a breath.

I crossed my arms and waited. She had been trying to tell me something for days, but she couldn't quite spit it out. "What happened on the other side of the island? Before you found us."

She shook her head. "That doesn't matter anymore. There was nothing I could do to stop it anyway."

"Whatever it is," I said, "just tell me."

"I put too much on you. You were fifteen. You needed to be a kid."

My arms dropped to my side. Something heavy lodged in my lungs. She didn't want to talk about the last few months. Or Felix going down into the sinkhole. Three years of silence on my missing childhood, and she chose *now* to apologize.

"You needed me to grow up," I said, the words feeling heavy in my mouth, like they weren't mine. "And at least I was doing something I love, rather than working in a tennis shoe factory or something."

For some reason this made her turn away. And then Mom's breath hitched.

"I shouldn't have done what I did," she said, still not looking at me. "But I was so lonely when your dad went away."

I stiffened, because we weren't talking about me growing up too fast anymore. We weren't talking about the three-tank days, seven days a week. We weren't talking about the late nights I spent studying, in a classroom of one, just me and my computer, when all the kids my age were going to football games and homecoming dances.

The diving trip to Texas, that's what we were talking about, back when you were fresh in the pen and we had all those years of waiting ahead of us.

"I shouldn't have," she said again. "I was . . . My head was in a weird place then. Can you understand that?"

I didn't answer at first, waiting for the cool breeze to calm me down, soothe my heated face. No such luck. My mind snapped three years back in time, that day we arrived at Clear Springs. We stepped out of the car, and her ex-boyfriend held her like you used to. Like he knew what she needed, had always known, and he had been waiting for her to come back to him. Waiting for her to come back to her senses and realize you had been nothing more than a terrible mistake.

So like I said, Dad, I promised you the truth. Her confession. And mine. Because I *knew*, before she spilled her guts on the beach, confessed like a woman does when she knows she's about to die or lose somebody. I knew everything, even before I picked up a pencil to write this letter to you. I looked you in the face a hundred times during our weekly visit, with this weight clinging to my bones like coral, and I said nothing. I'm so sorry.

Mom and her ex-boyfriend inside his tent, after she thought Felix and I had fallen asleep in ours. Talking and laughing. Until they went quiet.

I had nowhere to go, so I got my gear on, which felt so light compared to what was inside me, and I dove the Silo. A midnight dive into oblivion. My way of sticking a knife in memory. And my fear pulled apart the past and the future so that nothing would be left but the now.

"Can you forgive me?" she asked, her voice cracking on the last word.

I tried to wrap my mind around her question. Wondered what your answer would be. Wondered if you would forgive me. You know, for trying to forget everything. Everyone. Because forgetting is a kind of leaving, isn't it? And I want you to know I won't forget you, I swear. I will never leave you behind.

"Do you forgive me?" she asked.

"I'm not the one you need to ask."

"Please, Tasia."

I almost said no. Then I turned and looked up the beach, an instinct pulling my gaze away from my mother and the sea. The fire that had gone out long ago had been lit again. A girl with long black hair sat next to Felix, just inside the warm glow. Our eyes met, and a flash of understanding passed between us. Between me and me, I guess.

I turned back to Mom. "I forgave you a long time ago." I reached out my hand and found hers in the dark. "And I'm going with Felix. You can't stop me."

A murmur under her breath. "My brave girl." I could tell she meant it. She was proud of me. But I felt that hot flush of shame anyway.

You know why. Going back into the sinkhole was the least selfless thing. I needed to get away from the topside world, the heavy pull of gravity and the smell of the forest and the noise all of us made. Down in the dark, floating weightless in space, I can finally breathe.

She squeezed my hand. "I won't fight it. I guess me telling you what to do doesn't make sense anymore."

Dad, people do strange things when they're in pain, and Mom's affair doesn't mean what you think it does. It just means she's not perfect, which you already knew. But we all can't be together without you two talking about it, and she'll never bring it up. So consider this an intervention. Mom and I are going to make it home, and we're bringing Felix with us, and we're all going to be happy.

I don't care what the Sense says about it.

While Phil and Mom rigged the safety stop, I cut off a foot of neoprene from the arms and legs of a spare wet suit and helped Felix slip inside. When I strapped him into the smallest BC we owned and secured the last release, a drop of water fell onto my fingers. I looked up to find the clouds thick and gray, swollen. Ready to pop. After three weeks of nothing but bone sky blue, Mother Nature would give us rain. A good omen, you would say.

Felix's gaze went skyward, and when he took in the sky, his face broke into a smile. We were both thinking the same thing: rig the tarp to capture fresh water. There was no guarantee our plan would work, and something clean to drink would be a good consolation prize.

By the time Phil and Mom had added a few bungees to Felix's gear, the wind had picked up. A crack of thunder rolled across the island. Mom's face darkened, taking in the heavy clouds, the lightning in the distance. Another flash and crack had Felix burrowing into her side.

"That's just a storm, Felix," Mom said. But she picked up speed anyway, preparing for our big drop to the center of the earth.

Phil tightened Felix's gear while Steph distracted him with little kid jokes. Ben stood nearby, his expression pained.

I kneeled in front of Felix and attached the extra reg to the front of his BC.

"If your reg stops working, you can grab this." I put his hand on the backup.

"I know. Mom taught me in the pool."

I bit my lip. But it wasn't the time. "I'm sorry I forgot your birthday."

Felix tested the regulator, looking very grown-up. After his Darth Vader breath, he pulled it aside. "It's okay. You were busy."

"I was."

"When we get back home, you have to buy me extra presents."

"Just one extra present."

"A Supersoaker Soakzooka."

"Okay."

"And a morfboard, the one you can make into a scooter *and* a skateboard."

I cinched his vest tighter as he went on about the morfboard. Mom stood a few feet away, suited up and ready. She looked to Phil and he nodded. Felix played with the zipper pocket on the BC. The playful movement—something a little kid would do— made a bubble of panic rise in my chest. I grabbed him by the shoulders so he would look at me.

"You don't have to do this."

"Yes, I do," he said.

"I know what you're thinking. 'This is what Dad would do. He would save everybody.' And you think you have to be like that."

He took another breath from his regulator, pulled it away to speak again. "That wasn't what I was thinking."

"Then why?"

"I was thinking, 'This is what T would do. She would save everybody.'"

I hugged him then, so he wouldn't see me tear up.

When I pulled away, and Mom and Phil had slipped into the sinkhole. I helped Felix into the water, and his BC floated up around his ears. Steph kneeled by the edge and wrapped her arms around his neck, a tear making its way down her cheek.

Before I could look for Ben, he was kneeling next to me. His hands on either side of my face. "Don't take any extra risks down there, okay? Not this time. Just focus on your goal, what you're doing."

I nodded, and he kissed me. When he pulled away, I caught a glimmer of longing in his eyes. Warmth. Something more maybe. I almost said, "I love you." Before I could, he'd turned and walked away, past Steph, who didn't look up from her hands, clasped so hard in front of her the knuckles were white; past Graham, who gave me a brief nod before returning his attention to the perimeter.

I swam to Felix. Mom held his BC in a death grip. Phil floated a few feet away, his expression unreadable through his mask. I met Felix's eyes, and he held up a fist for me to bump. My throat constricted, and I forced a confident smile. Our knuckles met.

One more breath, and we descended.

Plummeting through the dark.

The sinkhole yawned beneath, swallowing us. The Vanessa Peters song played in my head.

I tell myself that . . . everything . . . will be okay from now on . . . if I just close my eyes . . . and believe it . . .

Four lights. Three steady, the fourth—Felix's—dangling from his wrist, his light skittering over the rough rock walls, the cored-out earth.

In my head there was a fifth light. Yours. But that light shone like a hot coal in my throat, lighting me up from inside. Then the last bit of the chorus came to me, the part I'd forgotten until now.

The unravelling of love . . . is sometimes hard . . .

but there's only so long . . . you can grieve it . . .

A glint of silver below caught in my beam. A railing. The lab.

Mom slowed, her hair floating around her face, like Yiayia's hair streaming out behind her when we dove for sponges. Which wasn't real. Or it was. I was no longer sure.

A rush of bubbles obscured Mom's mask as she gripped the edge of the catwalk and came to a stop. She gave me the okay. Phil's sign joined hers, his breathing slow and measured.

The four of us hovered there for a few breaths, taking stock. No green glow beneath us, just the honeycomb of blackness waiting beyond the railings, tunneling into the earth. Felix hung onto Mom like a barnacle, his body very still. A rush of bubbles came from his regulator, and then another. His breathing was fast, which meant he was scared. But I told myself Ben was right. We'd be in and out of there fast, before anything could go wrong.

I finned over to the entrance marked with the orange line, unspooling the wire Mom and Phil would connect to the last depth charge. We swam past the bomb that sat a few feet from the drop-off—one of Ben and Steph's Xs. Mom stayed a few feet behind me, her arm wrapped around Felix's thin waist. The silt had settled at the entrance to the lab, and my firefly dive light punched a clean hole through the dark, all the way to the end of the hallway.

Making my way into the blackness, I obsessively glanced over my shoulder. Three lights floating in the dark, two close together and one behind. Floating in space, our lights had become stars.

The orange line would take us right, then left, past a hallway, and left again. Deep in the heart of the labyrinth. Your voice stayed with me the whole way. Breathe in. Breathe out. *Keep your breath steady, Sia. Shallow and easy. Piece of seaweed cake.*

We passed a body. Mom turned Felix's face toward her chest, his light jittering. I made the last turn, skirting a dead guy in a white lab coat, and checked on my brother again. His grip on her BC had turned his knuckles white. I couldn't even imagine how frightened he was.

My dive light caught the silver of a depth charge ahead, sitting in the hallway like a promise, so much violence and destruction held inside that metal skin. And this whole place, flooded with seawater and secrets and some government's arrogant idea of progress. I reached the barrel and hung on to the metal handle that ringed the top, watching my bubbles rise and catch on the ceiling. Waited for Phil to help me roll the last bomb down the hall to the locked door. Thought about all those scientists screwing with Mother Nature, thinking there wouldn't be any consequences.

Phil's light joined mine. He made a hand signal in front of his dive light, silt particles moving through the beam. *Easy.*

Yeah, Phil, go easy with the two-hundred-pound depth charge. Got it.

I wedged myself against the corner, and we eased the barrel over to roll it. And then my hand slipped. Before I could catch it, *clang!* rang out through the hall.

My heart jumped, and my breathing stuttered. Phil did something I'd never heard him do—talked into his regulator. I think he was swearing. So was I. And I was so happy the depth charge hadn't exploded that I didn't think about the burst of sound traveling through the lab.

We slowly rolled the barrel down the hall. Mom and Felix followed behind us with the wire and the trigger. I directed my beam ahead, and as we swam, a door gradually materialized out of the dark. Phil stopped in front of it, his light sliding over its thick metal surface. Above the door was a small rectangle space. Just big enough for a child to crawl through.

I hooked an arm around Felix, my limbs heavy and slow, breathing too fast. His hair floated around his mask, and the regulator—way too big for him—made his mouth look huge, comic.

Phil swam up to the grate and produced a small screwdriver from a pocket at his waist. Mom unbuckled Felix from his BC and he slipped out, his mouth still connected to the regulator. Even in the wet suit, he was shivering. The grate fell with a dull clank to the floor.

Mom reached into her mesh bag and pulled out the pony bottle and its rig. She didn't hesitate. The time for doublethink was over.

Mom swam up to the small opening and slipped the pony bottle through. A muffled thud followed. Felix would swim into the hole, find the bottle with his dive light, and breathe for a precious few minutes. And open the door. If his hands were strong enough. If it wasn't locked with a key. I never hated a door so much in my life.

I shined my light in front of my hand and made the okay sign. A question. *Are you okay?*

Part of me wanted a headshake. I would grab him, get out of the lab. Go up. Stay on this broken island forever, stuck on an endless loop. Maybe the Bubble would break on its own.

Felix's small hand entered the beam of my dive light. Thumb

and forefinger together. An okay sign. His hand wasn't even shaking. I wished, at that moment, for your steel cage heart. I checked my gauge to give myself something to think about.

Mom pulled the regulator out of his mouth. He turned and swam up to the grate. A strong swimmer, the pale bottoms of his feet catching the light. He gripped the edge of the opening. I held my breath, something you told me never to do at depth. A bad habit that gets divers killed. And watched Felix disappear.

I counted to ten. Then twenty. Thirty.

Phil hovered an arm's length from the handle, his hands clasped, radiating calm. I directed my beam down the hall, a clear shot to the back wall.

God, forty seconds. I wanted to punch through that door. You would have. Mom floated beside me, her light trained on the handle. I pointed my light at the small opening Felix had slipped through. His bubbles still clung to the top edge.

Fifty seconds. Where was he?

Phil hovered by the door, his knees bent and his fins crossed. Mom glanced at her watch every two seconds.

I started to swim up to the crawlspace above the door, a bubble of panic hitting me hard in the chest. I would squeeze through. Even you, with your broad shoulders, would find a way to get through. Scrape a layer of skin off if you had to.

Then, in Phil's beam, the handle turned with a glint. And when the door swung open, the world wasn't dark anymore.

Green light. Oozing out of the rectangle Felix had opened.

FELIX'S DARK FORM, a silhouette. A child coming home after a long day, surrounded by bubbles and phosphorescence.

Phil pushed away from the wall, his fins stirring up silt. Mom dropped the spool of wire.

Dad, you don't know how the panic took hold of me, in a way it never has before. *Ever.* I grabbed Felix and pulled him to me. Stuck my regulator into his mouth. Turned to swim. Phil rushed past me in a blur of bubbles. A sharp elbow to my face knocked my mask sideways. It instantly filled with water.

Another hand on my arm stopped me. Mom, her iron grip. Two squeezes on my bicep.

Stay.

I struggled to free myself. My heart beat against the rocks filling my lungs, like wave crash in a storm. Stay. Go. Listen. Ignore. What would Dad do?

I stopped struggling and turned, holding tight to Felix. Through my flooded mask, the world had become a green haze. My hands shook, but I cleared the water out, took a few breaths from the regulator, and forced myself to look.

No beast slid through the doorway. But the green glow was *everywhere.* The phosphorescence came from the room itself, which was the size of a small house. Green light oozed from the gears of a machine that honeycombed the walls, like steampunk coral.

The word came to me again: *connected*. The thing out there circling the *Andrews*, and this room, this machine. They were both part of the same thing. But how?

Mom rolled the depth charge inside the room to set it on Ben's imaginary X. I followed, amazed at her steel nerves. Felix held on to me, his breathing as fast as a sprinter's.

I stopped swimming and put a pulse of air into my BC. Floated above the lab floor and hung on to my brother. Dim light bled out all around us in the water, seeped into the edges of my wet suit, stained my exposed skin green. On the edge of my vision, Mom worked to unscrew the panel on the depth charge.

Felix's body wasn't trembling. Neither was mine. I felt small, like a flower petal floating on the surface of the big blue, about to drop. So small that my fear disappeared.

A current, through the walls. Pushing against my face. The walls, moving, as if made of baleen.

The machine. We had floated into its heart. I could feel a whisper-thin tether reaching out—no, thousands of them, spreading into the world to grab on to what they could. The creature. The machine. Which one was the alpha? Which one the omega? I'll never know.

The walls shimmered. Expanded. And then the world turned into a kaleidoscope.

A diver appeared, floating on the other side of my mother as she wired the bomb. Two more, wearing my wet suit, with my long black hair, swimming toward me. Three others hovering over three other metal barrels. Six barrels. Then twelve. Three divers holding a child. More lying on the floor, dying.

Felix took two breaths, handed my reg back, clung to me again. The walls bowed as a current hit my face. A pull took its place, a gentle undertow. The walls had gills. The walls were breathing. In the soft glow of the room, Felix met my eyes, and I held on to him tighter.

The divers around me replicated, until hundreds of Sias and Felixes and a couple of Phils and several Grahams floated in the lungs of this strange machine. I turned in a circle. All around me, a kaleidoscope of possible realities. Zoe who'd never left the dock, she was there, wiring up the depth charge. That captain Mom hires sometimes to fill in, the one who didn't come with us on this trip, he was there too, helping her.

And the truth hit me. The bubble we'd been caught in was expanding, all the way into Key Largo, picking up people on shore and tossing them into my life again. So I looked for you. Of course I looked for you.

There I was, clinging to my brother and searching faces in a crowd, like a lost kid at the train station. As Mom worked and Felix and I shared breath, I sorted through the kaleidoscope images, eliminating them one by one until . . .

You weren't there.

Felix tapped me on the shoulder. I'd forgotten to give the regulator back, too busy wondering if my wet suit would keep my insides from spilling out. I gave it to him and focused on Mom, watching her wiring up the bomb to explode so we could make it back home.

Home. That word has always been tangled up in you. But floating there inside the heart of the machine, I realized something awful. No version of you exists that pulled his punches that night. No version of you walked away from the bar fight and came home to us.

No version of you exists that did the right thing.

It's the little moments that break us. That's what you said.

How could you? How could you leave us?

I decided not to write another word to you. No, I wouldn't pick up a pencil to scratch my sad "Daddy, please understand me" crap anymore.

You see how well that worked out for me.

Felix and I floated in that nexus, clinging to one another until my vision blurred, became so full of phosphorescence I couldn't think about anything else.

I almost didn't feel the tug on my arm. Lost in the soft green glow. A memory trying to rise. Of you. Me. A beach. A strange phosphorescent glow covering the sand.

Another tug. Harder this time.

Mom, pointing back down the hall. A wire trailed from the depth charge, out the door. Time to leave.

We slipped into the empty hall. While we pushed Felix back into his rig and bungeed him into place, I noticed Phil's mesh bag lying on the floor. He hadn't come back. He'd saved himself, left us behind.

Mom's beam moved between us. Her hand in the light. An okay sign. I returned it. Felix's fingers snuck into the circle to join ours.

Mom and Felix and me, in the sunken world of silt and rock and breath, finning our way through the labyrinth. We would find our way out. Together. Even without you, we're still a family.

Mom turned, her dive light running along the walls, and swam. I followed, Felix clutching to my side. We moved fast, stirring up the silt behind us like new divers. If everything worked out, we'd never come down here again. My light danced on the back wall.

Right turn. Down the hallway, past signs I couldn't read. Past doorways I didn't need to open anymore. Past the stores of food that would soon be blown up with all the rest. Past the flickering image of the metal walls shimmering like mercury, and a girl swimming into the sponge beds.

Left turn. Mom beside me, her beam on the wire and the orange line leading us out.

Right turn. The pale rectangle at the end of the hallway glowed with a gray light. The entrance to the sinkhole lay ahead. Beyond that, our escape and the world above. To Ben. And eventually, back home to Key Largo.

Felix took another breath from my regulator. Mom swam ahead, her slim form moving as easily as a dolphin.

The three of us shot out of the sinkhole onto the catwalk. I grabbed the railing, ready to head up.

A clamp on my arm forced me to still. Mom squeezed once and let go.

Just below the catwalk, in the dark maw of the sinkhole, a green glow rose.

Felix's grip tightened. I sank to the mesh of the catwalk. Mom covered her light with her hand. I did the same.

The mesh bit through my neoprene. Darkness. Breath. The soft green glow rising just beyond the railing.

Still. Be still.

My tank became just another part of the metal surrounding me. The bubbles just artifacts of nothing. We were small. Not worthy of notice. Your words came back to me. *Swim, little fish.* I pushed them out of my head.

But maybe you were right, and we should have made a break for it.

I stayed put. So did Mom. Felix hung from me, his fingers digging into my arm, his bubbles coming faster.

The phosphorescence rose and brightened. My eyes widened. Huge. Its body filled the sinkhole. And as I peered into the light, through the membrane I saw movement inside.

A skittering light bled from my hand, and I realized my fingers were shaking. I clamped a fist over the dive light.

A thrashing. Something inside its body. Its monster heart, beating.

The beast rose past the catwalk railing. Each breath became a vise upon my lungs. I silently begged it to sink, to go away, to head back to the threshold and out into open ocean.

Thump. Thump. Thump. A shudder, its heart jerking. I hoped the thing was sick. Maybe its heart would burst.

And then I saw what really moved inside the thing. The outline of a tank. A regulator. Something jerking. Legs and arms. Phil.

Felix realized it at the same time I did. He thrashed out of my arms, swimming awkwardly for the doorway. I reached for him. His leg slipped out of my grasp. Mom turned, her hand uncovering the light and sending a beacon into the black.

The glow swept up from the darkness, a long cord snaking toward me. Over the catwalk. I swam back in a panic, past the depth charge, toward the hallway.

A sting on my ankle. A cord cutting through. I fumbled for my dive knife.

A second and a third filament, snaking over the grill like glowing vines, seeking the rest of me. I didn't think about how it would react when I cut it. How it would spasm.

A quick slice and my ankle was free. The thing shuddered. Its tentacle wrapped around anything it could find. The railing. Metal dangling from the walls. Rocks that jutted from surfaces between the floors, that broke off and tumbled into the deep.

And the depth charge, sitting on the catwalk.

The tentacle, glowing in the darkness, slithered over the barrel and cinched tight on the bar that circled its crown. The metal casing of the depth charge scraped across the grill, to the edge of the catwalk, and caught for a moment on the railing. I swam for it, my fingers almost catching the end. Then it slid over the rim. Plummeted into the darkness.

I scrambled back toward the hallway.

Swim, little fish. This time I listened.

In my head, that depth charge falls on an endless loop, plummeting into the dark.

One hundred ten feet, one hundred twenty feet.

The green glow pierced the black hallway. I swam back into the lab.

One hundred fifty, one hundred sixty. Falling in space.

That thing, squeezing itself into the hallway, lengthening. Reaching its filaments along the floor to find us. I dropped my dive light, swimming into the dark.

One hundred eighty, one hundred ninety, the bomb spinning into the abyss.

I reach the back wall. A thousand nettles envelop me, cover my body like a second skin, break through the neoprene as the beast takes me into itself.

Swim little fish, your voice said again. And I knew, a split second before it happened, that the charge had fallen far enough to end us all.

Two hundred feet.

Boom.

I DON'T HAVE MUCH TIME, but I have to tell you. Record it. Everything changes now, all the time.

Truth. With a capital T. I've written that entry 153 times since we tried to blow up the machine. 153. Each time the Bubble blows, the last few pages go blank. And I write the last entry again. Every time. Because it's the only way to make myself remember.

Blowing up the time machine didn't work. Ha, ha. I guess that's obvious. But we did manage to break it a little more.

Four hours. That's what my life has become, a four-hour slide into a hurricane. Over and over.

Sometimes it starts with the dream of my grandmother. We swim down into the reef, past purple sea fans, the thick barrel sponges and brain coral. I follow her as she kicks forty, fifty, sixty feet down, her knife in her hand, and then the *drip, drip* of the storm begins. *Drip. Drip.*

Daybreak, and a storm coming. I don't realize it's a storm, and I kiss Ben, and sometimes that kiss lasts a thousand years. In that moment, we don't need to rig the bombs to explode. When he's kissing me, I don't remember that I die in the lab, becoming the most recent meal of our resident horror show. The time machine puts its big metal finger on the rewind button, and like puppets we all go back to the beginning, asleep on the sand in a shared nightmare.

As soon as the kiss ends, I remember. So does everyone else.

At first, we tried to blow the place again. That never worked. Then we stayed on the beach and watched the rain build in the distance, watched it sweep over the beaches. Sometimes I get to the *Last Chance* and pry the gun away from Phil before he can kill Ben. I guess I haven't told you about that version of things, when everything went to hell. Sometimes Phil shoots me, and I bleed out on the beach. But each time, that sinkhole eventually blows, whether we're there to pull the trigger or not, and the rubber band pops us back in time.

I've become a collection of splinters, a shattered window, a repeated breath in an endless loop, caught up in a whirlpool of I don't know where and I don't know when.

And Phil, Phil talks to himself more and more each time we pop back in time, humming to himself as he drags tanks around, his eyes on the palm forest, as if he wants to go in there and never come out. I wish he would—go away and never come out. In most of our realities, he finds the stash of morphine. Sits on the beach, high as a kite, and counts the cans like some sort of beach bum dragon curled around his gold, demanding that we ask him before we eat anything. I've thought about killing him, but each time I get ahold of myself and remember that's a bit of your dark side in me trying to get out. Phil would just pop back to life again anyway.

Four hours.

Our whole existence, for the rest of eternity, lived over and over inside the opening act of a hurricane.

I don't have much more time to write, because I have a plan. Graham's got the gear ready to go, and he's coming with me. We have to go back to the wreck, the USS *Andrews*, where this all started. We have to blow the second half of the machine, which lies inside a crate in the room with the rest of the depth charges. At least we don't have to move them this time. Convenient.

Felix is sitting beside me, and he's crying. He doesn't want me to go. He wants me to tell you he loves you, and he misses you. Mom is here too. She says she's sorry, and you know what for. Ben and Steph both asked me to send a message to their parents, that they love them. Graham's already suiting up. Everyone he knows back home died long ago.

When I finish my last entry, I'm putting the journal in a dry bag from the charter, inflating a BC, rigging it together with a dive flag, and sending it to you. Mom thinks it's a waste, but I don't care. Even if it ends up on the bottom of the ocean, it's okay. Besides, people don't send a message in a bottle thinking someone will ever find it. People throw the bottle into the waves just to watch it float out to sea.

And I want you to know one last thing, something I almost remembered inside the heart of that machine, covered in phosphorescence.

That trip to South Carolina, when we walked the beach after sunset at low tide. I was six, and the sand glowed, soft and green.

You told me the sand was alive, and you scooped it up into your palm. I looked closer and saw them. Tiny, each one. Small enough to fit on a fingertip. Thousands of little sea creatures, stranded, covering the beach for miles.

The way I felt then, I feel it now. A little sad, watching them expire on the sand. But awed at how death could be so beautiful.

The wind is picking up, so I have to go before the sea's too rough to dive. And I'm excited, I want you to know, to be floating in space again, because you'll be there with me. Always.

Dear Mr. Gianopoulos:

Sir, I'm Graham Fitch, and I'm writing to tell you what happened. I meant to come by, to tell you man to man. For the last
six months, I've taken the bus over to your apartment. But each
time, I stand a few feet from the stairs for a while, stare at your
closed door, then go wait at the bus stop.

You see, I don't know which journal you read. I hear over
a hundred washed up on the Florida shores. And they're all different. In some, I ain't the best guy. So I get on the bus and ride
back to the little apartment Steph's parents were good enough
to help me find. And sometimes I don't go straight home, just
ride the bus route over and over, through a world so shiny and
strange I don't recognize nothin'.

Sia made me promise. We were suiting up and putting tanks
on for our final trip down, and she turned to me and she said,
"Graham, I forgot to tell him something. You promise me. If I
don't come back from the *Andrews*, and you do, you make sure
he knows. You make sure, you hear me?"

I've spent a lot of time wondering what she meant by that.
She wasn't quite right in the head by then, considering what
happened after everything went sideways in the sinkhole, how
many times we'd tried to make the Bubble pop. Women in general, they ain't very specific sometimes, not that I know much
about women, spending so many years growing up on a ship.
Back in those days, ladies didn't sign up to be sailors or soldiers.
Apparently, they do now. Girls like Sia, I suppose. Strange new
world, but I'm getting myself used to things here.

I spent a lot a nights sitting on the Key Largo docks, watching the charters come in and out of the harbor, and I figured it

out. What Sia meant. So I'm writing you this letter to let you know, just like she made me promise.

Sia and I suited up on the edge of the sinkhole, the gray clouds above us angry and spitting. Coming for us personally. My hands shaking. Her hands shaking. Mine from fear. Hers from crossing that threshold more times than she could count. But Sia and me, we had a new idea.

Sia gave Felix and her mom a goodbye kiss. I thought about the people I wished were there, the guy who taught me to load the big guns. My mess buddies, the ones who hit the deck with me the moment the explosions began. But I had nothing, no goodbyes to take into the darkness with me except . . . I thought about my bunkmate, the best friend I ever had, what he done to me. But it's hard to hate someone who's dead, now that I know he'll never have a chance to say goodbye to his people back home. Somewhere in Kansas, I think. I always thought if you did enough good things, enough brave things, the world would rain down forgiveness on you for anything you didn't get right. It's a hard thing, learning that ain't true.

We slipped off the slippery, muddy edge and into the water, black as an oil slick. Sia and I floated for a moment, fiddling with cords.

"You ready?" she asked me.

"I was born ready," I said, although I wasn't.

"You should take that saying back with you, to 1943," she said, as if she knew she wasn't going to make it out of the sinkhole. And right then, I needed to know something, because maybe she was wrong, and *I* was the one who wasn't coming back.

"Who wins?" I asked her.

"Who wins what?"

"The war. Who wins?"

"We win, Graham."

I thought about that for a moment, floating next to her, why I didn't feel anything one way or another about that. "How?"

Her face went dark, and then she said something I didn't understand until later. "We just win, that's all. In a kind of everybody loses sort of way."

Hiroshima. Nagasaki. That's what she was thinking. But I didn't know yet what we'd done and she didn't want to say.

I reached over and fiddled with the strap of her mask, which was twisted. At that moment, we were friends, you know, real friends, the kind who do things for each other.

"When the Bubble breaks, you think we'll end up in my time or yours?" I asked.

She shrugged, and I could see she was pretty sure we weren't going to end up anywhere.

And then she said something I didn't understand. She got this faraway look and said, "Brand-new world, baby. Maybe you don't belong, but you're going there anyway." I thought she was talking about herself, but now I realize she meant me. She knew, even before we went in.

Somehow, I felt my head settle on my shoulders better, and I saw more clearly. Which was good, 'cause I was going into the darkness with Sia.

I fit the regulator into my mouth, let the air out of my vest, and we sank.

We reached the lab fast, the darkness and silt swallowing us up. The cold seeping into my wet suit, moving up my arms and legs.

Our lights found the entrance of the hallway, and we swam in, both of us kicking shallow.

We made our way through the darkness. Right at the first juncture. Then left. Bits of stuff drifted through my beam. The world turned colder. So dark, like the storage room on a submarine. Down one hall, and the next. I remember thinking, *This is what it's like to die.*

Ten minutes in, we hit the threshold.

Stretch, pop.

My stomach flipped, and a cold knife ran through all my veins. I gasped, choked. Stopped swimming, drifted. The darkness spun.

My light slid across gray walls of the USS *Andrews*, fell from my hand, dangled. Moved across the pile of bombs I'd stacked a year ago. No, seventy years. One year, seventy years, all of it the same.

My body hit the floor in a soft landing. A few feet away, the wooden crate hummed. Its shape blurred and sharpened and blurred, like I'd come back drunk from shore leave. The beam lay still, slanting across the metal deck.

I don't know how long we lay there, curled up on the floor of the armory of the *Andrews*, sucking down air. But when I came back to myself, my air needle was down a ways, and my whole body shook from the gut yanking that the time machine's threshold had given me.

I pushed myself up, fumbled for my light, and dragged the beam over the floor.

Sia lay a few feet away, and at first I thought she was dead. Then a cloud of bubbles pulsed from underneath her regulator.

I shook her awake. She moved slow, like she didn't own her hands or feet.

I pulled a spool of wire we'd hooked to my gear, and a screwdriver, and moved toward the pile of bombs. It took me six tries to unscrew the cover on the bottom one. I kept dropping the screwdriver. I wondered if we were sending out a special made-for-monsters Morse code. *We're here. Come get us.* As long as we got the place rigged to blow and it actually worked this time, I didn't care much.

Sia held the light while I finished attaching the wire, although I don't know how I managed, my fingers as cold as a dead fish. Remembered my time back in Lubbock, fixing engines to make pocket change. That time when I thought—I *knew*—the money would never be enough, and I had to leave it all behind and come halfway around the world to fight. Prove myself.

Then get caught. Then lose it all.

I finished wiring up the bomb; the voices of dead friends, the ones who taught me how to be a gunner's mate, those voices kept me company in the dark. And that was the moment I decided I don't regret what I did, signing up. Because to this day I know what I did was right and good and true. It's just that sometimes people grow up faster than they need to, and that's just the sacrifice they have to make, even if they're sacrificing everything.

I know I'm talking too much about myself, when really this should be me telling you about Sia. But I think this is the way to make you understand. What it's like.

Sia gave me a little nod, and we made our way back to the threshold. I prepared myself, my guts bunching up inside, knowing what was coming, how the knife would slide over my skin and my eyes and my whole body. We crossed the spot.

And nothing happened.

Nothing.

We floated for a bit, pointed our lights around the place. At first, I thought we'd gone to the wrong area of the room. Sia led me back over the invisible line, swam around in circles. Then she stopped and pulled out her slate and wrote with the little stub of a pencil.

It's gone.

I shook my head, swimming in circles again, searching for the threshold. She wrote again with the little pencil on the slate.

Get us out?

Out, through the rat maze of the USS *Andrews*, out into the drink. Which was full of five-foot waves and an honest to God sea monster.

I nodded—because what else was I gonna do?—and led her through the doorway.

Moving through our beautiful lady, wrecked at the bottom of the ocean like that, tore through me. All her hallways and quarters, the little bits of her that gave us comfort and peace on long days, and even longer nights. All of my past life dead and gone, a ghost of herself, a ghost of us, my years out in the South Pacific nothin' but a flat photograph, a record in Uncle Sam's file cabinet. It tore me up so much I can't write about it now without my hands shaking.

The wire spool was long, and as I let her out, floor by floor, toward the upper deck, I laid a copper thread behind me. Sia held both lights so I'd have my hands free. We'll blow her when we got up into the light, I remember thinking. Blow the whole tomato and take our chances with the storm and that thing that hunted us.

We reached the last door, and when we floated up the ladder, the darkness grayed, until a full-on parade of natural light lit us up, dim and soft, light so sweet I almost laughed. My chest eased up, and I had a feeling we'd be able to do this. That we'd blow it, and we'd swim back to shore, and the Coast Guard would come. Whether we were in Sia's time or mine, we'd all live.

Sia and I slipped up and out and hovered above the deck. I pulled the gear from my waist and rigged the end of the wire to the prongs, got ready to throw the switch.

And the light changed.

At first, I didn't notice. My attention was on the wire and the trigger. I floated a foot above the deck, the currents pulling me. But as I tightened the last screw into place, the light shifted. Slow, like a cloud had passed over the sun.

My finger stilled on the wire. I didn't want to look up, so I wasted two full seconds staring at my hands, which now glowed green.

Above us. That's where it floated. I tilted my head to look.

Its fat body stretched out so far on either side, her edges blurred in the distance. Water moving through her. A hundred tentacles and filaments spread out, stretched to either side of the deck, from the mizzenmast to the bowsprit, down to the crow's nest and beyond—so huge she was all I could see. The tentacles of the thing hanging down like roots into the earth. And an eye, huge and unblinking, focused on me.

I dropped the trigger and pulled Sia's arm so she'd look up. Then I bolted for the corridor that led back into the *Andrews*, swimming down into the darkness, Sia following right behind me. She still had both lights, the beams jagging and moving down the ladder, into the hallways. The darkness shut out the world, and I went through two compartments before I stopped and turned to Sia.

The copper wire and the trigger, in her hand. She'd had the sense to pick up what I'd dropped.

She held up her gauge and shone a light on it. Then grabbed mine. I blinked, focused on the needle to see how long I had. Mine sat on the red line.

We floated in the dark, face to face, both of us staring at the gauge. And I knew what I had to do. I'd draw that thing deep into the *Andrews* and blow the bombs and the machine. That thing and me. I'd die, but I'd take it with us. And Sia would head to the surface and back to your wife and son.

Then she did something I'll never forget. Her hands came up, and as I remember it, they came up slow, the beam of her light falling from her hand and dangling from her wrist and sliding across the wall and the floor. And she held my head between her two hands and pressed her mask to mine, like that day in the sinkhole when she wouldn't leave me behind. Everything around us dark and hollow and cold, and I thought it was her way of saying we were in this together. That we would go down together.

She slipped off her vest and tank, keeping the breathing part in her mouth. I didn't know what she was up to, but I trusted her, so I waited, watched, trying to figure it out. Then she pulled the screwdriver from my waist and pushed me through a doorway behind me, into an open storeroom. With the trigger in one hand and the screwdriver in the other, she started banging.

I lunged for the screwdriver. She needed to put her gear back on. If it came, she wouldn't have time. She needed to be ready. But Sia pushed me away and kept banging.

We struggled. One of her flashlights fell to the deck. I pulled the screwdriver out of her hand. She grabbed on to a bulkhead for purchase pushed me back again, toward the doorway to the storage room, and I didn't understand, Sir, I didn't, I swear I wouldn't have let her do what she was planning.

And then the darkness lit up. That thing, squeezing itself long and thin and making its way into the ship's corridors. After us.

And that was when my air ran out.

It wasn't like it fizzled out, like a balloon slowly letting off steam. It just cut off, as if someone had filled my throat with concrete.

Sia gave me one last push, and I floated back through the doorway. And she was gone, her and the trigger and one flashlight and no tank to keep her alive, swimming fast back down into the ship, slipping away from me. I started to swim out the storeroom, but the thing filled the hallway, squeezing through, following her. A green glow, its body thick and moving fast. And me, I was trapped in the storage closet, my mind burning for air, and black spots in my vision.

The glow faded until the flashlight was the only thing I could see, lying in the hallway. I slipped back and grabbed it. Found her gear a foot away and took the best breath of air I'd ever tasted. Then I slipped off my vest and put hers on, ready to go after her, but I was all thumbs and it took too long. Must of been two minutes since she'd left. Two minutes. Holding your breath that long just ain't natural. And that meant the trigger lay God knew where, somewhere inside the *Andrews*, useless. Our four hours would end, and we'd bounce back to the beginning. Which was fine by me, I remember thinking. Next time we'd do better. Next time we'd find a way for both us to get out and—

Boom.

Well, you know the rest. I guess everyone in Key Largo does, seeing as how the paper can't shut up about it. Shipwreck survivors, rescued after four years of being lost at sea, made the news all the way up in New York City.

I'm sitting here on the dock, and there's a band playing at a fish and chips place right on the water, next to the dive shop that's hired your wife. Just for a little while, till she gets money in her purse again to buy a new charter. People coming and going, smiling and laughing like every day is shore leave. The marina smells right to me, like ship oil and seaweed, and the air coming off the ocean nudges me like it remembers I chose it over the desert. I ain't important, but I feel like I'm a part of something here, so I'm staying, to make a life of it.

Steph's stuck herself in her house since we got back, so we haven't seen much of her. Shell-shocked, that's what I call her. Phil's still in the hospital, drying out, and none of us miss him much. Felix is waving to me across the parking lot. Ben's inside the scuba shop, renting himself some gear for his first dive. I'll never put that tank on my back again, but Ben, I guess he wants to see what all the fuss is about.

And Sia, she just drove up to the marina in her beat-up truck.

I hear from Ben that Sia hasn't come to see you yet. When she finally does knock on your door, she'll never tell you the real story. Maybe she don't remember it like I do. Besides, that girl is not one to blow her own horn. And she's stubborn. So I'm writing this letter to deliver her message, the one she gave me before we went under for the last time. A promise is a promise. So here it is.

She forgives you for what you did. She forgives you for leaving. She forgives you for everything.

That's it then. As my old captain used to say, I wish you fair winds and a following sea.

Sincerely,

Graham Fitch

THE COAST GUARD IS COMING.

The ship rising on the horizon is so small I could hold it on one fingertip. But it's growing. Even better, it's real. One hour, and they'll launch the small boats and rush the shore like freakin' Valkyries come to take us home.

One hour. Sixty minutes. Thirty-six hundred seconds. An actual movement forward in time.

Steph kneels in the surf, her head gripped in her hands, crying with relief and God knows what else. Ben's leg is strong enough to climb a ladder, so he's standing on the roof deck of the *Last Chance*, the place where I first saw him all those years ago. And when he meets my eyes, he looks calm and sure, like he knew this would happen.

The Bubble's gone. I can feel it. The Sense has gone deep, back into the secret places of the ocean, where I hope she stays.

Felix has climbed up on Mom's shoulders, and they're both staring out to sea. He's playing a drum on her head, and she's too happy to tell him to cut it out. Phil's gone off somewhere, wandering in the palm forest. I think he's still alive. At least most of him is.

And me, I found the notebook in the charter. It's blank now, all the way back to the beginning. Leftover math equations written in pencil cover the first two pages. My hands shake as I flip through the leaves, crisp with salt, dried out in the sun. Not one mark on any of it. My hands are shaking, ~~because I have to say this last thing to you. The one thing I was too lost to say when I was heading out for what I thought was the last time. I just want you to know~~

Ben's calling me to join him up on the roof deck. I don't want to miss it—watching our Coast Guard arrive in a cloud of diesel fumes and glory. Because I'll never have this moment again. Time moves in only one direction now. Forward. I can't live in your cell with you anymore, trying to keep you company. I get that now.

I've decided this is better done in person. I'll see you soon, Dad. I have so much to tell you.

ACKNOWLEDGMENTS

PEOPLE THINK OF WRITERS as solitary creatures, but most books don't happen without the help of a community. First of all, I want to thank the DFW Writers Workshop and DFWCon for all your support. This book would absolutely not have happened if I hadn't found you. You're the coolest bunch of writers around, and a lot of my acknowledgement space is dedicated to calling you out by name.

Thank you to my three DFWWW beta readers. Daryle McGinnis, your military experience and general awesomeness helped me shape this book on a microlevel. Brooke Fossey, you taught me so much about subtext. And John Bartell, your lessons on voice were indispensable. Thanks for keeping Sia from sounding like a forty-year-old soccer mom.

A big thank you to all those writers who gave me advice and support during the difficult publishing process: Brian Tracey, Melissa Lenhardt, Sally Hamilton, A. Lee Martinez, Rosemary Clement Moore, Larry Enmon, Dana Swift, Jenna Sutton, and so many more, I can't name them all. I'm really grateful or the generosity and kindness you all showed. Writing communities rock.

A big thanks to Amy Bishop at Dystel, Goderich, and Bourret for taking a chance on a new author and for handling everything that came our way with kindness and professionalism. Thank you also to the wonderful editors at Blink: Hannah Van

Vels, whose enthusiasm for the project helped me immensely; and Jacque Alberta, who has an amazing eye for detail. Thanks to Denise Froehlich, who designed the gorgeous interior. I also have to give a huge hug to all the marketing and PR folks who helped me navigate some very unknown waters: Michael Aulisio, Sara Merritt, Jessica Westra, Lauren Summerford, Dana Kaye, Julia Borcherts, Hailey Dezort, and Angela Melamud. Without you, my book would be hidden in the most obscure recesses of the internet.

Vanessa Peters, a wonderful singer-songwriter, let me use her brilliant lyrics as Sia's anthem, and I'm so happy to know someone this talented. I'd also like to send a big thank you Seimi Rurup and Sachi Mitchell, two excellent sensitivity readers on an earlier version of this book. I'll always be grateful for your support of the project, and your compassionate attitude toward writers who try to connect with cultures different from their own. And Tasia Fossey, thanks so much for lending me your beautiful name.

I needed to check a lot of technical details in *Fractured Tide*, so thank you to Chief and all the folks at Lone Star Diving in Fort Worth for answering my questions about decompression and wreck diving. Thanks, all you awesome writers at Writers in the Field who taught me about World War II–era weapons. And thanks, George Goldthwaite, for your advice about bombs and World War II destroyers.

To my friends who cheered me along the way: Adrienne Knutson, Zetta Brown, Alicia Druba, and Hannah Head. Thank you for listening to all my news—both the good and the bad—and helping me celebrate. And thanks to my family, both the Lutzes and the Browns, for reminding me what life is all about.

To Chris Brown, my actual real-life brother, I promise I will never drag you into a flooded sinkhole to face a giant sea monster and blow up the world. And to Dad, even though you're gone, you're not forgotten, because we don't leave anyone behind.

Most of all, thank you to my husband, Russell, and my lovely daughter, Robin. Russell, you are my friend, my sounding board, and a really great writer. And thank you, Robin, for inspiring the sweet character of Felix. All the love Sia has for her brother, I have for you.

BLINK®